THE CRIB

Paul Kent

BANTAM BOOKS
TORONTO • NEW YORK • LONDON • SYDNEY • AUCKLAND

THE CRIB

A Bantam Book / Seal Books

Bantam edition / April 1987

ISBN 0-553-26650-0

Published simultaneously in the United States and Canada

Bantam Books are published by Bantam Books, Inc. Its trade-
mark, consisting of the words "Bantam Books" and the portrayal
of a rooster, is Registered in U.S. Patent and Trademark Office
and in other countries. Marca Registrada. Bantam Books, Inc.,
666 Fifth Avenue, New York, New York 10103.

PRINTED IN CANADA
COVER PRINTED IN U S.A.

U   0 9 8 7 6 5 4 3 2 1

Pictures of horses and clowns hung gaily on the walls. The crib, dark and empty, still stood under the window, the changing table against the far wall. The room looked more like a child's nursery now than it had the morning of little Todd McEwen's death.

Absently Stuart ran his hand over the top rail of the crib. "Is this the crib Jill was talking about, Brian? She mentioned something about your uncle making a crib that the whole family uses."

Brian nodded. "Have you had a chance to look at it? It's really quite a work of art."

Stuart examined the names on the crib. Thayer, Jackson, Lasalle, Assad, Wellington, Bucknall, Harrison, McEwen . . . He looked back over the list. "Lasalle," "Wellington," he had seen those names before. The two vaguely familiar names he had noted on the computer list from the CDC.

He shivered slightly. A tiny finger of ice touched the back of his neck. . . .

WHAT *REALLY* HAPPENED
IN THE CRIB ON
THAT TRAGIC NIGHT?

THE CRIB

ABOUT THE AUTHOR

PAUL KENT patiently suppressed his writing urge through six years of medical school at the University of Toronto and ten hectic years of practice in various parts of British Columbia. He couldn't hold it any longer. His first novel, *The Crib*, was the result. He currently lives in Vancouver with his wife and two children. When he is not writing, playing piano, skiing, playing squash, tennis, golf or basketball, he works as a physician in family and sportsmedicine.

Herb
This one's for you.
P.G.

Prologue
April 20

It had stopped snowing. Almost stopped. Occasional flakes appeared suddenly, trapped in the glare of the headlights; horizontal tracers of white, slicing at the grille, veering at the last second, vanishing in the swirl as they passed.

He turned off the wipers. The face of the woman beside him reflected in the mirror of the windshield. A stranger. Yet her eyes, the desolation, the quiet form in her arms, the tragedy so familiar now. When had it begun? One thousand? Two thousand years ago? For him it was a year. Exactly one year . . .

Chapter One
April 1

Something had awakened her: instinct, a sense of urgency. Her eyes scanned the darkened room, the phosphorous glow of the clock radio: 6:21. A muted ringing filtered under the door.

"The phone," she whispered. Something in the ring of a telephone after midnight, mixed with the chemistry of sleep; half-awakened, a pervasive, irrational hint of panic. She slipped her husband's arm off her breast and slid quietly from the bed. Padding into the kitchen, she interrupted the fourth ring.

"Hel—"

"Marnie? Oh Jesus Marnie, it's Jill McEwen, from across the street." The words spilled out, panicked, terrified. "It's the baby, I don't think he's . . . You said your husband is a doctor. . . . I don't know anyone to call. Can you, can he come over?" The voice broke into sobs.

It had been more than seven years since they'd had a call like this. While her husband was in practice she had frequently taken calls from terrified parents. Not once had the child's illness been serious enough to justify the panic. She had been able to defuse most of them herself, with reassurance, common sense. But this one was different. Something in the voice; a terror, vibrating over the wire. Even after seven years she knew it was different. She placed her hand over the mouthpiece.

"Stuart," she called to the open bedroom door. Then into the phone, "Jill, what's the baby . . . Jill? . . . *Jill!*" she yelled.

The sobbing stopped.

"Jill, what's happened? What's wrong with the baby?"

"I don't know. Marnie, I don't think he's breathing. He

2

usually cries to be fed around six. He didn't, but I woke up anyway, just a few minutes ago. He's just lying there, Marnie. I don't know what to do. . . ."

She put the phone to her hip. "*Stuart!*" She half-screamed this time.

"Jill, we'll be right over. Listen to me. As soon as you hang up I want you to unlock your front door. Then go back to the baby; turn him onto his side and wipe off his face, if he's vomited I mean. And inside his mouth, clean it out. I'll hurry Stuart up. Now go on."

She winced as Jill crashed her telephone onto the cradle. The old responses were returning. The initial panic giving way to an organized calm as she hurried back to the bedroom. Her husband was sitting, half-asleep, on the edge of the bed.

"Stuart, get up. Come on. It's Jill, the new couple across the street, the McEwens. There's a problem with the baby and it sounds serious."

This early in the morning Stuart Rice shared none of his wife's sensitivity or intuition. "Shit, Marnie, can't this wait? I don't do this any . . ."

She cut off his protest, throwing a grey sweatsuit at him. "Come on, Stuart, something's wrong, really wrong. She says the baby isn't breathing." She flicked on the light. "Get dressed and go on over. I'll get your box and meet you there."

He winced at the light. He resented being awakened like this, hated it. During his years in practice everything from infant colic to head injuries had taken precedence over his sleep. It was the worst of several irritants he thought he had left behind. He tied the oversized pants at his waist and shrugged into a grey sweatshirt. At the door he slid his bare feet into tennis shoes and left the house. The door slammed behind him.

It had been raining most of the night but had slowed now to a drizzle. The cold and the moisture tugged at him, washed the remaining haze of sleep from his mind. He organized his thoughts as he crossed the cul-de-sac. It had been so long since he had been confronted with a real emergency that he wasn't at all sure he'd know what to do. Airway, Breathing, Circulation . . . he rehearsed the ABCs of basic life support. Just four months ago he had taken the mandatory refresher course to keep his hospital privileges—and access to chart information—intact. But as a full-time epidemiologist, it hardly applied to his daily routine. What little he had absorbed was long forgotten. As he climbed the stairs at the McEwen house he wished he had paid more attention.

He knocked, then pushed the door open. "Jane? It's Stuart Rice. From across the street . . . Jane?"

"It's Jill." Marnie pushed around him, leading him to the stairs. "She'll be upstairs, in the nursery." She handed him a dusty fishing-tackle box.

At one time he had carried his emergency supplies in a custom-built, black leather case. It had cost him more than five hundred dollars and looked impressive. Too impressive. Someone had stolen it and the twelve hundred dollars' worth of emergency equipment inside. Wiser, he had replaced it with a large, cheap, plastic tackle box, the compartments modified and held together with contact cement. It looked like hell, but no one would suspect the value of its contents. That had been twelve years ago. He hadn't touched it for the past six.

Muffled sobs led them to a small room at the end of the upstairs hall. Jill McEwen, desperate eyes rimmed with tears, looked up as they entered. Marnie moved to her side as Stuart crossed the room to where a small, quiet form lay on a change table.

He turned the baby onto its back, silently recording his observations. The skin blue, mottled, cold. Small flecks of dried foam at the corners of the mouth. He fished a stethoscope from the box and held the bell to the baby's chest. Nothing. He lifted an eyelid. No reaction; the pupil remained dilated, fixed. The cornea was dry and dull; he touched it gently. No blink response. He listened again for a heartbeat as he moved the baby's arms and legs. Silence. The limbs had already developed the first traces of rigor. He looked up at his wife, at the mother.

Marnie's eyes moistened. "Stuart, is there anything you can do?" she asked softly, knowing the answer.

As he shook his head, Jill's control broke. She buried

her head in Marnie's shoulder, sobbing uncontrollably. Marnie looked at her husband, pleading.

"He's been dead for some time, Marnie." His unused, forgotten responses surfaced. Always with death, a sense of impotence, a defensiveness. "Three or four hours anyway. There's nothing anyone can do at this point."

Marnie held the mother's head against her shoulder, rocking her. Stuart turned back to the baby, looking for more detail: signs, clues to the cause of death.

As the sobbing eased Marnie asked, "What happened, Stu? Can you tell?"

He shook his head. "There's nothing I can see—no marks or bruising I mean. . . ." She glared a warning. Chastened, he continued, "I'm sorry, Jill, that was careless. It wasn't meant as an accusation. I don't know why this happened. Has he been sick? With a cold or the flu I mean? Or vomiting, anything like that?"

Jill looked at him, shaking her head. "No, no, nothing. There was nothing wrong with him. He's never been sick, ever." Her voice faltered again, barely controlled.

"It's hard to say," he continued, groping for words, reasons. "When a baby dies suddenly like this, unexpectedly, there often isn't any apparent cause. Sudden infant death syndrome it's called, crib death. I don't think anyone really knows what causes it, but—"

"Stu?" his wife interrupted gently, aware of his growing discomfort. "Is there someone we should call? The hospital? Would they send an ambulance?"

He nodded, grateful for the distraction. "I'm sorry, Jill." He shrugged, helpless. "There just isn't anything anyone can do. Maybe we should call."

Fresh tears welled as she raised her hands to her face. Marnie held her, mouthing to Stuart, "Downstairs."

He nodded and left.

Using the telephone in the den, he began dialing the hospital's emergency dispatch number, but stopped after the fourth digit.

What the hell am I doing? he thought. He was thinking more rationally now, logic replacing the mixture of emotions that had dominated his reactions until that point. State legislation required a postmortem examination on all unexplained deaths. And the time between death and autopsy, especially in an infant, could be critical. Tissue destruction began as soon as oxygen-starved cells released their toxic enzymes. Early decomposition would already have started. Even if the autopsy wasn't performed immediately, at least refrigerating the body would retard the decay process.

I need a morgue, not an ambulance, he thought, and completed the call, substituting the pathology department number. It answered on the first ring.

"Novak."

"Wally, Stuart."

"Stu! Good Christ, you haven't been up this early since you stopped working for a living. To what do we owe the pleasure?"

Waldimir Novak had been a consultant pathologist for twelve years, chief of the hospital's pathology department for the past eight. During his combined years of residency training in Czechoslovakia, London, and Baltimore, his work days had started at 6:00 A.M. Though his present duties did not require him to be at work that early, he had never relearned how to sleep in. Their professional paths had crossed frequently since Stuart's switch to epidemiology. Similarly, their friendship, born of common interests, had flourished.

"Actually, Wally, I have a problem. I'm at a neighbour's house, and from what I can tell they've had a crib death." He described the situation briefly, including his concern over the delay in autopsy.

Novak's joviality disappeared. "Tough problem to wake up to, Stu. As far as the delay goes, I'm not all that concerned. The big studies on crib death are doing all kinds of chemical assays—sugars, neurotransmitters, the works—and a big delay there really screws them up. But we're not involved with them here. We just do a drug screen and a gross postmortem, with microscopics on anything suspicious. The time-related changes are usually pretty obvious.

"In fact, your problem sounds more logistical than clinical. I agree you don't need an ambulance. This time of the morning, for a nonurgent call, Christ, you'd be waiting for two hours. And you'd just get caught in the out-patient crush once you got here. If you think the parents would go for it, why don't you bring the baby down in the car yourself, straight to me I mean. I'll call the coroner and she and I can take it from there. You'll have to sign the death certificate, and we'll need a release from the parents. But there's no hurry for that. With the holiday weekend we won't be doing anything but toxicology till Monday or Tuesday anyway."

Stuart sighed, relieved. "Thanks, Wally. I knew you'd help. I don't think I could take any bureaucratic hassles right now. Unless there's a problem, we should be there well before eight."

As he returned to the nursery his concern shifted from the immediate task of delivering the baby's body to the morgue to the support role he and Marnie were about to assume. From the physician's perspective, a crib death was the ultimate tragedy. It involved, demanded, an unbelievable amount of counseling and emotional support— the weakest elements in his own practice, and something he had never been any good at, never enjoyed.

He had never really enjoyed patients at all for that matter, not on an individual basis anyway. He had all the right motives when he entered medical school: concern, caring, empathy, all the right stuff. And the warmth and understanding even carried over into his practice, for a while. But after six or seven years the shine faded. He realized that what his patients mistook for sympathy was really little more than a finely tuned act. A convincing act, but progessively less satisfying. He needed a change.

At first he considered staying in clinical medicine, but specializing in surgery, until he began asking his consultant friends about their specialties, about their personal lives. Not one was any happier in his work than he was in his.

He began a search, his "midlife dabble" he called it, attending courses and workshops in anything that looked interesting: hypnosis, acupuncture, orthomolecular medicine, industrial medicine. But each was no more than a different shade of the same clinical colour. He even considered abandoning medicine altogether, until he discovered epidemiology.

It had enough exposure to diagnosis and clinical medicine to satisfy him intellectually, but none of the one-on-one encounters that left him so drained and frustrated. It was like a switch had been thrown as he immediately felt a greater affinity for sick populations than for sick people.

Still, the change was difficult, personally more than professionally. It had taken him a full year to resolve the guilt he had felt about his preference for statistics over a stethoscope. But once he had accepted it as being right for him, the move to epidemiology was natural.

The sound of running water distracted him as he returned to the nursery. Marnie was there alone with the baby.

"Jill's just freshening up." She shook her head slowly as she took her husband's hand. "Her husband isn't even here yet. In fact he's supposed to be arriving today from Pennsylvania. We're all the support they have here, Stu. Believe me, I know how you feel about this. I can handle Jill, but I need your help, as a facilitator, a support role, that's all. You don't have to solve anything."

She paused, then asked, "I overheard you talking to Wally Novak. What happens next?"

Stuart explained the procedure, that it would be easiest if all three of them took the baby to the hospital. That they could avoid a lot of red-tape delays by going straight to Novak in pathology.

But traces of resentment remained. "Marnie, I gave up trying to be the great comforter years ago. I'm no good at it, I don't enjoy it. I don't want it."

She cut him off, the edge of her own anger and frustration showing. "Nobody wants it or enjoys it, Stuart. None of us can undo what's happened, so forget about the resentment and the guilt. Just feel a little natural human sympathy."

He looked away, at the baby. The water stopped.

"I'll explain it to Jill," Marnie said, gently now, squeezing his hand, "if you'll get the baby ready." She left him alone in the nursery.

He draped a small blanket over the change table, placed the baby on it and wrapped it, leaving the head exposed but coverable with one corner. He could hear his wife quietly explaining their plans to Jill in the hall as he took his first look around the room.

It was obvious that the McEwens had just moved in. Packing boxes lined the walls. Bare hardwood floors waited for the throw rug, still rolled and taped, standing in the corner. A bright-coloured quilt hung awkwardly over the window. The change table and the crib were the only functioning pieces in the room.

The crib. He moved towards it, studying it. It had a handmade, crafted feel to it; solid, and finished. Less than three feet long, considerably smaller than a commercial crib. All wood, very dark, streaked-looking. He reached out to touch it, his hand withdrawing instantly, reflexively, as a sudden spark of static leaped from the crib. He licked his finger, rubbing sensation back to the tip. He touched the crib again, cautiously this time. The wood was cold, and hard, almost rock hard. Not painted, just sanded and oiled—or stained, he couldn't decide which. Uniform vertical slats ran from top to bottom rails on all four sides. The center slat on each side was wider than the rest, and roughened. He bent over, looking closer at the wider slats. The roughness was carved into the wood. Each of the slats was filled with names and dates. At the head of the crib, the wide slat held only four names. The last, the most recently carved, was TODD McEWEN. Beside it, one of the narrow slats on the headboard was different, lighter in colour, not as well finished. *A patch job*, he thought. *It shows*.

Marnie interrupted his thoughts. "We're ready, Stu."

He turned. Jill, more composed now, was holding the baby, the free corner of the blanket draped loosely over the infant's face, a tiny chin just visible. Marnie took her arm and led her from the room. Stuart followed, but before he left he took a final look around the nursery. The small wooden crib, the empty walls, the bare hardwood floor. Something was wrong, out of place, inconsistent. It teased at him, floated, just beyond his grasp. At the door he reached for the light switch, tentatively, expecting another shock.

Nothing.

He shivered slightly and left.

Chapter Two
April 15

"Subject is identified as a male infant, 2 months of age. Subject is dressed in a diaper, wrapped in a blanket. Weight 1400 grams, crown-heel 55 cm., crown-rump 41 cm."

Stuart continued down the autopsy report on the McEwen baby. Each organ was listed in turn, its weight followed by a comment on its gross appearance.

". . . Brain: 575 grams; basal vessels, meninges, C.S.F.: normal. Lungs: combined weight 100 grams; external surfaces, bronchi and cut surfaces show no abnormality. Thymus: 16 grams . . . normal. Heart: 33 grams . . . normal. . . ."

The gross examination was followed by a tediously detailed description of each organ's microscopic appearance, and this by a list of biochemical tests done on blood, urine, cerebrospinal fluid, and vitreous specimens. The entire seven-page report was summarized in two tersely worded concluding sentences: "The investigation, including gross, microscopic, and toxicological findings, fails to reveal a definitive cause of death. It is concluded that this two-month-old male died as a result of sudden infant death syndrome."

As he read the final paragraph, Stuart remarked, "This sounds a lot more involved than the routine postmortem you described on the phone, Wally?"

The pathologist crossed his ankles on his desk and sipped his coffee, nodding. "It's more than we usually do."

"Any particular reason?" Stuart asked.

Novak fingered the report. "Your being personally involved was part of it. But there was something else. I couldn't quite put a finger on it, but it seemed almost too clean."

"Everything being normal, you mean? I thought that's what crib death was all about."

"It is, but this kid had absolutely nothing. I mean not even the time-related postmortem changes you were so concerned about last week when you first called. But even if we ignore that, more and more of the new tissue markers they're turning up on these infant deaths—brain stem changes, carotid body changes, arteriolar thickening, there's nearly a dozen of them now—they're all anoxic or hypoxic tissue changes that have most of the prevailing theories on SIDS suggesting some degree of chronic oxygen lack. And they've come up with some weird fucking hypotheses, looking for things you'd never expect. But this kid had nothing like that. I mean literally nothing. Christ, we even took his neck apart."

"His neck? His spine you mean?"

"Right. Some hot shot in Boston—Giles or Gilles or something—found an abnormal skull-spine configuration in some of these kids. In certain positions the first cervical vertebra inverts into the foramen. So both vertebral arteries get compressed when the neck is extended, potentially anyway. Which shuts off the brain-stem blood flow, and zap. But this kid's neck was normal.

"And all the biochemistry. If anything, we'd expect chloride or magnesium or urea nitrogen changes in the vitreous. But they were bang-on normal."

"Why not serum changes?"

"That's another thing." Novak shifted in his chair. "The serum values usually aren't worth piss-all. You'd expect them to change so much anyway after death you can't rely on them. But even they were normal. It's like the kid hadn't even died—like he was just hibernating or something. Cultures, the same. Not even the usual postmortem flourish of pathogens. You know, some of the studies suggested botulism as a cause of male infant death. I think they blamed it on contaminated honey. But this little guy was spotless. We don't have all the viral studies back yet, but the ones we do have are all normal."

Novak sipped again his drink, looking at Stuart. "So the

ball's back in your court, my friend. I may not like the feeling it gives me, but from a pathology perspective this kid was anatomically and physiologically clean. If it's any help, some of the papers I've read describe kids at risk for SIDS, based on family background and habits, or socioeconomic status, or birth trauma. The list goes on and on. None of the methods they use are more than twenty-percent sensitive, and they all give a barnful of false positives, but it may help to go over some of the items with the parents."

Stuart nodded absently.

"Stu?"

"I heard you, Wally." He folded the report, slapping it against his thigh. "Two things are bugging me about this now. First of all, I dread the prospect of talking to the parents at all. Marnie's really on my case. I've tried to be philosophical about it, but it sticks in my craw. I hated counseling when I was in practice and I hate it even more now. About ten years ago one of my patients had a crib death. A year and a half later she was still bringing me articles from lay magazines. And we'd go through the same process all over again, rehashing the whole goddamn thing. She'd relive the torture and I'd end up licking antacid off the shelves of my sample cupboard. Christ, I used to get heartburn just seeing her name on the appointment sheet."

"And?"

"And what?"

"You said there were two things bugging you."

Stuart laughed and flopped into a chair. "It's a good thing you went into pathology, Wally. An insensitive prick like you would never survive in the real world. Christ, I could be choking on a fucking hot dog and you'd ask me to pass the mustard."

Novak just grinned. "So what's number two?"

"The same thing you mentioned: it's too clean. Look at this report. Everything in it is normal, every single item. That in itself, especially in the light of the research you've been quoting, is abnormal."

"Nothing is what we found, Stu." Novak's voice had a slight edge to it.

"Relax, Wally. You may be an asshole but you're the best pathologist in California. Well, in Davis anyway." He grinned. "If you found nothing, it's because there was nothing to find. I guess just hearing you voice the same thing reinforced my concern about the lack of findings."

"That was off the record, Stu. Officially this kid died a crib death. It may be inconsistent with what I've been reading, but there was nothing in the autopsy to suggest otherwise."

"I know that, Wally. It's just that there was something, a feeling I had in the baby's nursery. . . ." His voice trailed off. He brightened suddenly and stood up. "But as a pathologist, Wally, you wouldn't know anything about feelings."

"Not true, Stuart. I had a feeling just last year."

Stuart chuckled, waving the report in front of him. "Can I get a copy of this?"

"It is a copy. Take it."

Stuart opened the door. "About that feeling you had last year . . ."

Novak finished the thought for him: "I think I just had to take a crap."

"We really know so little, don't we, Stu?"

Stuart was toweling off after his shower. He had briefed Marnie on the autopsy results when he arrived home from work, omitting the unease he still felt about the report being so completely negative. She had scanned it while he showered and was sitting on the bed now, the report on her lap.

He replied, "It's been a poorly understood, poorly studied problem for a long time, Marnie. They're just starting to put together—"

But she cut him off. "No, I don't mean that. Oh sure, we've got ways of researching and investigating events to the *nth* degree. But here we have one little baby, alive one minute, and dead the next. Gone, just like that. No warning, nothing. Even if the autopsy had shown a cause of death, it's unlikely anything would have prevented it. It seems so inevitable, almost like it's part of some prearranged plan. . . ." Her voice trailed off. "Anyway, I told

Jill we'd be over before eight. I know how you feel about encounters like this, but they're coping really well. Their gloom is giving way more and more now to curiosity. They don't want sympathy as much as they want answers. They want to know what happened. And why."

Stuart nodded absently. That was just the problem. Even with the report and all the reading he had done, he had no idea what had happened. Or why.

Brian McEwen answered the door. It was the first time Stuart had seen him. He was huge. At least six and a half feet tall, and solid. As they shook hands, Stuart was amazed that his grip was so gentle. McEwen detected his guest's surprise.

"Force of habit." He grinned, holding up his oversized hands. "The first time I met Jill's mother I was so nervous I broke one of the bones in her hand. Now I shake hands like a wimp."

The comment was so natural, so unexpected, that Stuart's tension began to evaporate.

McEwen led them into the den. Jill, legs tucked beneath her, looked up from the corner of the couch. Her face, her whole body, seemed tired but more relaxed since he had last seen her. She smiled as Marnie joined her on the couch. Stuart settled on the hearth; the fire hissed softly at his back. Brian turned to Marnie.

"There's fresh coffee on, or whatever you'd like." He looked at Stuart. "Beer, Stuart? Or brandy?"

"Coffee's fine, thanks," he replied.

Marnie smiled, shaking her head. "I'll pass for now, thanks, Brian."

With coffee served, McEwen sank into a large rocker. He took several sips from his cup, allowing time for his guests to relax before beginning.

"Stuart, I really appreciate the help you and Marnie gave Jill two weeks ago. I know you're not involved in this kind of medicine anymore, so we're all the more grateful for your offer to come over tonight."

Offer! Stuart could feel his wife's eyes burning into the side of his face.

Brian continued, "We've just got so damn many questions about this whole thing we don't know where to begin. . . ."

Stuart interrupted, surprising even himself with his gentleness. "Maybe it's best if I start it off, Brian. I'll run down what we know about crib death, and how it applies in this, ah, in Todd's case. And we'll see where we can go from there."

It was the first time he had used the baby's first name. What had been just a statistic and a source of stress for him to that point had taken on a new dimension. Todd McEwen, a baby boy, dead, but still very much alive in the memories of his parents. First the natural warmth of the father, and now this personification of the infant son; his task was suddenly easier, infinitely easier. He began.

"It's wrong, isn't it, Stu?"

She had awakened to find him staring at the ceiling. It was 3:00 A.M. The evening with the McEwens had ended at midnight. Both Brian and Jill had picked up immediately on the absence of abnormal autopsy findings. He had reassurred them that in the majority of sudden infant deaths, that was the rule rather than the exception; that no consistent cause had yet been identified. It was mostly the truth and they accepted it. He hadn't mentioned his own unease about the lack of findings. Not to them or to his wife. Yet she knew. Instinctively she knew.

He turned to look at her, then back at the ceiling. "I don't know how you do it, Marnie," he said. "Yes, it's wrong. I don't know what it is, but there's something missing."

Chapter Three
June 18

Mid-June: that pupal time, no longer spring yet not quite summer. A season for preparation, full of hidden activity, energy wrapped in a cocoon of warm gentle breezes.

Two months had passed since Todd McEwen's death. The tragedy had followed its natural course; Stuart's memory of the event had faded, the edges already blurred. After that first meeting with the parents he had replayed the events of the evening over and over in his mind, trying in vain to find the source of his unease, the missing piece. And gradually the combination of other interests and his responsibilities at work had driven the incident from his mind. It had been a full month since he had last thought of it.

He had seen Brian McEwen several times since the death, each time no more than a friendly wave. But the months, or the tragedy—or both—had cemented the friendship between the two women. They spent time together almost daily, shopping or running, but mostly in quiet, comfortable conversation. Their talks at first centered around the baby's death. But as Jill's grief slowly appeared to resolve, the topics lightened. They laughed easily together.

The two were sharing thoughts and morning coffee on the back deck. It was Saturday, and Stuart had slept late. As he puttered about the kitchen preparing breakfast, snatches of the women's conversation drifted through the open screen. Jill was talking.

". . . interesting how we keep bouncing from crisis to crisis. Two years ago, when Brian's nephew died, they had the whole family around them. And even then it seemed like everyone was still wiped from his cousin's problem the year before. They were incredible, his family I mean.

They have this old uncle who just seemed to show up about a week after, almost out of nowhere. And all of a sudden everything changed. He just radiated reassurance. He walks into a room and everyone's problems just melt away. . . ."

Stuart hadn't been following the conversation. But something had clicked in him; an alarm sounding somewhere. "What was that, Jill?" he called through the screen.

"Oh hi, Stuart," she replied. "I thought I heard you banging away in there. I was just telling Marnie about this old uncle of Brian's who—"

"No, sorry, not that. You were saying something about your cousin, I think."

"Oh, right. The two other crib deaths. Brian's brother, and a cousin back in Pennsylvania."

Stuart's mind raced back to the evening with the McEwens. They had asked all the questions, and he had given all the answers. Despite Novak's suggestion, it hadn't occurred to him at the time to ask if there had been other, similar infant deaths in the family. Patterns of disease. Probabilities.

Toast and coffee in hand, he opened the screen door with his foot and joined the women on the deck. He looked at his wife, then at Jill. "Mind if I butt in for a minute?"

Both women smiled a welcome. He settled onto a chaise-longue.

"You might not want to talk about this, Jill, open old wounds sort of, but can I ask you some questions about those other crib deaths? Three in one family in the past, what is it, four years? Considering the expected incidence is only one in five hundred, that's pretty unusual."

Jill shrugged. "No, I don't mind." She laughed nervously, glancing at Marnie. "But I think Marnie might be getting pretty sick of listening to this."

She told him everything she could remember about the two events. The first, the cousin's, had occurred under circumstances very similar to her own. The mother had discovered the baby dead at four in the morning. Totally unexpected, totally devastating. The baby, only six weeks old, was being double-diapered for a minor problem with one of its hips but was otherwise the picture of health. Jill remembered holding the baby just a week before his death, laughing with his mother at the wad of diapers wedging his legs apart. She also recalled the parents' anger and frustration when the postmortem examination failed to reveal a cause of death.

She continued, articulate, her voice expressive, but the tone, the timbre, changed. A crack had opened, a wound etched on the surface. "You know, that was the worst part for us, too. Not knowing what caused it. It's like you go through all this grief and anguish and you feel someone owes you an explanation. Like a consolation prize. And when you don't get it you feel cheated . . . again."

She shook her hair from her eyes and smiled quickly, shrugging again at Marnie. She continued.

The cousin had since had two other children, a boy and a girl, both normal and healthy.

The other death, Brian's nephew, was slightly different. They had already had a child—a boy, born just after the cousin's baby. The following year their second child was born, also a boy. He was two weeks early, but not premature according to his eight-and-a-half-pound birth weight. He was like a rock, completely healthy, until his death at eight months. Jamie, Brian's brother, and his wife, Theresa, had been out for the evening, returning home just after midnight. Jamie had driven the babysitter home while Theresa got ready for bed and checked on the children. She found the baby in his crib, unresponsive but still warm. Not waiting for her husband to return, she had rushed the baby to the hospital, where a full arrest resuscitation procedure had been carried out. Without success. Jill recalled the subsequent police investigation of the babysitter, the negative autopsy report, the lack of trauma or other apparent cause of death. Jamie and Theresa had had another child since then, a girl, now one year old and healthy.

Something was there, something she hadn't mentioned. Stuart's questions were becoming more direct, more insistent. "Did you know them well enough to know if they had any prenatal problems? Your sister-in-law or your cousin, I mean. Like toxemia? Or infections? Anything?"

Jill hesitated before answering. "Yes and no. I mean Theresa I was pretty close with; but no, she had a pretty routine pregnancy. The usual morning sickness, but as far as I'm aware nothing serious. I didn't know Debbie all that well, the cousin I mean. But she and Theresa were pregnant at the same time with Theresa's first baby, and they spent a lot of time together. Theresa didn't mention any problems with Debbie. I think they were both more concerned about winning the race than about their pregnancies."

"Winning the race?" Stuart asked. "You mean who was going to deliver first?"

"Right." Jill paused. "Well, sort of. But it was more than that. They were racing for the crib."

"The crib?" He was lost now.

"Well, it's pretty silly actually," she explained. "Jamie and his cousin had agreed that whichever baby was born first would get to use the crib. It's an old crib Brian's uncle made during the war." She looked over at Marnie. "The same uncle I was telling you about, Marnie, with all the vibes. Anyway, it's kind of a tradition to pass it around within the family whenever a baby is born. But with Theresa and Debbie both expecting at the same time, they couldn't both use it. So they decided first come first served. And Debbie won, sort of. . . ." Her voice faltered again. She cleared her throat and continued, quieter now, her eyes downcast, "As it turned out, when Debbie's baby died they sent the crib to Jamie and Theresa. So they both got to use it."

Marnie had been silent, intent, watching and listening as her friend related the stories of the infant deaths. She coughed quietly. On some silent cue, she rose, gathering the empty cups. "Stu, Jill and I have a ten-thirty court."

Stuart frowned up at her, annoyed. But his protest died as quickly as her eyes met his, their message unmistakable: *Enough, Stuart. Enough for now.*

Jill too looked up, the wound fading from her eyes. Her tension had dissolved with the distraction. She stood and smiled at Stuart. "I personally don't need it, but her creaky old frame has to have at least a twenty-minute stretch before she steps on the court." She nudged Marnie playfully. Both women disappeared into the kitchen.

Stuart leaned back in the chaise. Racing for the crib. A shrouded image of the dark, solid crib formed in his mind and just as quickly was gone, leaving only a mist of questions and shadows. He shivered and looked up. For just a brief second a thin puff of cloud hid the morning sun.

Chapter Four
July 6

Two weeks had passed. Once again Stuart Rice was passing his coffee break with Novak in the pathologist's office. He poured two cups and relaxed in the chair beside Novak's desk.

"I've got a great one for you this time, Wally," he began.

A large part of Stuart's job as chief public health officer involved tracking down the sources of various disease outbreaks in the area. Too often they discussed one of these miniepidemics over the autopsy on one of its victims. But today's item was much more benign.

"You know Steve Chenowith? Been doing general practice in the suburbs for the past fifteen or so years? Busy practice; killing himself with work."

Novak nodded.

"Well, he decides to take two weeks with his wife in Hawaii. Can you believe it? This time of year? His first holiday in fifteen years and he goes to Hawaii. Anyway, he gets a locum in to do his practice—a kid straight out of his internship. Shows him around, makes sure everything is smooth, and off he goes.

"Well, the kid's doin' great. After the first two days he's about six inches shorter trying to keep up with Steve's volume. But he's holding his own.

"Then he sees this little guy in the office; seven months old, fever, off his food. Sounds acute, infectious, probably viral. So he looks in the kid's mouth and sees a white membrane all over the kid's uvula and soft palate. 'Aha', he says. 'Diphtheria.'

"So he packs the kid and its parents—who are scared shitless by now—off to the university hospital for isolation

21

and treatment. He phones the infectious diseases unit, talks with the head nurse, gives her the diagnosis and a whole raft of orders, and asks her to get the pediatrician on call to see the kid.

"The message finally filters through to the pediatrician, who hears the word *diphtheria*. He calls his chief resident. 'Get all the house staff you can find to examine this kid's throat,' he says, ' 'cause they'll probably never see another case.' And before you know it the hospital's damn near bankrupt supplying isolation gowns for every goddamned medical student in the university while they take turns sticking tongue depressors down the little guy's throat.

"Meanwhile, the whiz kid in the suburbs has announced to a whole waiting room full of patients that because of a recently discovered case of diphtheria he feels it's prudent to close the office for the day, just as a precaution. That was more than a week ago. He hasn't seen a patient since."

He paused, shifting himself in the chair. Novak was chuckling, and about to speak, but Stuart continued. "Wait now, Wally. It gets better.

"I get the message from some frazzled local public-health nurse that a diphtheria epidemic is upon us. So I start my whole goddamn team in on it. Contacts, quarantines, checking up on immunization status, organizing booster stations—have you any fucking idea how many kids there are in the suburbs? You wouldn't believe the lineups for booster shots.

"Anyway, two days ago a candy striper at the hospital is bringing the kid's supper to him on a paper plate. A nurse is in the room at the time and the candy striper is curious about all the commotion so she asks the nurse if she can see what diphtheria looks like. The nurse says sure, why not. The kid opens his mouth—like a robot by now—and the striper says, 'Gee, just like my little sister's thrush.'

"The nurse just about shits herself. She checks back through the pages and pages of orders and, sure enough, no one has ordered a throat swab on the kid. They all assumed the admitting G.P. had done it prior to sending him in."

Novak's sides were shaking now.

"You guessed it, Wally. The kid had monilial stomatitis—fucking thrush. His mouth cleared up completely after twenty-four hours on Nystatin. Christ, if that candy striper hadn't made that stupid comment, the poor little guy would have been there till Christmas with his 'diphtheria.' Christ. With the extra staff, overtime, vaccines, media reports, we've put out more than twenty grand, all for a fucking case of thrush."

Novak got up to fill his cup. "Twenty grand. You should send the bill to the whiz. What happened to him, by the way?"

"He's still there, but like I said he hasn't seen a soul since the whole thing began. Poor Steve Chenowith. When he gets back and finds the fan so full of shit, it'll be another fifteen years before he takes another holiday."

Both men were silent for a moment. "Speaking of fans and excrement, Stu, whatever happened with your neighbour, McEwen I think it was, with the crib death? Has the dust settled there yet?"

Rice had been so preoccupied with the mistaken diphtheria case that the crib deaths had been pushed from his mind. Now, with the so-called epidemic resolved, Novak's comment brought back all the questions, the puzzles.

"Pretty well," he replied. "At least they seem to have resolved most of it. Actually it's turned out to be quite an interesting event, Wally, from my perspective I mean. Apparently they've had two other crib deaths—not them, but in the family—over the last four years. Way more than the stats would predict. I haven't had a chance to give it much thought over the last week and a half, but if I get the opportunity I think I might check into it a bit more. You never know. I might get my name up in lights yet."

The opportunity arrived a lot sooner than he expected.

A truckload of topsoil lay in a mound on the McEwens' driveway.

"Shit, Marnie, why doesn't he just hire a front-end loader for an hour?" Stuart complained as he laced his sneakers. His wife had volunteered him to help Brian move the dirt to the back of the house.

"Stuart Rice, you've hardly seen Brian since the baby died. You said yourself the only thing that made the evening tolerable was the strength of his personality. Besides, you could use the exercise."

In fact, Stuart's protests were largely ceremonial. He didn't mind helping, and though he preferred getting his exercise on a tennis court, shoveling topsoil was a mindless, automatic task requiring little or no mental input. It was just what he needed after the last two weeks of stress working on the nonexistent diphtheria crisis. And his wife was right about Brian McEwen. He had been looking for an opportunity to get together with him again. And not just for the pleasure of his company. It might be a chance to get more information about the family's infant death problem.

It hadn't rained in more than two weeks. When delivered, the topsoil had sat black and pasture-fresh. Now, after five days in the midsummer sun, all traces of moisture had vanished. It was like dust. Shoveling it into wheelbarrows and transporting and spreading it were easy, almost effortless. Still, the difference in the two men's styles was remarkable. Stuart, working with a standard spade, took small, rapid bites from the pile, fifteen or twenty to the load. Brian, enormous and glistening in the morning heat, used an aluminum snow shovel he had brought from Pennsylvania. Slow, methodical. Four huge scoops filled his wheelbarrow. He reminded Stuart of the killer whale at the public aquarium, with himself the diminutive porpoise swimming alongside. An easy person to be with. Quiet, agreeable, a gentle humour about him. Even long periods of silence were comfortable. *The gentle giant,* Stuart mused.

McEwen broke the silence. "Time for a brew, Stuart?" They had been working steadily for more than two hours.

Stuart wiped a glove across his forehead. "Christ, I thought you'd never ask," he replied in mock complaint.

The two men sat on the steps nursing their drinks. The scraps of conversation they had shared until then consisted mainly of safe talk: sports, the weather, their jobs. With their beers half-finished and the conversation stilled, Stuart on an impulse moved it to another level.

"Brian, I don't want to fan old flames, so tell me if I'm out of line bringing this up, but a few weeks ago Jill was over and happened to mention that your brother had a problem two or three years back. Similar to yours I mean. A crib death."

McEwen's gaze dropped to the ground.

"And a cousin a year after that," Stuart pressed.

Brian nodded, staring off past the drive. "The other way around, actually. Don, that's my cousin, and Debbie lost their boy first. Then Jamie the next year." He flipped soil back and forth from hand to hand. Looking up at Stuart, he asked, "When did Jill tell you this?" His voice was puzzled, concerned.

"It must have been two weekends ago." Stuart was worried that he had trespassed on some forbidden territory. "Listen, Brian, I'm sorry I brought this up. If you'd rather not talk about it I understand."

Brian leaned back on his elbows, relaxed. "As a matter of fact I don't mind talking about it at all. Todd's death is history. I've come to terms with it, and it's time to move on. But I think it must be a lot easier for me, maybe for fathers in general, to accept something like that than it is for the mother. For Jill anyway. I'm surprised she was able to talk to you about it. She puts on a pretty brave face, but it's eating her up inside. I know it takes time, but she's still devastated by the whole thing. Maybe this is a good sign, her talking to you and Marnie about it I mean."

He paused and took another swallow from his bottle. "Anyway, the other ones you mentioned, why do you ask?"

"I'm not sure, actually. I thought it was just curiosity at first, but now it's piqued my professional interest. Part of my job involves putting together individual pieces of information to see if some kind of pattern emerges. Pieces like these three cases. Three sudden infant deaths in one family in four or five years is unusual."

"Four, actually," Brian interrupted.

"Four years, then," Stuart agreed. "I missed the first part of the conversation when Jill was talking about it. I don't think I got the dates quite right."

"No," Brian interrupted again. "Four crib deaths I mean. Counting our own."

Stuart was confused now. "That's even more significant, but I could swear Jill only mentioned two others— your brother and a cousin."

"Well it goes back a few years. Hell, I think it was 1970 or '69. Before Jill and I met, anyway. A second or third cousin had a crib death. Don knew them quite well. We get a Christmas card every year but I don't know them at all. Theirs was a boy too, I think. In fact I'm sure it was. They named him after an uncle."

Stuart probed further. "Brian, is there any way I could get some information on your brother and cousins? Just names and addresses would be all I'd need."

Brian thought for a moment. "That's no problem with Jamie and Theresa. Don and his wife, though, they might be another story. They were really crushed when their boy died. They're still really overprotective of their other two kids. Don's cousin, Peter I think it is, Jill has their address somewhere. I don't know how they've adjusted to it. But it's been so long for them I can't see it being a problem."

"Actually it wouldn't involve any personal contact with them at all. With the parents' names and addresses I can get all the clinical information I'd need through the Centers for Disease Control in Atlanta. Collating health stats is something we do all the time."

McEwen raised his eyebrows. "You mean a crib death four or ten or fourteen years ago? You have enough information on file on something like that to come to some kind of conclusion about it? That's a little hard to believe."

"It's all filed under your social security number, Brian. You'd be amazed at the data being collected about us under those innocent little numbers. And all of it available to anyone with 'justifiable access,' they call it."

Brian shrugged. "If it's just names and addresses you need then I can't see the harm." He drained his bottle and stood up. "Got the energy to spread the rest of this?"

Stuart rose and picked up his shovel. "Is Jamie your only brother, Brian."

Brian's shovel sank into the pile. "Nope," he grunted.

"One older brother, Michael. We call him 'the Rabbit.' Five kids. He's with the state department. Gets consulate postings all over the world. None of his kids have been born in the same country. Great kids. Wild horses. Even Mickey, the oldest. Has some kind of arthritis, like his mother, but nothing keeps him down. Apparently. We hardly ever see them."

His wheelbarrow loaded, Brian dropped the shovel, lifted the handles, and disappeared around the side of the house. His own load only half-full, Stuart struggled to keep up. *One family, four crib deaths, all boys,* he thought. *It's a start.*

Chapter Five
July 12

"Donald Thayer and Peter Thayer. Are they brothers, Brian?"

As he had promised, Brian had provided Stuart with the names and addresses of his brother and two cousins.

"No," he replied. "Cousins. First cousins, I think. They're my cousins too, for that matter, two or three times removed, something like that."

Stuart looked at the first name on the list. "Is your brother Jamie or James? The CDC computer gets fussy."

"James. Sorry about that."

Although he knew a lot of people, Stuart had never developed a relationship that was both close and comfortable with anyone other than his wife. He was introspective, almost secretive by nature. And this, combined with a natural impatience that at times bordered on intolerance, served him poorly in his relationships with others. But since his morning of shared labour with Brian McEwen a week ago, their friendship had matured into an easy, natural bond. There was something different about this "gentle giant." A warmth. A direct, open honesty that invited closeness.

He waved the list as he departed. "Thanks, Brian. If I get a chance I'll crunch these through today. I'll keep you posted."

Later that day, with the pressing part of his work out of the way, Stuart turned to the monitor and keyboard on the console beside his desk. It never ceased to amaze him how completely he had adapted to this electronic presence in his work. Any hesitation and fear he had once harboured towards computers had long vanished.

During his introductory period with the machines his instructor had boasted that within two minutes he could have a list of all the left-handed, brown-haired, blue-eyed, female diabetics with herpes in the country, along with the names, sex, and ages of all their relatives going forward and backward three generations. The first- and second-year secretaries in the class had been impressed, but Stuart personally had written the comment off as part of the hard sell. Despite his cynicism, he had been sufficiently intrigued to try it out after the class had left. The instructor was wrong. It had taken almost four minutes. Nevertheless, he had been impressed enough to give the machine a chance. Now he couldn't function without it, and it staggered him at times to imagine how his predecessors in epidemiology had ever survived.

Personal medical data had been collected and centralized for decades. But with the twin emergence of a standardized medical nomenclature and vastly improved computer technology, the amount of information and its accessibility had literally exploded. Now, virtually all the major public-health facilities in the country had interconnected communication systems, all linked through a massive mainframe at the Centers for Disease Control in Georgia.

Since all the health data at the CDC was stored under individual social security numbers, his first task was to get those numbers for the four names on his list. To do so, he keyed in the four names, then linked up with the central demographic data bank in Washington, D.C. Within seconds he had the numbers. He then switched to the CDC link, repeated the numbers, and entered the information categories he was interested in. For each of the four men he wanted the names, dates of birth, and sexes of all offspring. In addition, he needed the identification numbers of all of the children and their current health status at level one, which simply meant whether they were alive or dead. He wanted to examine the children who had died in relation to their surviving siblings. A family health search such as this, a genealogy trace in which the end point was not pre-established, could be an enormously complex task.

He had learned from experience to accumulate and digest his data in gradual, logical bits.

The screen blanked momentarily, then filled. The information given was identical to what Brian had described.

McEwen, Brian David	M/11/20/82-d	824644
McEwen, James Robert	M/1/27/77-a	771129
	M/4/10/78-d	783461
	F/8/11/80-a	805818
Thayer, Donald Michael	M/1/14/77-d	771033
	F/8/1/79-a	799635
	M/4/14/83-a	8321162
Thayer, Peter Graham	M/8/30/69-d	6995738
	F/15/7/71-a	7113117
	F/9/28/74-a	7457529

Stuart looked at the first entry. That would be Todd, he thought.

There was nothing new or startling. Just as Brian had said, each man had had at least one child, and one of the children in each family group was dead. Concentrating for the moment on the living children, he asked for the status of health for each child at the second, third, and fourth levels. He was looking for life-threatening diseases, serious illnesses, and other illnesses, respectively. The screen returned the information that none of the surviving children had ever had a reported significant illness.

Noting the identity numbers of the four deceased children, he blanked the screen, reentered the numbers, and requested primary causes of death on each. All four entries were immediately returned, followed by the same letters: SIDS-A+. He requested secondary and tertiary causes of death (precipitating illness or other conditions contributing to death) and received again: SIDS-A+. Even fourth-level causes of death, any significant premorbid medical problem, produced the same result. All four had died of sudden infant death syndrome. None had had any reported health problems at any time prior to his death. And all four had been autopsied (A+). Noting this last point, he requested and copied the names of the institutions where the postmortem examinations had been done. He would need copies of those reports.

He wasn't surprised or disappointed by the information he had gathered so far. It matched what Brian had told him and reinforced his faith in the digital tools of his trade. But the search now would become more involved. For each of the dead children he needed to construct a genealogy. Tracing even the simplest of family trees back through two or three generations was extremely complex, especially if individual generation searches were required. Done manually, it could take weeks, even months. He entered Todd McEwen's identity number and asked for a level-one search. The result should be a list of all of Todd McEwen's first cousins. Seconds later the monitor presented him with a list of eight names, each with sex, birthdate, and primary health status. All but one was alive.

That's Jamie's three kids and "the Rabbit's" five, he thought. As Brian had told him, Jamie's second son was the only SIDS victim. He tried Todd's number at the second level in the same generation—second cousins. No additional names resulted. This implied simply that the McEwen family was relatively small. Any connection between it and the Thayers was at least at the third-cousin level.

He turned next to Peter Thayer's son. A level-one search produced four first cousins, none with SIDS. At the second level he expected to see Donald Thayer's son as the only second cousin having died of crib death. But when he keyed in the request, the screen remained blank. Stuart cursed, expecting an error signal or a link interruption. After several minutes the monitor beeped softly, and Stuart's eyes widened as the screen quickly filled with twenty-two entries. As he had expected, Donald Thayer's son was there, with SIDS following his name. But there were four other names on the list followed by the same letters, one with the code G-1. More startling than their numbers was the fact that all four new crib deaths were males.

"Jesus Christ. Four more kids in the same family. All boys."

He asked for an explanation of the G-1 code. It referred

to generation minus one, the preceding generation. Requesting an identity on this entry, Stuart discovered that it was Peter Thayer's brother, Gregory P. Thayer, born 9/30/45.

"Nineteen forty-five. You're going too fast, Rice. Slow down. One step at a time." He returned to Todd McEwen. He wanted to confirm the relationship between him and the Thayer children. He wasn't surprised when the screen replied "level 3."

"Third cousins. Okay, third cousins, let's see how far back you go." He was talking out loud to himself now.

He checked the entire Thayer family back through three generations, including all the crib death infants previously discovered. No additional cases emerged. Checking at the fourth generation level, he wasn't surprised to get an ODR signal—out of data range.

"Dr. Rice, line two," his secretary called through the open door.

"Not now, Jean. Take a number, would you?"

"It's your wife."

"Shit," he muttered. He knew better than to ignore Marnie's calls.

"Hi, hon," he said, tucking the receiver between his ear and shoulder, greeting his wife while continuing his search. He asked for fourth-level causes of death on each of the four new crib death cases. For each the monitor returned the same message: SIDS-A+.

". . . and, Stu, we're invited over to Jill and Brian's for dinner tonight. Stop off and get some wine on your way home, would you?" Marnie was saying.

"What kind of autopsies?" he replied. All five children had been autopsied. Again he requested the names of the hospitals where they had been performed.

"What? Stuart? Are you there?"

"Oh sure, Marnie, sorry. What was that?"

"Which? The autopsies or the wine?" she asked.

"What wine?"

Marnie clucked at him over the phone, recognizing his distraction. She repeated her request, making sure he understood it this time. "See you at home, professor." She chuckled, blowing a kiss over the line before hanging up.

As he put down the phone, Stuart realized his concentration was shattered. It was closing time anyway. He made sure that he had a printed copy of the list of crib death infants before terminating the CDC link. He straightened his desk and rose to leave. Before giving the list to Jean to send for the autopsy reports, he looked at it once more. Eight names in all. Two McEwens, four Thayers, one Lasalle, one Wellington. McEwen and Thayer he recognized. The other two were new, but strangely, vaguely familiar.

His hand trembled slightly, barely noticeable, as he dropped the paper onto the desk.

"Could we send for these in the morning, Jean?" he asked.

He left the office quickly to escape the air-conditioned chill. Despite the warmth of the afternoon sun, he was still shivering when he reached his car. *This is all I need*, he thought as he turned on the heater. *A goddamn summer cold*.

Chapter Six
July 13

By the time Stuart arrived home his shivering had stopped. Bad luck; he had forgotten the wine and could have used his symptoms as an excuse. Marnie, convincingly angry over his forgetful behaviour, criticized him constantly while they dressed, only to reach into the refrigerator as they left the house, extracting a chilled bottle of domestic white.

Stuart looked at the wine, frowning. "If you were so sure I'd forget, why did you bother phoning in the first place?"

She took his elbow, leading him down the steps. "I wasn't sure you'd forget until I did phone." She squeezed his arm. "Not to worry, darling. They say the mind is the first to go. And it's not that part of you I'm interested in anyway."

Dinner with the McEwens was a quiet, relaxed affair. The attachment between the women was natural. They shared their feelings and activities much as sisters would. And, to Stuart's continuing surprise and delight, his friendship with Brian continued to deepen. They were both naturally quiet, private men, ill at ease in crowds. But the long periods of silence together were neither forced nor uncomfortable.

The silences were few that evening, however, due in large part to three bottles of wine, consumed in the main by the two men, before- and after-dinner liqueurs, and a dessert heavily laced with brandy.

The meal itself was accompanied by a raucous succession of anecdotes. As they finished dessert, Stuart recounted the story of the diphtheria epidemic, slightly embellished in the retelling. Marnie had heard it before, but Brian, happily drunk, listened in amazement. Especially as Stuart added the epilogue: the young doctor who had started the whole crisis had ended up in a mobile government medical clinic serving the south coast of Alaska.

"And the irony if it," Stuart concluded, "is that it's very likely he'll run into a kid with diphtheria while he's up there. But he's so gunshy now he'll probably end up treating it as a thrush."

The women, Irish coffees in hand, pushed their chairs from the table and moved to the den. One at each end of the sofa, legs curled under, they were soon lost in their own conversation.

The men were silent, each content in his own solitude.

After a few minutes Brian asked, "Word has it you're a hot-shot tennis player, Stuart. Your skill wouldn't extend to the table version, would it?"

"Ping-Pong you mean?"

His host nodded, a glint in his eye.

"The glove has been dropped, I take it?" Stuart asked.

"It has indeed," his host replied, rising. "Come along. Time for a lesson."

They continued their banter as they made their way upstairs. The house had originally boasted six bedrooms, but the previous owner had converted two adjoining rooms on the second floor into one large activity area. A centrally placed table-tennis table now dominated the room.

"Choose your weapon, Dr. Rice," Brian offered.

Stuart shrugged and picked up the nearest rubber-coated racquet. "This'll do," he said nonchalantly.

The contest was on.

Despite his enthusiasm, Brian's size was too great a handicap. Stuart, even with the alcohol affecting his coordination, easily dominated his host. He snapped a winner past Brian's backhand for the match. Casually tossing the racquet onto the table, he nodded solemnly, his face serious. "Interesting game, table tennis. You should try it sometime, Brian."

McEwen smiled. "Brave words, for a dwarf," he countered. "I'll meet you downstairs, Stuart. Nature calls." He turned into the master bedroom.

Stuart, still feeling the effects of the wine, turned in the wrong direction as he left the room. He reached the end of the hall before he realized his mistake. As he turned again, he noticed the open door to the nursery.

Curious, he looked in, then entered, cautious, aware of a vague sense of trespass. The packing boxes were gone, and the carpet was unrolled on the floor. Pictures of horses and clowns hung gaily on the walls. The crib, dark and empty, still stood under the window, the change table against the far wall, a half-empty package of disposable diapers beside it. The room looked more like a child's nursery now than it had the morning of Todd McEwen's death.

Stuart was startled by the voice behind him.

"She just can't let it go." Brian stood leaning against the door frame, his arms crossed in front of him.

"She still spends hours every day in here, just standing, looking at the crib, out the window. Not crying or talking or anything. I've gotten up at four in the morning and found her in here, just standing, staring."

Stuart nodded. It was the kind of encounter he ordinarily would have tried to avoid. But with Brian's gentle, open manner he felt comfortable, unpressured. Absently he ran his hand over the top rail of the crib.

"Is this the crib Jill was talking about, Brian? She mentioned something about your uncle making a crib that the whole family uses."

Brian nodded. "Have you had a chance to look at it? It's really quite a work of art."

He snapped on the overhead light, crossed the room, and pulled the crib under the light.

"Apparently he built it in his spare time during the war. Hardware must have been scarce back then—there are no nails or screws in it anywhere. It all just snaps together. I think he must have cut the fasteners out of plate metal of some kind. The damn thing is solid as a rock." He shook the crib gently. "In fact I've squeezed into it myself, if you can believe it. It didn't budge." He rapped a knuckle against the top rail. "I'm not sure what kind of wood it's made of. It's so hard it almost feels like granite."

Stuart was fingering the mismatched slat on the headboard.

"In fact," Brian continued, "the original slat there was broken when I got the crib from Jamie. He sent it wrapped up in cardboard, but I think the post office must have dropped it out of an airplane somewhere. I thought I'd break my wrists getting the broken pieces out. There was a big notch or hole in it, which I guess must have weakened it. I doubt it would have broken otherwise. Anyway, what's left of it is now out in the garage wedging the door spring away from the wall, and doing quite well. It's tough as steel. That spring snapped an ax handle on me."

He was silent for a moment, rubbing his hand over the names carved into the side of the crib.

"I've been meaning to crate it up and send it off to a cousin somewhere up in Oregon. But Jill's been so hung up on it and the room, I've been afraid to change anything just yet. They aren't expecting their baby until around Christmas anyway, so I guess there's no rush."

Stuart was examining the names on the crib. The quality of the carving varied with the fathers' skill. Thayer, Jackson, Lasalle, Assad, Wellington, Bucknall, Harrison, McEwen . . . He looked back over the list. *Lasalle, Wellington,* he had seen those names before: the two vaguely familiar names he had noted on the computer list from the CDC. He must have registered them subconsciously the morning he had first examined Todd McEwen's body. He shivered slightly. A tiny finger of ice touched the back of his neck.

"Who are these people, Brian?" he asked, indicating the other names: Jackson, Assad, Harrison, Bucknall.

"No idea. Cousins I guess. Harrison is the name of the couple I'm supposed to be sending the crib off to. Maybe it's the same one. The whole thing is a Thayer tradition actually, and I'm not all that close to them. My cousin Don Thayer, the one whose name I gave you the other day, he and Jamie are quite close, even though they're only second or third cousins. Jamie used the crib for his kids, and he still had it when Jill got pregnant. We figured if he was closely related enough to use it, then we were too. So we asked him to send it on to us."

Still fogged from the alcohol, Stuart's attention was too

fragile to concentrate for long on the crib or the names. He rubbed his hands over his arms.

"I'm freezing. What kind of host are you anyway, McEwen?"

Brian smiled. "Poor fellow. Need a little more warmth in your veins, do you?" He turned and left the room, waiting for his guest in the hall.

Stuart followed. At the door he paused and scanned the room a final time. Again it registered, even through the alcohol haze. An inconsistency. An intangible, impalpable doubt. The icy finger worked its way past his collar, tracing its nail over his shoulder, down his back. Again he noticed the tremor as he reached for the light.

Chapter Seven
July 14

"I hope you brought cash, Rice. I don't take credit cards."

Wally Novak had just won the second set of their weekly tennis game, six love. Ordinarily the score would have been reversed, but Rice's overindulgence the night before had taken its toll. His ground strokes were erratic, his first serve rarely in. It felt like an adventure every time he rushed the net. Adding insult to injury, Novak had taken the final point on a second-service ace.

"You'll probably never forget this, will you, Wally? And you'll make damn sure I never do either." Stuart tossed his racquet and slumped onto the bench, disgusted.

"I seem to recall you being a gracious loser the last time I beat you." Novak was enjoying himself, savouring his victory. "Come along. To the showers with you. Then we'll drown your sorrow with a pint, on you of course."

"Christ, it was the demon rum that did me in already," Stuart protested, gathering his equipment. "I just might never drink again."

The two men were dressing after their shower. Novak, no longer gloating over his win, had changed the subject. "Any results yet on your SIDS investigation, Stuart?" he asked.

"In fact yes, now that you mention it," Stuart replied. "Did I tell you there were three other crib deaths in the family, before the McEwen one I mean?"

Novak nodded.

"As it turned out, when I ran Todd's and the three new names, the CDC files gave me four more infant deaths in the same family."

Eyebrows arched, Novak looked around from the mirror

where he was brushing his hair. "You bloodhound. That's what—seven? eight crib deaths? All in the same generation?"

"Eight. And no, the earliest one was the preceding generation, back in the mid-forties. I haven't worked out the full genealogy yet, but with the generation jump there's a good chance we're looking at something genetic. There's not a lot on file at CDC as far as clinical detail is concerned, so I sent for the postmortems. I might lean on you for an interpretation, by the way, if I get stuck.

"There's something else about this though, Wally. Last night Marnie and I were over at . . ."

Stuart was about to comment on finding the same names on the crib in the McEwens' nursery as were on the CDC list of infant deaths when he was interrupted by the arrival of Andrew Turpin, one of Novak's pathology co-workers at the hospital. Turpin had just come off the court.

"You're just in time, Andy," Novak greeted his colleague.

Stuart knew the worst was yet to come.

"Our epidemiologist friend is buying today. Poor lad claims to have had his entrails pickled last night. If you ask me, he played his usual brilliant game. He was simply outclassed."

Stuart rolled his eyes and winked at Turpin, who in turn clucked in mock sympathy. The three headed for the lounge, all thoughts of crib deaths gone from Stuart's mind.

Until the following day.

Stuart rushed through the urgent correspondence on his desk, setting aside everything that could wait. He was too eager to trace the new names he had seen on the McEwens' crib to concentrate on the more mundane aspects of his work. As it was, he was unable to re-establish his computer link with Atlanta until mid-afternoon.

He could remember only three of the four new names he had seen on the crib: Harrison, Jackson, and Bucknall. Harrison had already shown up on the CDC list as a same-generation cousin of Brian McEwen, but not as a crib death. Which left only two names to cross-reference. The fact that neither Bucknall nor Jackson nor the missing third name had shown up as crib deaths suggested that the deaths were probably related to some closed, genetically inherited disorder that affected only a small portion of the family tree, the Thayer-McEwen branch. But to prove this he had to trace the Thayer-McEwen family back to its origin, then run a prospective trace on the two new names from that point. Depending on where the new names married into the family, the connection between the two family groups would be either genetically familial or nonfamilial. If, as he suspected, it was nonfamilial—that is, with no common, shared genetic background—then the basis for his theory would be firm. Provided, of course, he did not turn up any more crib deaths with the new names.

Using the CDC genealogy files, he quickly found the link between the Thayer and McEwen branches of the family. Brian McEwen's paternal grandmother and Donald Thayer's paternal grandfather were sister and brother. He used this as his index point to cross-reference the two new names. He asked first for a familial, genetic search. Nothing. There were no Jacksons or Bucknalls with a direct genetic link to the Thayer-McEwen side of the family. So far so good.

As he expected, the nonfamilial link between the Jacksons and the Thayer-McEwens occurred at the same generation level as Brian McEwen's parents, the generation before the first known crib death. In fact, Peter Thayer's mother, May, was the first Jackson in the family.

As the significance of that sank in, a faint, uneasy chill settled over Stuart. Not only was Peter Thayer's brother Gregory the earliest of the discovered crib deaths, his son too had suffered the same fate. They were May Jackson's son and grandson. It was still consistent with a nonfamilial link, but it was close. Too close.

He traced the Jackson link laterally and forward from May's marriage into the Thayer family. She had had two brothers. They in turn had produced six children and seven grandchildren. Of the grandchildren, three were Jacksons, three were Bucknalls. The seventh was Assad.

"Assad," Stuart said aloud. The missing fourth name from the crib.

The Jackson and Thayer families were tied together by

May Jackson's marriage to Walter Thayer. The Thayer and McEwen families, however, were linked through a completely separate branch of the family tree, a full generation before the Thayer-Jackson marriage. The Thayer-McEwens shared all the known crib deaths. All that remained now was to confirm that no one in the Jackson branch of the family had suffered the same fate.

Rather than proceed with the time-consuming health-status searches he had used for the initial names, he simply keyed in a request for crib death occurrences in the Jackson-Bucknall-Assad complex. Again the screen cleared and remained blank for more than a minute. Stuart's unease resurfaced. With each request for a search, specific codes were looked for in the data files. If the codes were not present, the search proceeded quickly, almost instantaneously. As the code was identified in the data, however, the software was constructed to arrange the information in logical sequence, collate it with each previous and subsequent occurrence of the code, and eventually present the data collected. Even for an instrument of this power, this took time. And the more occurrences of the code in the data, the more time it took.

Stuart leaned back in his chair, rocking gently, his arms folded in front of him. The monitor beeped softly, new information on line. Five names filled the top portion of the screen: three Jacksons, one Bucknall, one Assad, each followed by the same letters: SIDS-A+.

"Sweet Jesus. What the fuck is going on with this family?"

Stuart just stared at the screen, trying to absorb, rationalize the new information. His hereditary-transmission theory was dead. There was no genetic link between the Jackson and the McEwen branches of the family. Yet, both displayed an abnormally high incidence of sudden infant death. Coincidence? Possibly. But he knew it wasn't just pure chance. He was on to something. He had no working hypothesis now, no rationale. Nothing but a shadowy gut feeling that he had uncovered something . . . different.

Automatically now he requested information on health status and cause of death on all the Jackson, Bucknall, and Assad members of the family. None of the survivors had any significant health problems. None of the deceased had a reported contributing cause of death. All had died of sudden infant death syndrome. All had been autopsied. Again he called for the names of the hospitals where the postmortem examinations had been done.

As he handed the list to his secretary, a familiar chill crept over him. Todd McEwen's death had unlocked a door. But now, as he peered into the shadows beyond, he found not a room with windows and familiar walls, but a hall. A hall dark and seemingly endless, lined with doors, all of them locked.

But more than that. A cold energy had enveloped him. Some unseen momentum had moved him through the first door. And had closed it behind him. He was committed.

Chapter Eight
July 26

Gentle summer days and nights ran into weeks. Stuart tried to push the SIDS investigation from his thoughts as he concentrated on his work. But as each of the crib death autopsy reports arrived his interest was rekindled. More than just interest, more than just professional curiosity. His involvement in the deaths, passive, even reluctant at first, had shaken something in him, awakened long-dormant feelings: the compassion he had felt as a medical student and in his first few years of practice, the excitement and concern smothered by the crushing patient load as his practice expanded, demanding ever more of his time and energy just to stay in control. A passion never aroused since, never stimulated by the methodical tedium of epidemiological research and administration. Until now. Each report was like an intoxicant. He read each one immediately.

When all thirteen reports had arrived he devoted an entire afternoon to reading them again. Two of the reports— Gregory Thayer and one of the Jacksons—were more than thirty years old. Besides a relative lack of detail, they contained several rarely used, unfamiliar terms. A brief phone call to Novak for an interpretation solved that problem.

Other than reaffirming that all the children were males, he could find no other feature common to each. He went through the reports again, and then a third time, making copious notes as he read. He recorded heights and weights, ages at death, organ sizes, tissue histology, biochemical and toxicology results. He broke each category down into smaller and smaller subunits, making separate lists of positive and negative findings.

When he had finished, his negative list ran to more than

twenty tightly scribbled pages of tables, arrows, and aster-
isks. The positive findings were disappointingly few. All
were males of varying ages less than one year old. Two
had an undescended testicle; two others had a small benign ventricular septal defect. One had a minor syndactyly
with his third and fourth toes joined, and one, Todd
McEwen, had a birthmark, a hemangioma. He flipped the
list onto the desk; all fluff, nothing significant, nothing
causative.

He rubbed the fatigue from his eyes. He was missing
something. "It's probably staring me in the face," he muttered as he pushed his chair back from the desk.

He took the reports and his notes to Wally Novak, who
offered to review the cases. But when Stuart returned the
next day the pathologist simply shook his head.

"Sorry, Stuart. These are pretty bland cookies. I'm not
totally current on all the latest as far as crib death goes,
but I can't see anything exciting here at all. One of the
reports is from Mass. General, from one of the big national studies I told you about. One of the Jackson cases, I
think. Shit, they did everything on him. Vitreous assays,
neurotransmitters, carotid body histology, the works. But
they found nothing.

"I noticed that only five or six had references to the
length of the pregnancy. But wherever it was mentioned
the gestation was normal. I'm not sure that's much help
anyway. I only got part way through your notes, but it was
pretty obvious you were sifting things out finer and finer.
Trying to analyze data like that manually can turn you into
a vegetable. Can't the geniuses in Atlanta help?"

Stuart shook his head. "Not much. They can only corre-
late the data they're given. It's mainly epidemiological and
I've got all that from them already. I could feed the
clinical stuff back in, but their reference categories are too
broad for such a small study population anyway. I need
something a lot more refined. I thought about getting
someone to rework one of the spreadsheet programs at the
department head office, but they're built right into the
hardware. And getting an outside consultant to come up
with a custom-built program costs an arm and a leg."

Novak crossed his ankles on his desk. "This might be way over their heads," he said, "but have you thought of trying the computer science faculty at the university? Andy Turpin's niece is doing a summer semester and was looking for a project for a paper. I think she found one, but apparently, according to Andy anyway, they're always looking for real-life stuff for the students to practice on."

Stuart was skeptical. "Your first comment was probably closer to the mark, Wally. It's probably over their heads." He fingered the reports. "This is pretty technical stuff. Without a fairly intimate grounding in medicine and pathology I can't see a second- or third-year computer science student being much help."

Novak thought for a moment and nodded sagely. "You're probably right," he said as he leaned back in his chair, sipping his coffee. "After all, if two great white doctors like us look this thing over six ways from Sunday and don't come up with sweet fuck-all, what could a mere candy striper do?"

"Dr. Rice? Oh good, Dr. Hamilton is expecting you."

The secretary led him through a door into an adjoining office. Following Novak's suggestion, Stuart had arranged to meet with the assistant dean of the faculty of science, a Dr. T. R. Hamilton. All week he had formed a mental impression of a tweed-jacketed, rumpled-looking older man, the stereotypical university professor. The real Dr. Hamilton was none of these. The tweed jacket was a crisply tailored grey suit and tie. The rumpled professor looked more like a Wall Street executive. A tall, attractive, stern-looking blond woman in her mid-thirties shook Stuart's hand with a surprisingly firm grasp. She motioned him to a chair.

"Dr. Rice. You're an epidemiologist with the department of public health?" It was more statement than question. "We don't have a rat problem. How can we help you?"

Stuart wasn't sure if she was joking. With her low, almost masculine voice and stern, emasculating stare, he decided to ignore the remark.

"I'm not sure if you can help me or not," he began.

He tried to describe his problem, the crib death investigation, the unusually high incidence of so many cases of SIDS in one family, and, tapping the briefcase on his lap, the increasingly complex mass of data he had compiled. He tried to outline some of the problems he was having in analyzing his data manually, describing some of the technical details involved in each case.

She cut him off. "Dr. Rice, my understanding of the medical significance of your problem is hardly relevant. You are obviously looking for some means of analyzing your data electronically. Otherwise you wouldn't be here." Her voice and manner remained unchanged. "I'm not sure how much you understand about data-processing, but it really doesn't matter whether your problem pertains to medicine or market research or whatever. Complexity and technicality are irrelevant. Any data base can be broken down into its component parts. Processing and comparing those component parts then becomes a simple matter of system design."

Her condescending manner was becoming more irritating. "Actually, I'm fairly familiar with the available applications, Dr. Hamilton. I guess my main concern is whether or not this is the kind of project you might be interested in. I'm not a programmer by any means, but I was concerned that the technical medical aspects of the information here might make the whole project too complex for your students." He immediately regretted his words.

Hamilton bristled. "Quite frankly, Dr. Rice, my concern is just the opposite: that your project might be too simple. As I just pointed out, the technical medical issue is moot, trivial in fact. All that's involved is the creation of a program with enough boxes to accommodate each of the pieces of information in your files. Then we simply start shuffling the boxes. The shuffling can be as basic or as complex as you like. If each box has six sides, then each side can be matched with each side of six other boxes. Or we can give each box eight sides, or twenty, or a hundred, depending on the statistical parameters you indicate."

She sighed. Stuart was about to speak, but she contin-

ued. "All things considered, I suppose this is the kind of
practical application we're looking for, although it might
not be as challenging as we usually like. I should point
out, however, that there are conditions to our accepting
project applications such as this.

"If it's to be valid as a student project, then the student
herself . . . or himself," she added, "must do all the
material analysis and breakdown. She must enter all the
data herself, fill all the boxes that is, and create all
the cross-referencing commands in the system. We welcome
an outline from the applicant, from yourself, indicating the
kind of processed information you're looking for. But it's
important that you understand that we will be looking at
this as a student project only. We can't guarantee it will
give you the answers you're looking for, or even that it
will necessarily be accurate. Although when the assign-
ments are handed in for marking we usually recommend
revisions and corrections. I should add that if past perfor-
mance is an indication, the resulting system will be within
one or two percent of the accuracy of anything you're
likely to get from a . . . professional." Her emphasis on
the word punctuated her disdain for anyone not associated
with the university, Stuart included.

"How long does something like this usually take?" he
asked.

"Well, these are summer students. If you can leave the
material here with me now, I'll assign a student to it. The
papers must be in by the second to last week in August.
With marking and revisions, it should be ready by the end
of August."

He tried to hide his disappointment. "That's four weeks!"

"If you took this to a professional, Dr. Rice, you'd be
fortunate to get anything at all within four months. And
for an outrageous fee, I might add."

He nodded, not wanting to press the issue. His manual
analysis was stonewalled anyway. And since it wasn't cost-
ing him anything, he had nothing to lose. He rose.

"Well, I'm grateful for all the help I can get at this
stage," he said lamely. "Thank you, Dr. Hamilton. I'll
leave the files with your secretary, shall I?"

She nodded, and smiled, the first time she had done so since he arrived. "You're still skeptical, Dr. Rice." She walked him to the door. "It's a fairly predictable initial reaction. We can't promise you anything, but I do think you'll be pleasantly surprised with the results." She extended her hand.

Stuart took it, squeezing harder than he usually would a woman's hand. He smiled, turned, and left. *Four fucking weeks,* he mouthed silently.

Chapter Nine
August

For Stuart, those four weeks were well occupied. At least as much as one could expect four late summer, weather-perfect weeks to be, they were well occupied. Cloudless skies, the temperatures hovering in the low eighties by day, cooling off comfortably at night. A childhood summer of seven-day weekends and relaxed, unpressured fun. Stuart and Marnie continued to trade evenings with the McEwens; usually impromptu backyard affairs of charcoal and beer.

Late in the evening, after Brian and Jill had left, Stuart was carrying dishes back to the kitchen. "Has Jill been on a diet, Marn?" he called over his shoulder.

She didn't answer.

Returning for a second load, he repeated the question. "Marnie? What's with Jill? She looks like she's lost a few pounds."

Marnie was still in the chaise, her arms wrapped around herself against the evening chill. Tears had welled up in her eyes.

"Marnie?" Stuart pulled up a stool beside her, concerned. "What's going on, hon?"

She sighed, wiping a thumb across her eyes. "I don't know what to do, Stu. About Jill. She and Brian have turned into the closest friends we've ever had and it's just tearing me apart to see her like this."

"Like what?" he asked, lost. "She looks great to me. All I said was she looks like she's lost a little weight."

"No." She shook her head. "You don't understand. It's the baby, still. And it seems to be getting worse. She's still so ripped up inside about Todd. She's not eating, or sleeping. She's lost about fifteen pounds, and that's just in the last three weeks. She's sick, Stu, and I don't know what to do about it."

Stuart looked off across the yard, nodding. "Brian mentioned something about it the first night we went over for dinner. That was more than a month ago, but even then he said she was still moping around the nursery, like she was expecting the baby to come back. He hasn't brought it up since, though. I thought things were healing over." He paused for a moment. "Do you think there's anything I can do, Marnie? I mean I'm no good at the counseling end, but can I turn them on to any of the people downtown? I hear this new gal, Lorraine . . . something, has made quite an impact on the local psychiatric scene."

"I've tried that, Stu. But every time I bring it up she just refuses to talk to anyone about it, professionally I mean. She figures it just has to run its course. But with the way things are accelerating I'm really worried." She looked up at him. The tears had disappeared. The worry was still there, but the desperation was gone, replaced by a resolute concern.

She stood up and gathered the rest of the dishes. "I'm not sure there's anything anyone can do. I think that's part of the problem; I myself feel so powerless. I don't know what, but something's gotta happen."

Something happened.

On the tenth of August the McEwens had a houseguest.

Brian had called Stuart at work. "You've gotta meet this guy to believe him, Stu," he said. "Jill's already talked to Marnie about it; you're coming over for dinner around seven. Don't bother with wine, we've got lots. Talk to you later." He hung up.

The "guy" was Walter Thayer, a distant uncle. A widower, in his mid-seventies, who lived alone in a house he had built himself more than thirty years ago. Every year he embarked on what he called his "tour de famille": a cross-continental pilgrimage during which he visited as many of his relatives as he could. He allotted two months per year to the task, and a strict, inflexible three days per visit. This year it was the West, and Jill and Brian were on his route.

Despite his neighbour's enthusiasm, Stuart was apprehensive. He had adapted quickly and naturally to Brian's personality and sense of humour, but Brian was an exception. As a rule he made friends slowly, and rarely. He avoided parties, even small social gatherings with strangers. The discomfort of strained smiles and small talk never seemed worth the effort.

For once his concern was not justified, his apprehension short-lived. On the patio, before-dinner drinks just poured, Stuart, reserved and polite, asked Thayer where he was from and what his actual relationship was to Brian.

"Brian who?" came the reply, apparently serious.

His host chuckled softly. "Careful, Stuart. He bites."

The old man continued. "Seriously, I'm from a small town, which you've probably never heard of, back in Ontario, Canada. I'm what's-his-name's uncle two or three times removed, I think—I'm not really sure and I don't particularly care. The real reason I'm here is to freeload some of the best damn steaks in the West out of what's-her-name." He jerked a thumb at Jill.

It was her turn to laugh. She reached over and pinched his thigh.

Grinning, he turned to Stuart and winked. "That's the other reason."

As the evening progressed, Stuart relaxed completely. Thayer, complimentary to a fault, mixed his charm with a delightful aura of mischief. He knew precisely when to jab or feint and when to be sincere.

If it's an act, thought Stuart, *it's the best damned act I've ever seen.* The old man had him mesmerized.

. A late evening drizzle forced the party indoors. While the two women prepared coffee in the kitchen, the men traded stories in front of the fire in the den. Thayer was just finishing his as Marnie and Jill returned.

It was the story of the underendowed man who had searched all over the world for someone to perform a penis transplant. He finally found a surgeon in South Africa who was using elephant trunks for the purpose, and who, as luck would have it, just happened to need volunteers for his revolutionary operation. The man offered himself immediately. After the surgery, however, he was warned that under no circumstances was he to allow himself to become sexually aroused for the next six weeks. Alas, his girl friend couldn't wait. Sitting together in a pub one evening she began stroking his thigh. The man felt an awful surge in his loins as the zipper of his trousers ripped open. An enormous trunk-shaped organ lifted above the bar, grabbed a bowl of peanuts, and just as quickly disappeared. His girl friend couldn't believe her eyes. She had to see it again.

The women walked into the room. Thayer couldn't stop now.

"So this poor guy's sitting there with tears streaming down his cheeks, pleading with her not to touch him again.

" 'Whyever not, dear?' she asks. 'I just want to look at it.'

" 'I don't mind you looking at it' he says. 'I just can't take another bowl of peanuts rammed . . .' "

He stopped at this point, grinning sheepishly at the women. "Sorry, girls. Must have been the devil made me do it."

Brian and Stuart, filling in the punch line themselves, collapsed in laughter on the hearth. The women placed their coffees beside them and settled on the couch, one on each side of the old man. He put an arm around each of them.

"Well, we've taken care of those two. What say the three of us go out on the town."

The laughter settled slowly. Over the next hour the conversation seemed to ramble from one topic to the next, usually at Thayer's instigation.

Something stirred in Stuart's mind. A veiled pattern seemed to emerge as the subject matter slowly, subtly touched on closer, more personal items. *He's getting at something,* he thought. He looked at Marnie. She shrugged, acknowledging his concern. *She's noticed it too,* he thought.

As if reading his mind, Thayer looked at him, his face impassive, but his eyes boring into him.

This is getting weird, Stuart puzzled. *What does he want?*

Brian interrupted the flow. "Do you really have to go

tomorrow, Walter? You know you're welcome to stay as long as you like." His invitation was genuine.

"Like forever, you mean?" Thayer quipped. "No, it's one of my few absolute commandments, Brian. Visitors are like fish. After three days they start to stink. Besides, I wouldn't want to deprive the rest of the family, now would I?

"Actually I told my daughter Steffie I'd be there the day after tomorrow. She's way the hell up in Oregon, which for an old goat like me will probably take all week, what with pit stops every hour."

He looked directly at Stuart again, his eyes pleading, belying the lightness of his tone. "I'd like to see her before she gets so big I won't recognize her."

Stuart's mind was a frenzy of conflicts. *He wants me to say something. Something about his daughter. Stay on the topic. What about his daughter? Getting big. What does that mean, getting big?*

But the moment passed. The message remained just beneath the surface. As the fire slowly died, so too did the conversation. During a still moment, Brian asked, "This is where you're supposed to fill in the gaps with war stories, Walter."

The old man looked up. "Sorry to disappoint you, Brian, but there's not much excitement there."

Jill persisted. "Oh, come on, Walter. Every old soldier has a war story."

Thayer shook his head. "That was 1940," he replied. "I was in the army, but by then I was too old to go overseas. I got stuck with shore patrol in the Maritimes, looking for German U-boats. I never did see a damn sub. In fact, in the five years I was there, only two or three guys ever saw one. We spent most of our time playing poker and making . . . oh, making knickknack sort of stuff. Not exactly the kind of thing war stories are made of, Jilly. By the time the war ended we were damn near numb with boredom."

Stuart caught Thayer's hesitation. Again he could feel the old man's thoughts burning into him: *Ask me. Ask me. Ask him what?* Stuart thought. *He wants me to prompt him, to bring something up. What? Knickknacks? Poker? The war? His daughter?*

Determined not to let the opportunity pass this time, Stuart asked, "There must be something there, Walter. Five years is a long time for cards and crafts."

He was on the right track. Thayer's eyes took on a different tone. Grateful. More than grateful, they were earnest now, acknowledging Stuart's effort, prompting him further, leading him.

"Well, true. It wasn't all letters and lonely nights. We had family around, some of us did anyway. So it wasn't as big a bust as I let on. But for some of us it got pretty dull when the family wasn't there. Then we'd spend a lot of time just keeping our hands busy, makin' things. I had always been pretty handy with tools, and with the time available I managed to turn out some pretty handsome pieces, if I dare say so." A false smugness grinned playfully over his face.

It was there. Something about family. The contradiction: the family there, then not there. Tools, handsome pieces . . . the briefest glimpse of an image, a vision, unbidden and unreasoned, flashed in Stuart's mind. A collage of past events, conversations. His words were out before he could think about them.

"One of those handsome pieces wouldn't just happen to be a crib, would it, Walter?" He looked at Brian. "The one upstairs, with the names on it."

At the word *crib,* Jill seemed to stiffen. Brian looked quickly from Stuart to his wife to the old man. A subtle change came over Thayer's expression. Beneath the warmth and tenderness, something deeper emerged. It seemed to brush with thanks against Stuart, then moved to Brian and Jill, spreading over them with a comfort, an empathy. It was as though a gate had been there, a gate Thayer had wanted to use but needed someone, Stuart, to unlock for him.

He nodded slowly, just barely smiling at Stuart. "It would indeed. In fact, in all the time I spent at the coast, making that crib was about the most exciting thing that happened to me. There's an interesting story to it actually. . . ."

He looked around at the others, for the first time unsure whether to proceed. His gaze locked on Marnie. She understood exactly what he was doing. Her eyes pleaded with him to continue.

He looked at Brian. "For another scotch, of course," he said, holding up his glass.

Thayer glanced briefly again at Stuart before reaching down to take Jill's hand. She remained silent beside him, withdrawn, her eyes fixed on her lap, her thoughts anchored on the shoals of some dark memory.

When Brian returned with his drink, the old man leaned back on the couch, his hands folded behind his head. He began.

ORIGINS
Part One

Halifax, Nova Scotia: A.D. 1943

*"It's empty!" Thayer was drenched and fuming. "Carter,
you bastard. You brought me all the way to hell out here
on the worst fucking day of the year, and the place is
empty."*

*As if punctuating his fury, a long roll of thunder rum-
bled, threatening, out of the mist. The two men had rowed
the three miles from the mainland in a driving rain—Thayer
had done the rowing while Carter sat smoking in the
stern. Soaked with spray, they had climbed the fifty-foot
cliffs surrounding the island and scratched their way along
an overgrown trail to the fort. Once there, Carter, who
had traveled the route before, led them to the munitions
storage shaft.*

*Thayer shone his light around the room. The fort had
been erected by the British in the mid-eighteenth century.
Built as it was, on the windward side of the island facing
the Atlantic, it was ideally located to defend their New
World prize against seafaring invaders. Unfortunately, as
with all coastal fortifications, it had fared better against
its human enemies than against the ravages of the maritime climate. After two centuries of gales and spray, little
remained of the towers and walls.*

*During the fort's occupation, the munitions, the powder
and balls, were especially vulnerable to the corrosive effects of moisture and salt. For protection they were stored
in specially constructed, moisture-resistant artillery shafts,
large, unventilated rooms near the periphery of the fort,
lined completely with maritime teak. The teak, originally*

imported by the shipload from Burma, was the target of Thayer's expedition. But as he shone his light around the shaft his hopes sank. All that remained in the room were the splintered, unusable remnants of a half-dozen boards, and in the corner a squat, narrow, six-foot bench.

He leaned against the wall and lit a cigarette, inhaling deeply. He wanted teak. There was lots of maritime spruce and pine on the mainland. Even maple was available, as much as he needed. But he wanted something more exotic, more durable. He wanted teak.

He crossed the room. Small clouds of dust billowed as he kicked aside the fragments of wood. He settled onto the bench, his shoulders hunched as he surveyed the empty shaft. When he had overheard Carter in the pub bragging about teak-lined rooms in the island fort, he had thought his problem was solved. A carton of army-ration cigarettes was all it had taken to bribe the little miner into leading him to the place. But apparently the trip was wasted.

He stubbed the cigarette under his foot, drumming his fingers on the bench. He looked down, curious. He rapped a knuckle against one of the boards. Solid. He stood and faced the bench, measuring it, analyzing it. Two six-foot lengths of solid dark wood, planks actually, each about two inches by four. He kicked it onto its side. The boards were fastened together on their undersurface with two narrow strips of fir. Two rough-hewn blocks of spruce were braced at the ends as legs. He knelt, running his hand over the wood, tilting it towards the light. While the top had been worn smooth with use over the years, the underside still bore the serrations of a hand ripping blade. It wasn't teak. It had a vaguely familiar grain, almost a cross between cypress and cedar, but he couldn't place it. It was streaked, as though stained with some dark pigment.

He extracted a small bar from his pack. To his surprise it took all his strength to remove the nails holding the fir slats. The wood was hard, much harder than teak; harder and darker than anything he had ever worked with.

With the bench disassembled he turned the planks over, examining the surfaces for flaws. Except for the saw marks and a squarish hole near the end of one of the boards they were clean. It wasn't teak, he thought as he hoisted one plank onto his shoulder, and it wasn't much, but it was better than going home empty-handed.

He called out, "Grab this other fucker, Carter. You've done piss-all else to earn your smokes."

Carter was a cocky, irritating little . . . prick was the best word Thayer could think of to describe him. He had connections with all the seamier aspects of life. Alcohol, drugs, whores; he could get or do anything, for a price. When the war erupted in Europe, the maritime defense base in Halifax became a major staging area for Canadian overseas forces. For Carter, the constant supply of entertainment-starved troops was a dream come true. A renewable resource, a ready market for his services. This was the first time Thayer had actually used him. And would be the last.

"Fuck you, Lieutenant. You want that shit, you carry it. I'm just the guide, remember?"

Thayer's mood blackened further, but his face remained blank. He ambled across the shaft, stopping at the door. He unshouldered the plank and rested it carefully on the ground. Impassively, he gazed out at the ruins of the fort, and farther, to the rain lashing the open sea. Without turning he asked quietly, almost nonchalantly, "Can you swim, Carter?"

"What?" The miner's insolent expression changed slowly to puzzlement, then to fear as understanding suddenly dawned. "Aw come on, Lieutenant. You wouldn't." The pleading in his voice was edged now with panic.

Thayer lifted the plank again and glared at him. "Don't tempt me, Carter. I'm pissed enough as it is. If I have to carry both of these myself there'll be just me and two pieces of wood makin' the return trip. And they'll make a helluva lot better company than anything else I've seen today. If you have any intention of seeing the city tonight, you little asshole, you'll be sitting in the boat when I get there with that fucking board on your lap."

Carter sat in the bow this time, sulking, as Thayer rowed back to the mainland. The rain had stopped and the wind eased, but after the effort of the overland hike and carrying the wood back to the boat, the return trip seemed twice as far. The boards had been stowed along the gun-

wales under the benches. Thayer looked down at them as
he pulled on the oars. It wasn't the teak he had come for,
but it was good. Perhaps even better. If he could split the
planks into three-eighths-inch boards or, better, quarter-
inch, he should have enough. It would be hard work. If
the difficulty he had had pulling those nails was any indication, it would be harder than any of the woods he was
accustomed to working with. Too hard to split with his few
hand tools. It would probably take another carton of cigarettes to bribe his way into the base carpentry shop with
its power equipment. Only a few cuts would be necessary,
but each cut would be critical. There would be very little
to spare, and that hole in one of the planks might be
awkward.

The wood turned out to be even harder than he had
expected. Splitting it into boards had destroyed the blade
in the power shop, and the shaping and planing quickly
dulled his hand tools. But once accustomed to the slower
pace and the daily blade-sharpening, he enjoyed the
challenge.

His plans called for no nails or screws of any kind. It
was to be fully collapsible for storage and shipping, yet
easily assembled, held together by an ingenious system of
handmade metal dowels and plates of his own design. It
was to be sturdy enough to hold an adult, yet light enough
to be moved about easily.

It took six months to finish, three times longer than it
would have had he used teak. But the result was well
worth the extra effort. He still hadn't been able to identify
the wood. What he at first had thought was a dark stain on
the surface turned out to be some kind of natural pigment
that permeated the wood throughout. He found it was too
hard to take any kind of finish. But it didn't need it
anyway. After fine-sanding and buffing, it literally gleamed.
In the end, the dark, mysterious wood was far more
attractive than teak. And more durable. With its incredible hardness it was likely to last forever. The only flaw was
the square spike hole, which he had managed to partially
conceal at the bottom of one of the end slats. It added a
touch of rustic charm, he rationalized.

Ever since his wife, May, had surprised him with the

news of her first pregnancy, Thayer had been consumed with the idea of building something for his children. Something permanent for them, and for their children, and their children after that. He built a crib.

But before it was finished, circumstance had forced his wife to move back in with her parents, more than a thousand miles away. He managed to complete the crib just two weeks before the baby was born. It arrived at the grandparents' intact and in time. Just.

The coastal defense station at Halifax closed shortly after the end of the war in 1945. A total of three submarine sightings had been reported.

In November 1954 a mine shaft in Cape Breton Island collapsed, killing thirty-seven miners. Austin Carter's body was never found.

When Walter Thayer returned to his family in northern Ontario in November 1945, his firstborn, Peter Graham, was two years old. By then his second son, Gregory Paul, had been using the crib for two months. He carved the names of both his sons onto the side of the crib. The tradition was established.

In the early morning of April 1, 1946, Gregory Paul Thayer was found dead in his crib.

Chapter Ten
August 12

The four listeners sat spellbound as the story unfolded. Thayer's recollection of the events was flawless, as if they had happened just yesterday. He had a knack for detail— intimacy was more the word—which drew them, even Jill, into the tale, involving them all. By the time he had finished, a warm unity had settled over the room. Each was lost in his own little corner of contentment, yet all were united by the closeness only shared experience can generate.

Marnie broke the silence. "I don't think I could take the separation that events like that impose on people. The war I mean."

Thayer replied, "It wasn't as bad for me as it was for some of the guys. I remember some of them were from the prairies; farmers, born and raised on the same land, with three or four kids. They'd get seasick just lookin' at the ocean. That was during the day. At night they'd cry themselves to sleep, some of them, till they got used to the idea of bein' so far from home. And then the fellas overseas, that was a whole different thing altogether.

"But for me it really wasn't all that rough. Up until she got pregnant, May lived right on the base with me. But they wouldn't allow any kids at all. And with money as tight as it was we couldn't afford an off-base residence. So when she was gettin' on in the pregnancy we both figured it was best if she moved back in with her folks.

"But it wasn't like we never saw each other. Once Petey was born and May could travel a bit, then every time I could I'd get a seventy-two-hour pass and we'd meet in Montreal. And we'd do that four or five times a year. Hell, the first time I laid eyes on Pete was in Montreal, at

Easter in forty-three. I can still see him, two months old and sleepin' in a dresser drawer, while me and May were . . . gettin' reacquainted, so to speak.

"It don't sound like such a big deal now, but I remember bein' pretty disappointed at the time. I damn near destroyed every tool I owned makin' that crib for Pete and I never did get to see him sleepin' in it. By the time I got home he was well into his terrible twos, and little Greg was usin' it."

Whenever Stuart thought back to that night, he would remember best what happened next. He would try to compare the old man's story to a game; a closely fought match in which, over the course of one or two pivotal rallies, the momentum would swing in one unalterable direction. Or even to a finely crafted film, all its energy, and even the outcome, revolving around one critical scene. It was as though Thayer's story was a pivot point, a fulcrum, a sun around which Jill's emotions would circle. Her depression would reach its greatest depths on the dark side, then dissolve on the return, cleansed somehow by the orbit. But none of his comparisons would ever be quite adequate, ever quite describe the intensity of what followed next, the emotional energy that seemed to flow through the room.

Still leaning back on the couch, his hands still clasped behind his head, the old man turned to Jill.

"We lost Greg when he was six months, Jill," he said gently. "Little fella just died in his sleep. No reason, no warning. No time to prepare—not that you can prepare for it anyway, any more than you can do anything about it after it's happened. Other than cry a lot, and remember."

Her shoulders stiffened slightly. She looked at Thayer. Her eyes moistened as they met his; her body relaxed as she nestled her head against his shoulder. They were alone in the room now. The others were just bystanders, uninvolved spectators.

"Just like your Todd, Jill. Greg was there one day, and gone the next. And there's been nothing, nothing in the years before or the forty years since that's ever quite matched the anger and the guilt and the just plain sadness of him leavin' like that."

She looked up at him again, desperation in her eyes. He read her fear immediately.

"No, you won't feel like this for forty years," he said. "None of us could take that. Todd's only been gone five months, Jill. Give yourself time.

"It's not long before the hurt goes away. All of it. I don't mean the memory disappears. I don't think that ever happens. But it's like the edges get softer somehow, so it all seems to fit better.

"And when the grief stops eatin' away inside you like a cancer, you find there's all kinds of room left. You find it's done something to you, changed you, for the better. You start drawing strength from it, rather than the other way around.

"Like Greg, he's still in here." He tapped himself on the side his head. "Sort of a beacon for me now. A reminder of just how irreplaceably precious my family really is. He's the reason I go on my little tour every year, just touching bases, reassuring myself. Little Greg is gone, like your Todd, but the rest of us, we're still here."

In the quiet that followed, Stuart could feel the change. All the fury, all the desperately controlled anger, the oppressive burden of guilt Jill had borne since her son's death lifted. It was gone, dissolved in the compassion of the old man's words. It would never return.

Thayer left the following morning. Stuart and Marnie joined the McEwens to say goodbye. Next on his list was a homestead thirty miles from Adrian, Oregon—"wherever the hell that is," he said. His daughter Stephanie lived there with her husband and ". . . a huge dog that shits all over the place and about four million chickens. She's due around Christmas, and I'd like to see her before she gets too far along." He winked at Stuart. "Missed that one last night, didn't you, Stu? As much as I admire ladies heavy with child," he threw a friendly arm around Marnie's waist, "I do prefer them lean and mean."

"One of the many advantages of being seventy-five." Stuart returned the wink. "You can be as lecherous as you want and get away with it."

Thayer laughed. He shook hands with each of the men.

"Stuart, it's been a pleasure. I've forgotten your jokes already. Another one of the advantages of being seventy-five."

He turned to his host. "And, Brian, you've turned out all right, for a McEwen. Thanks for making me feel so welcome. I've never been so tempted to break my three-day rule."

He gave Marnie an affectionate hug. "I think you're the only one who really understood what was happening last night," he said quietly, none of the others overhearing. "Jill's done all right by you."

He turned last to Jill. She held her embrace with him, her arms tight around his neck. She kissed his cheek and looked into his eyes. Gently he touched her hair, nodding almost imperceptibly.

"You'll be fine," he whispered.

Tears of gratitude shone in her eyes. She smiled and squeezed his hand.

And so he left them, better than when he had arrived; more in touch with themselves and one another. But as he backed out of the driveway, a faint, pebbled rash of goose-flesh shivered over Stuart's arms. He could see two pieces of soft-sided luggage on the rear seat of Thayer's car. And stacked under them, dark and unmistakable, the pieces of the disassembled crib.

Chapter Eleven
Late August

What remained of the summer passed. As it did, Stuart managed to redirect his enthusiasm, diverting it into different channels. Unable to proceed with the crib death investigation, he had set his mind to other tasks. So much so that by late August the call from Dr. Hamilton's secretary came not just as a surprise; it felt more like an intrusion into his comfortably reorganized priorities.

"Oh, and, Dr. Rice," she added, "Dr. Hamilton probably didn't tell you, she never does. The program is free of charge, as you know. But in return for the service, we ask that a small donation be made to the science faculty student fund. I'll have a receipt ready for you when you arrive."

As he drove back to his office, he glanced at the package on the seat beside him. "Nothing much," he mimicked the secretary, pursing his lips, his resentment now rage. "A hundred and fifty dollars is the usual."

The program was accompanied by an eighty-page manual describing the details of the programming code, formatting, and command instructions. It even included multiple appendices of explanatory message codes and error signals, and a list of statistical problem tables. He had made a point of getting the name and telephone number of the student who had designed the program. It would take him days to read the manual and probably weeks to understand it. Much easier to get a verbal explanatory overview from the student.

"Dr. who?"

"Rice, Stuart Rice. We've never met, but you've been working all summer on a computer program based on data

I submitted to the science faculty. I thought I'd call and congratulate you on the results. It looks very, ah, professional—though I doubt Dr. Hamilton would approve of the word." He was at his diplomatic best. "I was wondering if you might give me your impression of the results." He paused, hoping the student would take the bait.

"In other words, you're having problems with the manual," came the reply.

Shit. Then aloud, "Well, it is kind of intimidating to a novice, I guess. But also I was sort of hoping to learn what you found when you ran it."

"Found? Like what? I had no idea what you were looking for. Christ, all I got was this pile of morbid shit on dead kids. The instructions were to categorize the information and create a cross-referencing program with enough built-in windows and stats equations to analyze the shit to death. I damn near threw up reading that shit. I mean cross-sectional brain slices and intestinal contents. And fecal analysis, that was the fucking end, man. I put in five weeks of nights on that shit. All I got was a C-minus and a case of terminal nausea. And the fucker's probably useless anyway."

Useless! Stuart was trying to contain himself. "Ah, what do you mean by useless?"

"I mean the consistency of the data was off, way off. Shit, two of the reports were ancient; like one was from 1945. The terminology was so different from the rest I wasn't sure where the hell it should go. And there was one that just went on for fucking ever. It had so much extra shit in it that the others didn't have I thought for a while it must have been included by mistake. I was tempted to leave all three of them out, but that would have really fucked me with Too Right. So I had to create separate categories just for those three reports."

Stuart was comfortable with the practical applications of computers in his work, but he understood very little of the technical intricacies of programming.

"That sounds like a reasonable solution," he said. He still hoped to tap the student for more information.

A loud snicker forced its way over the line. "Oh sure, reasonable. Too Right just loved it. That's what got me a

fucking C-minus, man. It sounds innocent, but as soon as
you add that kind of extra category—partially framed quan-
tifiers they're called, PFQs—it really screws the system
up. There was an incompatibility between the data, the
program language, and the stats equations to begin with.
There's no problem doing spot data analysis. But once you
start doing analytical searches the PFQs show up. At the
top end the poor fucker starts looking at the categories
themselves rather than the data that's in them. It'll throw
all the probability curves off at the upper end. Anything
above ninety percent is just a shot in the dark.

"Look, I'm right in the middle of semester finals and
I'm cramming my ass off. Too Right's got my balls in a vise
as it is. If I don't pass these exams I'm history. The manual
is pretty clear once you get into it. Just give me five more
days. If you're still in trouble call me back then."

Stuart resigned himself to reading through the manual.
"Sure, no problem," he lied. "I'm sure it'll all fall into
place once I get started. By the way, Randall is it? What's
a tourite?"

"It's Too Right, capital T, capital R, two words. It's not
a what, it's a who. T. R. Hamilton, ball-buster supreme.
Too Right, Testicular Remnants, Tits Renounced; fuck,
the list is endless. Five days. I've gotta run."

Stuart replaced the phone on the cradle. "Four weeks
and a hundred and fifty bucks," he groaned. "For a C-minus
program that doesn't work."

But it did work. After three nights of study and hours of
trial and error he finally got the program to load and run
smoothly. In fact, it was surprisingly simple to use once he
had mastered the commands format.

The program had eight of the more common probability
equations built into it and contained entry windows by
which the user could insert any other equation with which
to analyze the data. The data itself could be added to or
deleted at will. Any number of information bits from one
to infinity could be analyzed and subjected to any combination of probability equations. The results were presented numerically on the screen and, if desired, in graphic
form as probability curves. He was familiar with some of

the statistical references in the manual—P values, chi square tests—but most of it was advanced far beyond his understanding. Grudgingly he conceded that by appearances it was an extremely versatile, intricate program. "Elegant" his instructor would have said.

To test its reliability he began with the obvious analyses based on sex, age, organ weights; the same ones he had done manually. The results were identical to his own. He broke the categories into smaller units, dividing the ages into three-, then two-, then one-month subgroups. Eye colour, head circumference, urine acidity; he chose subcategories at random. Each time the program returned an analysis of the data requested, along with the probability of those results based on the particular equation being used. None of the results was surprising. The number of available searches was infinite. He realized it would take forever to go through them all individually. He returned to the manual.

To accommodate this problem, the student had included an infinite search function in the program. All the user had to do was specify the incidence limits, and any searches that satisfied those limits would be identified. An incidence limit of one hundred would identify all those instances in which the data was one hundred percent conforming. Since all the crib deaths had occurred in boys in their first year, he knew the age and sex factors would satisfy an incidence limit of one hundred. The only catch in performing an infinite search was the time required. For the amount of data he had it would take almost four hours. But since it was late afternoon anyway, he decided simply to leave the computer on and working overnight.

He entered the incidence limits at fifty, then paused. Better to check it out first, he thought, as he changed it to one hundred. If the results confirmed his findings, he would have more confidence in subsequent searches. He keyed in the infinite search command, watched as the screen blanked momentarily, then chuckled as a song title filled the screen:

ON A CLEAR DAY . . . YOU CAN SEE FOREVER . . .

INFINITE SEARCH ON

When his alarm sounded the following day, his normally lethargic morning routine was energized by anticipation. Eager to check the search results, he arrived at the office a half-hour early. He expected to find two entries on the screen—age and sex. Instead there were eleven.

NA 100
IN 100
TI 100
HC 100
CR 100
WT 100
MD 100
MA 100
MR 100
AG 100
SX 100

He reached for the manual. He knew AG and SX were the space-saving program abbreviations for age and sex. The number 100 referred to the one hundred percent incidence limits. But, according to the results on the screen, there were nine other features besides age and sex that were common to all the autopsy reports. He found all the abbreviations listed in an appendix at the back of the manual.

NA: name; IN: institution; TI: time; HC: head circumference; CR: crown-rump length; WT: weight; MD: month of death; MA: month of autopsy; MR: month of report.

He sat staring at the screen, pulling at his upper lip. Name, institution, time. It made no sense. None of the children had the same name. None had been autopsied in the same hospital. Their weights, lengths, dates of death, all were different. He searched the index of the manual for an explanation. Nothing. The introduction listed only the purpose and scope of the exercise. He finally found his answer, an appended note on the last page:

NOTE: The user is advised that due to errors in data categorization, incidence limits in excess of ninety percent are unreliable and may reflect clerical rather than data consistency.

He recalled his conversation with the student: "Anything above ninety percent is a shot in the dark." All the results meant was that each of the autopsy reports had a name, an institution, a time, and so on. Not necessarily the same name, just *a* name. Instead of information consistency, for probability searches above ninety percent the program recognized clerical consistency. If all the "name" boxes were filled, that was recognized as one hundred percent consistency regardless of the actual names in the boxes.

For the rest of the week he continued to experiment with the program, setting the incidence limits progressively lower. As the limits approached ninety percent the number of conforming categories increased dramatically. At the ninety percent level there were more than two hundred entries awaiting him when he arrived in the morning. Except for age and sex, all of them denoted clerical conformity.

At eighty-nine percent, however, the situation changed dramatically. He was back to the original eleven categories. At eighty-five percent it was down to nine. At eighty percent he was still left with five categories: age, sex, month of death, autopsy, and report.

It was a classical catch-22 dilemma. Even at eighty percent limits the program was still confusing the categories with the information they contained. Setting the limits lower would presumably eliminate the problem, but at those lower levels the results would lose both statistical and clinical significance. Either way it was unreliable. "Useless," just as the student had predicted.

By this time two weeks had passed. Stuart braved a second call. "Randall? Dr. Rice again. How did the exams go?"

The change in tone was remarkable. "Oh, hi ya, Doc. Fucking awesome. Ended up with a C-plus. So Too Right's back in her cave for another year. How's the program running?"

"Well, that's why I'm calling, actually. As you predicted, I'm having a lot of trouble with searches at the top end. The problem is that by the time I eliminate the clerical trivia I'm so far down the probability curve that the clinical results aren't worth anything. Any suggestions?"

"Like I said before, it's those three oddball reports, the two old ones and the really detailed one. Get rid of those and it should run like a judge in a cathouse."

"I thought of that," Stuart replied. "The problem is that my study is so small to begin with that eliminating three out of the thirteen cases doesn't leave me with enough to work with. What if I went through those three reports myself and recategorized the data. You know, make them conform to the format of the others. Would that eliminate the problem?"

The student was silent for a moment. "You'd solve the problem you have now, but you'd end up with a worse one."

Stuart was getting discouraged. "How does that work?"

"It's kind of tough to explain. Let's see. When you went in to see Too Right, did she give you her stock condescension shit about your project being too easy for us? About making and shuffling a bunch of little boxes?"

"Yes."

"Okay. And you understand the concept she was getting at, about the boxes I mean, putting information into slots and then moving them around?"

"I think so, yes."

"Okay. So there's no problem adding or removing data from the boxes. The trouble starts when you empty out a box completely, which you'd be doing by recategorizing those three files. Even though you'd be reinserting the information, it'd be going back into different boxes, and you'd be leaving a whole lot of empty ones just lying around, sort of. That wouldn't be a problem with Fortran or Cobal, but with this new shit Too Right wants us to use it'd be like throwing a fucking leper in a bathhouse. It's almost like those empty boxes would get homesick. They'd start matching up with other categories at random. You wouldn't be able to trust a search even at the zero level. Does all that make any sense?"

"It doesn't sound like there's anything I can do about it then."

"Not unless you change the program."

Stuart was confused now. "I guess I didn't understand, then. I thought you just said reorganizing the data wouldn't work."

"The data, no. The program, yes. It would mean accessing the software itself."

"Is there a difference? I mean, is it something I could do myself?" Stuart asked.

"You could," Randall replied. "But it's like walking on glass. Once you start changing commands with this shit, the whole thing can just crash on you. And there's no way to recover the information once you've lost it."

"The way things have gone so far, Randall, I don't think I've got a whole lot to lose."

Stuart could hear a rustling of papers. "Okay," the student said. "But remember, there's no disk copy of the program. I've got the printed program here, but I'm sure as hell not interested in logging all that autopsy shit again. If you want, I can read you the commands over the phone. It's not really as difficult as I make it out to be. Those three reports are off in a data list all by themselves, with separate entry slots and all. Write this down, exactly as I read it."

Stuart copied down a surprisingly short sequence of commands, then repeated them for accuracy. "And that's it?" he asked.

"That's it. Key that in and press the shifted return and those three reports are history. Not just the information in them but even the categories they occupied. Actually, that's not quite true. There'll still be the shit from those reports that conformed to the regular categories, but you want that in anyway. When you reassign the information later, don't worry about duplication. Each bit of data has an identifier to it. If you try to enter the same thing twice the program just ignores the second entry."

"And that's it?" Stuart repeated.

"That's it."

Stuart's spirits had risen considerably. He thanked the student for the help and was about to hang up when a

loud, desperate shout came over the line: "Dr. Rice . . .
Dr. Rice . . ."

Quickly he raised the phone to his ear. "Yes?"

"Fuck, I thought you'd hung up. I forgot the most
important part. You can't get at the program without the
password. It's kind of like an electronic lock to keep pi-
rates out of the software, like exactly what you're doing.

"Get into the infinite search mode first. When it asks for
incidence limits, type in one thousand and one. It'll clear
for about ten seconds, then the cursor will start blinking.
When it does, type in 'Twat's Revenge.' Capital T, capital
R."

Chapter Twelve
September 18

MD	100
MA	100
MR	100
AG	100
SX	100

He had spent the entire weekend at the office rearranging the data in the three reports to conform to the others. He had erased the information boxes, following the student's instructions exactly. Re-entering the data had been a frustrating, time-consuming task. And it still didn't work. Out of desperation he had even tried running a search at the twenty percent level. It identified many of the similarities he expected—last names for example—and weight approximations started to appear. But the program was still including the same clerical trivia concerning the dates of death. The frustration wasn't worth it. Yet, if he abandoned the electronic search, all he could do was return to the same systematic manual study. Or wait for another idea to crop up.

He didn't have to wait long.

". . . so I'm telling you this was insane. Here we had a hundred and eighty rats. Identical. I mean they're clones, right? So we start injecting them, and if it works we've got graft-rejection licked. So what happens? Half the little fuckers just kick off. Like after microdoses they just roll over dead. The rest of them we keep increasing the dose, increasing the dose. Nothing. Doesn't faze 'em a bit . . ."

Saul Pezim was the archetypal Bronx Jew. His look, his dress, his speech, his movement, everything about him reminded Stuart of Woody Allen. The only difference was Woody Allen was funny. Saul Pezim was just obnoxious.

Fortunately, Pezim's mentors in medical school had recognized his personality flaws early and steered him away from clinical medicine and into pure research. Cloistered away in the impersonal, reclusive confines of the laboratory, Saul Pezim shone. He had already made major breakthroughs in several widely divergent areas: chemotherapy, immunofluorescent antigen markers for preclinical disease, even a Nobel nomination for his work in intracellular transport mechanisms.

His current work with recombinant DNA had produced a prototype antirejection agent that, in his initial trials, had proven to be infinitely superior to combination steroids or even the more recently popularized cyclosporin-A. Unfortunately, his work was all Pezim ever talked about. When he had joined Rice, Novak, and Andrew Turpin at their table in the hospital cafeteria, each of them knew the conversation would be dominated by the little researcher and his rats.

"Anyway, naturally we did posts on them, and nothing. Gross and histology, zero. But biochem, we just about shit. Their blood sugars were unrecordable. All of them. I mean, they had diet blood in their veins, their sugars were so low." He chuckled at his own joke.

The other three just looked at one another.

Pezim continued, oblivious. "But everything else was normal, I mean everything. We even did testicular assays on them. You ever try to dissect a rat's balls? Wally? Andy?"

Before either could answer he continued. "So what the hell. We couldn't find anything to account for the low sugars in the dead rats, so we autopsied the rest of 'em. And they turned out to be the sick ones. They all had chromosome breaks in their pancreatic islet beta cells— you know, preclinical diabetes. The only reason they survived was because they couldn't manufacture enough insulin to respond normally to the drug. Their sugars just stayed right up there. We may not have a graft-rejection inhibitor that's worth piss-all, but I'm telling you we sure have one hell of an insulin stimulator."

Stuart had been only half-listening, but a bell had suddenly sounded somewhere. "Excuse me, Saul." He touched him on the arm. Pezim frowned at the interrruption. "What was that you said about the rats with the low blood sugars?"

"Christ, Rice, where have you been? I'm talking about a drug that's going to revolutionize the treatment of diabetes and you're . . ."

"Come on, Rabbi, spare us the polemics," Stuart interrupted again. He knew the insult would bounce off unnoticed. "You said something about autopsying the rest of the rats. You mean the dead rats?"

"No, the survivors. We sacrificed the survivors and posted them. They all had . . ."

But Stuart had tuned out. *Examine the survivors. Examine the survivors.* It was the opening he was looking for. His investigation of the crib deaths had stalled. He had dissected the autopsy reports on the dead children as much as he could and had reached a dead end. What about the rest of the children in the family, the survivors? Why had they survived? Better, *what* had they survived? Were they like Saul Pezim's rats, protected somehow by some abnormality? Some genetic or latent chemical flaw? But protected from what? It was a totally different approach.

Again he felt himself standing at the end of the hall, shaded, locked doors lining both walls. The dark silence was interrupted by the soft sliding of a bolt. One of the doors had opened. The momentum that had initially forced him into the hall resurfaced, moving him towards that now-open door. He had no idea where it would lead. Nor could he have resisted the momentum in any event.

"Examine the survivors," he said softly as he rose, absently stacking the used dishes on his tray.

"Stuart?" Novak called quietly, concerned.

"It's okay, Wally," he replied, focusing again. "Just something I remembered to do."

He needed a control group. Just as Pezim had solved his problem by studying the apparently unaffected rats, Stuart could duplicate the methodology by analyzing de-

tailed health data from the surviving family members. But
which ones? The CDC had given him a list of over ninety
names spread over four generations. Doing an entire population study was out of the question. Besides the time
involved, it would skew his results unacceptably. For the
study to be valid, he needed a subgroup, matched with
the crib deaths by age and sex and numbers. Detailed
health questionnaires sent to members of the family, fifteen, twenty at the most, to allow for nonreturns. But
whom to include?

The question dominated his thoughts as he sat musing
over his files in his study. The original list of names he had
received from Brian McEwen lay on the desk, each name
now circled, surrounded by hastily penciled annotations of
addresses, parents' names, postal codes. His thoughts flashed
back to the morning he had examined Todd McEwen in
his nursery; to the evening they had spent with the
McEwens, and to his conversation with Brian in the nursery that night. An image of the nursery formed in his
mind. The prints on the wall, the gaily patterned curtains,
the dark, solid crib with its history and heritage of names
engraved on its sides . . .

The crib. Four sides, seven or eight names carved into
each side . . . thirty, thirty-five names in all . . . it was
ideal. Some of the dead children would be among them,
but that would leave close to twenty names to work with.
A perfectly matched control group.

Not as perfect as he would have liked. Jill McEwen had
copied the names from the crib shortly after Todd was
born, intending it to be only one of many entries in his
baby book. She gave Stuart a copy of the list.

Twenty-nine names in all, seventeen boys, twelve girls.
He recognized some of the names from the autopsy list,
but when he compared the names of the dead children
with the crib list, a curious fact emerged. He had expected some, perhaps even most, of the dead children's
names to be on the list, but they were all there. At one
time, all of the dead children had used the crib. He wasn't
sure why he was so surprised. After all, they were from

the same extended family, a family in which all the children traditionally used the same crib. But not all. He recalled Brian McEwen's brother, the Rabbit. None of his five children had used the crib. None of them were on the list. Either list.

Coincidence, Stuart. Examine the survivors, he thought. He was falling into the same trap. He had already picked apart the autopsy files. He concentrated on the new names.

As a control group it was only fair. The ages and numbers were acceptable, but the sex factor was unmatched. All of the thirteen dead infants had been boys. But of the sixteen survivors, only four were male. Since they constituted the most logical subgroup, he started with them, preparing genealogy summaries on each.

Peter Thayer, the first name on the crib. Both his brother, Gregory, and his son, Jonathan, had died.

Stephen Jackson, born May 12, 1951. His twin brother, Scott, was one of the crib death victims. Stuart underlined the name several times. The value of twins, especially identical twins, in clinical research was incalculable. Given the same genetic and environmental backgrounds, why would one twin die while the other lived?

Maurice Lasalle, born May 29, 1958. His older brother had died two years earlier at three months of age.

Andrew McEwen, born January 27, 1977. His brother had died one year later at eleven months of age. He recalled Jill McEwen's story of the race for the crib. Andrew's cousin, Paul Thayer, born two weeks earlier, got to use the crib. Ironically it was Andrew, ostensibly the loser in the race, who ended up using the crib the longest.

He leaned back in his chair and stretched, arching his spine. Out of twenty-nine children, only four surviving males. Each of them had a sibling, a brother, on the autopsy list. There was no apparent pattern to the births and deaths, no logical sequence to the names on the crib. It was simply used by whichever infant was around at the time. If there was more than one eligible child, as in the case of Andrew McEwen, the firstborn used the crib.

But what if the children were separated by more than just weeks? Six or even twelve months, for example. Was the crib sent on after a certain specified time to the next child? And the size of the crib: it was so small that by the time a child could pull himself up he would risk climbing or falling out. Ten or twelve months would be the maximum in any case. In the case of the Jackson twins, both names were on the crib. But Scott Jackson had died when he was nearly a year old. Two eleven-month-old babies could hardly sleep together in a crib that size without disturbing each other. Were they sleeping in separate cribs by then?

Stuart caught himself. Fatigue was distracting him onto tangents. Who used the crib and when and for how long were irrelevant. The only important feature to note was the lack of a consistent sequence in the births and deaths. He had just enough energy left to draft a letter to the parents of the surviving children, or to the survivors themselves as their ages warranted. He explained the purpose of his study and included a detailed medical and genetic questionnaire. He would get their addresses from the demographic data bank in Washington and mail them in the morning.

But later, as he lay in bed waiting for sleep, persistent, unformed questions nagged at him. Like shapes moving behind a misted window, the forms familiar but not quite recognizable. An unseen hand wiped a streak of mist from the window. One of the faces stared in.

He sat up, suddenly wide awake, suddenly cold. The window was gone, but the questions remained. On impulse he padded back to his study. Who had died? How had they died? Why had they died? Never "where" had they died. He scanned the autopsy reports again. It was logical that a crib death should occur in a crib, but he had never actually considered it. From the times of death— all between midnight and eight A.M.—and the brief clinical notes at the beginning of most of the reports, it was apparent that in all likelihood the babies were in their crib when they died.

He closed the files. So what? He had probably known or at least assumed that all along, though he had never actually verified it. Why the compulsion now to confirm it? Another tangent, born of fatigue? Where the deaths had occurred was meaningless. Even if all the children had died in the one crib, there was no causal or temporal signifiance to the fact. Sixteen other infants had used the same crib, and none of them had died.

But as sleep finally overtook him the image returned. The window was more transparent now, as though discovering where the children had died had cleared away the outermost layer of frost. The questions, the shapes beyond, were less obscure, yet somehow more menacing.

How had the children died? And why?

ORIGINS
Part Two

North Atlantic: A.D. 1765

One hundred and eighty nautical miles off the coast of Nova Scotia, the British packet Essex-Leigh *hove to in the driving rain. Captain Thomas Cleethorpe stood on the stern deck swearing softly to himself as he thumbed through the dog-eared pages of his Bible. He glanced at the rain-soaked shroud outlining the small form at his feet. The grim maritime reaper was an unwelcome but inevitable passenger on virtually all extended voyages. Death at sea was accepted as a matter of course. But not the death of a cabin boy; this was different. It rang the same dark, superstitious knell over a ship as would an albatross, or a woman on board. It was the worst kind of luck, and all the more that it had occurred on a holy day, Easter Friday.*

Cleethorpe found the passage. He cleared his throat and began, his concentration divided between his reading and worrying over the events of the voyage.

"The Lord is my Shepherd . . ."

Eight months and twenty thousand miles earlier, the Essex-Leigh *lay at anchor off Burma, in the East Indies. Cleethorpe was getting quietly drunk in his cabin while the first mate supervised the on-loading of their cargo. Textiles, oils, spices, tea; but mainly wood, teak. Even blunted as it was by his alcoholic fuzz, the endless, irregular jarring and clattering as the logs fell and settled into the hold was intolerable to the captain.*

From Burma, around the Cape, and on to England, the passage was relatively uneventful. Only two hands lost at sea, another bled to death in a knife fight on shore at the Cape; fewer than average. But once in Portsmouth, with the luxury items, the oils and textiles and such, off-loaded, Cleethorpe's discomfort began.

The teak remained on board for the second leg of the trip. But as well as the wood, his agent had contracted additional freight for him to carry. Artillery supplies— powder, balls, cannons, muskets—and building and cloth- ing materials; all destined for the coastal garrison in Halifax, Nova Scotia.

That made the Essex-Leigh a munitions ship, and fair game for the heavily armed American schooners plying their Atlantic coast. Loaded down as she was, the Leigh could scarcely outrun a canoe, let alone the Yanks. Even the French, still smarting over their recent expulsion from Acadia, presented a threat with their lumbering frigates. But the commission was attractive, nearly treble that of a nonmilitary cargo. It would bring him that much closer to retirement. He would trust his luck.

To amplify his worries, his agent had miscalculated the Leigh's carrying capacity. With all the holds filled to overflowing, dozens of crates of powder and nails and heavy woolens remained on the wharf. The surplus cargo was eventually stacked against the gunwales in the 'tween- decks, space ordinarily reserved as a sheltered area for the crew, and at night as sleeping quarters for the galley staff. But there were no battens, no irons to belay the freight. Nothing to prevent it from shifting in the heavy winter seas.

Improvising as best he could, he devised a temporary restraining system. The freight was stacked along each wall behind makeshift wooden staves. The staves in turn were braced apart by six-foot beams. The result was a six-foot-wide corridor in the 'tween-decks, lined with planks and interrupted at the floor and four-foot levels by irregu- larly spaced cross-beams. To add even further to the frustration and confusion, there were inadequate supplies of extra bracing materials. The crew spent two long rainy days scouring the beaches and rocky shoreline to the east for driftwood suitable for the purpose. Every few hours they would return, soaked and furious, with scavenged bits of wreckage: a torn mast, a splintered mainsail boom, various lengths of planking and rotted timbers, each of which required cutting and trimming to size. With one exception: a curiously dark, hard, wooden beam, smoothed and rounded by the sea, exactly the right length for a cross-beam. It needed no cutting at all. The perfect beam, thought Cleethorpe. One out of seventy.

With the extra cargo stored and secured, the remaining space in the 'tween-decks was unusable for anything but a seating or sleeping area. But the galley crew, not looking forward to constantly banging their heads on the cross-beams, and uneasy with the prospect of shifting cargo crushing them in their sleep, moved into makeshift quarters farther aft.

But it was ideal for Jeremy. The diminutive cabin boy could walk unimpeded under the upper beams. And the promise of spending the entire trip in a separate area away from the belching, leering, snoring older men was a luxury he couldn't resist. Happily risking the perils of shifting cargo, he strung his hammock between two of the beams; the splintered, pointed remnants of a bowsprit at one end, the dark, "perfect" beam at the other.

The transatlantic leg of the journey proceeded uneventfully. The seas remained surprisingly calm for so late in the winter, the winds never rising above force five or six. Although the galley crew complained of their new, overly crowded quarters, and the regular seamen complained of the cabin boy's absence at night, all in all Cleethorpe was satisfied.

Until this morning when the cook brought him his breakfast. It was ordinarily the cabin boy's duty to deliver his breakfast to him in his cabin each morning at seven. But Jeremy had not yet reported to the galley. Cleethorpe ordered the cook to fetch him, to bring him to the cabin at once. They found Jeremy still in his hammock. Dead.

Cleethorpe immediately suspected foul play. The boy had often rebuffed the sexual advances of several of the crew, and the longer the time between ports, the more persistent their efforts to seduce him. He could understand their simply raping him and then guaranteeing his silence with threats of violence. But to kill him, to kill a cabin boy, was unthinkable.

However, when Cleethorpe examined Jeremy's body there was no evidence of violence. He was fully clothed. There were no bruises, no rope or gag burns, no genital contusions or anal lacerations. Nothing to indicate any kind of rape or struggle. He had simply died in his sleep.

Cleethorpe shivered against an unexpected chill in the temporary hold. Not given to philosophy or supposition, he immediately, pragmatically considered the inevitable effect of the boy's death on the crew. The longer he delayed, the greater would be their concern. He ordered the body brought topside. They would hold the burial service that morning.

". . . shall dwell in the house of the Lord forever. Amen."

He nodded to the bos'n, who lifted the body onto the rail. Securing the shroud with one hand, he pushed the limp form overboard with the other. It slipped neatly from beneath the shroud, splashed softly into the Atlantic, and sank immediately. Cleethorpe closed his Bible, exchanged glances with the crew, and returned to his cabin. The concern on their faces was unmistakable. He would be lucky if ten percent stayed with him when they reached Halifax.

As if to belie the omen of the cabin boy's death, the rest of the voyage, brief as it was, was uneventful. The seas and winds remained fair. His navigation had been accurate; only 120 miles north of Halifax at first landfall. And never a sign of the Americans or the French. Even the off-loading of the cargo proceeded without incident.

Nevertheless, he had overestimated the loyalty of his crew. Of a complement of forty-five, only the mate, the bos'n, and one hand remained. The rest opted for other, ostensibly luckier vessels. But such were the vagaries of eighteenth-century maritime commerce. A replacement crew would be only difficult to find, not impossible. Many stranded sailors were desperate to return to England. They would sign on with any ship, regardless of her reputation. Within ten days his new crew was weighing anchor. His destination: the village of Quebec, in lower Canada, there to take on a full load of furs for the nobility of Europe.

As the Essex-Leigh made way out of Halifax, Cleethorpe leaned against the rail and watched the island guarding the harbour entrance. A fort had been erected there to defend against seafaring invaders. The teak, near-perfect moisture-resistant protection for the powder and balls, would be milled into one-inch boards with which to line the fort's artillery shafts. As he turned, heading north, his last view was of the barges transporting the logs to the island. Pilings holding the teak in place poked high in the air above the barges. He could identify several of the pilings as the salvaged ship remnants his crew had scoured from the beaches of Portsmouth. He recognized the sharp end of the bowsprit that had held one end of the cabin boy's hammock. And beside it, blinking unmistakably in the morning sun, the dark, "perfect," six-foot beam.

By 1768 Captain Thomas Cleethorpe had saved enough to leave the sea forever. His retirement was brief. He died two years later of the pox, syphilis.

The cargo of teak Cleethorpe delivered to Halifax served its purpose well. Two hundred years later, scattered fragments would be all that remained in the artillery shafts, the rest having been scavenged for use elsewhere.

The dark wooden beam that had served so well as a cross-brace on the Essex-Leigh was split once by the carpenters on the harbour island. Hard as rock, it damaged their saws beyond repair. The resulting two-inch planks were fashioned into a rough bench. A natural, conveniently placed square hole in one of the planks served as a useful belaying point for securing powder barrels.

The Essex-Leigh burned to the waterline in 1781. All hands perished with her. Dated April 4, 1765, a two-sentence entry in the ship's log would be the only recorded reference to the life and death of Jeremy Burrows.

Chapter Thirteen
October 8

"Christ but you're tedious, Rice. When you're not cutting up my tennis game, all you ever talk about these days is dead kids."

Novak plunked his empty glass on the table. He was just getting some of his own back. The two men, finishing their drinks, had just come off the court. Playing indoors this time—"pure tennis" Stuart called it—the pathologist had lost badly. Rice's constant patter of on-court sarcasm had only added to the punishment.

"Accept it, Wally," said Rice. "You're on the dark side, over the hill. The only thing slower than your serve these days is your urinary stream. And not by a whole helluva lot. Give me your glass, old scout. I'll pay for your audience with a refill."

Stuart rose, collected the empties, and returned to the bar. He was only too aware of his increasing obsession with the crib death study. It was like a rebirth, a rejuvenation. At one point he tried to compare it to the past and forgotten stimulation of clinical practice. But it was even better. There were none of the frustrating vagaries of vague symptom histories. None of the agony and discomfort he had once felt while delving into the intimacies of his patients' lives.

Over the past three weeks detailed replies had arrived from all but two of the control group. Separated physically from the "patients," protected from them he thought, he could analyze them with a kind of professional detachment on one hand, yet with a welcomed, refreshing sense of empathy on the other. He didn't know where his commitment had sprung from—perhaps from his involvement with the McEwens. He sometimes felt it was a morbid way to regain a sense of compassion. But he didn't care. For the first time in years he was honestly enjoying his work, even though the replies had been disappointingly negative.

With the exception of one girl who had developed diabetes and another with a seizure disorder, they were all normal, healthy. None of the surviving boys—two of them now adults—had any medical problems whatever. He had tabulated the results and run them through the CDC for conformity to statistical averages. But there was nothing there. He was back where he had begun, except for the questions. The same haunting questions of how and why the babies had died, now that he had confirmed that they all had died while sleeping in the family crib.

To presume a causal relationship between the crib and the deaths involved a quantum leap of logic. Yet it was there. The shapes behind the window, the faces once so blurred, so obscure . . . the past six weeks had given them form, substance. Irrational as it seemed, the crib was somehow involved.

He had tried to argue that not all the children who had slept in the crib had died. In fact, not even most of them, not even all the boys. But the inconsistency served only to reinforce his feelings. Such was the case with any epidemiological phenomenon. Only rarely did a disease affect one hundred percent of a given population. The current AIDS epidemic was a perfect example. Homosexuals and hemophiliacs seemed especially vulnerable to contracting the disease. But not all homosexuals, for example, developed it. Each class formed a major sub-group of victims, with only one identifiable predisposing agent common to both. The only common denominator was that they had been exposed to contaminated blood.

In his case, there were thirteen children, born at different times to different parents in different parts of the country, all dead for no apparent reason. The only features common to all thirteen were their sex, an often-distant familial relationship, and the use of the same crib when they died. It was tenuous and illogical, but the face was still there.

When Stuart returned with the second round of drinks,

he continued. "I know you must be getting pretty sick of this by now, Wally, but bear with me. I can't get this thing off my mind."

Quickly he summarized his facts. "So, thirteen kids in the same extended family, all boys, all dead. The only other positive thing I've come up with is that they were all sleeping in the same crib when they died. That's it. Period.

"But there are sixteen controls—twelve of them girls, by the way—who also used the crib. All of them are alive and healthy, or almost healthy. One of them, incidentally, is an identical twin to one of the dead kids."

Novak's eyebrows shot up.

"That's right, Wally. Identical. Alive and well. His twin brother died when they were both eleven months old. According to the parents, they were in separate cribs by then. And guess who was in the family crib, the one the other kids died in?"

Novak's interest was rising now. "Any studies done on the surviving twin?" he asked.

"No. Well, sort of, I guess. This was back in 1952. The parents couldn't recall exactly what was done. They remember something about blood sugars and X rays and keeping him in the hospital for a few weeks. But nothing came of it. Apnea monitors and telemetry weren't available back then. Anyway, he grew up happy as a clam."

"So what's your point?"

"Well, I know this sounds crazy, Wally, but I just can't get rid of the feeling that somehow the crib and the deaths are related."

"Well, they are. You just said all the kids were in the crib when they died."

"No, not just temporally, or geographically. I mean causally related. That there's some etiological connection."

Novak snickered. "I'm glad it's just my tennis game that's turned to mush, Stuart." He took a long draft from his glass.

But Rice wouldn't give in. "Come on, Wally, try it on. Have you ever heard of some kind of genetic factor, some sex-linked recessive kind of trait, that might predispose a baby to a sort of delayed hypersensitivity kind of reaction? Like the guinea pigs in med school. Remember how we'd sensitize them to a specific antigen and then reinject them a week later? They'd just twitch a few times and roll over dead. Like that. Only something in the crib, in the wood I mean, or the stain. The kids get sensitized to it, then depending on some genetic flaw some of them die. Possible?"

The pathologist shook his head. "Not even remotely, Stu. Any reaction like that, severe enough to cause death, would have to be anaphylactic. You know, bronchospasm, cardiac arrhythmias. Massive histamine release, anyway. And even if all the gross changes had reversed by the time the kids were autopsied, which is bloody fucking unlikely, histology would still show all kinds of changes. Incredible mass cell degranulation, for example. And anoxic changes. I can't speak for the other kids, but you read the PM I did on the McEwen baby. He sure didn't have anything like that."

"Okay, maybe not as an anaphylactic reaction," Rice conceded. "But what about some kind of humoral response? IgE-mediated, or some other immunoglobulin. Something we wouldn't ordinarily look for."

"Forget it, Stu. Sure, anything's possible with immunology.
But nothing you're proposing is even remotely as likely as some of the prevailing theories on SIDS. Christ, you read the literature. There's all kinds of shit coming out now on autonomic dysfunction and apnea and lower respiratory infection. . . ."

"Sure, sure, I know. And the hyperplastic pulmonary smooth muscle and the astrogliosis and on and on. Fuck, I read it all. But that's just the point, Wally. None of these kids had any of that. Nothing at all. That in itself is incredible, don't you think?"

"There's a lot we don't know yet about SIDS, Stu, but there's a lot we do know, too. And none of it points to any kind of hypersensitivity or immunological reaction, genetically triggered or otherwise."

Novak's last comment was made with such finality that Stuart could think of no reply. He drained his glass and rose again.

"To the showers. You're probably right, Wally. As usual.

"I can't believe I've become so obsessed with this thing. It seems like every waking minute it's always in the back of my mind. It's making me crazy. Shit, it's even affecting my sex life." Turning, he added, "For the better, of course."

Novak threw a consoling arm over his friend's shoulder. "Of course. From what I hear it couldn't get much worse."

Chapter Fourteen
November 29

"Would this afternoon be more convenient, Dr. Rice?" Dixon's voice was an insistent, obsequious whine now. Gone was the patronizing, overbearing tone so evident during their first encounter five weeks earlier.

"I guess that'll be all right," Stuart replied, his curiosity boiling. "Can't you give me some idea now what you've found?"

"Only that your little piece of wood has my entire department in a flap. I'm sorry, Dr. Rice, I don't mean to sound so secretive. But I really think you'd rather hear about this in person. Shall we say two o'clock?"

Stuart cleared his schedule of unessential tasks and left work shortly after lunch. Seven weeks ago, Wally Novak's coldly logical arguments against it had persuaded him to dismiss his theory of a causal relationship between the crib and the deaths of the children. For two weeks he had continued the investigation, rearranging his data, subjecting it to different statistical formulas, but always with the same results. He was the first to admit that he had no rational evidence even to suggest that the crib, or the wood in it, was somehow responsible for the infant deaths. But the less his conventional research succeeded, the more his suspicions returned. Something—intuition? instinct?—was there. He had smiled at himself at the time. Perhaps it was simple panic. He had exhausted every other angle he could think of.

Brian had agreed immediately when asked about the crib slat that had been broken in transit. It was still wedging the garage door spring away from the wall.

He had handed him the slat, replacing it with a piece of

firewood. "You're welcome to it. You know, Stuart, you've become so damned obsessed with this whole thing." The concern was evident in Brian's voice. "I don't think I need to tell you how much Jill and I appreciate all you've done for us already. Especially when you were sort of forced into the situation from the beginning. If any of what you're doing now is out of what you feel is an obligation to us, then I want you to just drop it. Seriously."

"I think this is probably my last gasp, Brian," Rice admitted. "And a pretty desperate one at that. For the number of times this has happened in your family, you'd think I'd have found something by now. But the results so far have been pretty discouraging. The fact that all the children died in the one crib is probably nothing more than coincidence. But who knows, maybe there is some pathologically reactive substance in the wood. I've exhausted all the statistical approaches. All I've got left now are wild cards."

He held the wood to the light, noting again the dark, streaked finish, the symmetrical square notch at one end. "By the way, I'm not too sure just what they do when they analyze these things. There may not be much left. Do you want any of it back?"

Brian shook his head. "It's all yours."

The following day he had taken the crib slat to the associate dean of geology at the university. *First computer science, now this*, he thought.

"With all the legitimate requests we receive for artifact identification, Dr. Rice, you really can't expect us to give this much priority."

Gerard Dixon had turned out to be his second typecasting failure. Far from the fit, gregarious, plaid-shirted outdoorsman he had expected, Dixon was short, fat, bald, and rude. Worse than rude. He had an imperial snottiness about him, an annoying patronizing air. Stuart was tempted to comment something about the whole world being run by assholes but checked himself.

"Well, I'd certainly appreciate anything you can do." Hoping to reinforce his request, he added, "As I mentioned, this piece of wood might have played an important role in the deaths of— "

"Yes, yes, yes, you did mention that, didn't you." Dixon sighed, resigned. "I suppose we do have a responsibility to our colleagues in the public-health domain." He paused, turning the wood in his hand. "I presume you'll want a full AIP on this?"

"AIP? I'm afraid I don't . . ."

"Artifact identification protocol," Dixon replied impatiently. "Surely you don't want us to simply tell you what kind of wood it is. That's hardly likely to be of much help in a medical investigation. There's not a lot to work with, but we'll identify the species, and date it of course. Get some cultures started." He held the wood up to the window. "This stain looks interesting. We'll track that down of course. And if there's enough left we'll do pollens and spectro on it, if we need them of course."

"Yes, of course." Stuart tried to hide his confusion. "An API sounds fine, Mr. Dixon."

"A . . . I . . . P." Dixon emphasized each letter. "Artifact identification protocol."

He rose. The interview was over. Without offering his hand he walked Stuart to the door. "Good day, Dr. Rice. I'll have my staff call you when we have something to report. Don't hold your breath on it. Three weeks at least; probably closer to six.

"And incidentally," he glared at Stuart, "it's *Doctor* Dixon."

Five weeks ago it was Doctor *Dixon. This morning it was* Gerry Dixon from Geology, Stuart thought with a smile as he passed through the university gates. *Somebody must have pulled the burr out of his ass.*

And it was Gerry Dixon who met him in the waiting room, with a huge smile and a handshake. He directed Stuart into his office. Before closing the door he said to his secretary, "Mrs. Anderson, would you inform the others that Dr. Rice is here."

Stuart noticed there were three additional chairs in the room since his last visit. He picked the most comfortable as Dixon settled behind his desk.

"I've asked some of my, ah, staff to join us, Dr. Rice. They shouldn't be long. Would you care for some coffee?"

The change in Dixon's manner was incredible. He was all smiles. The dour arrogance was completely gone, replaced by an almost boyish enthusiasm. As he brought Stuart a steaming cup, the door opened. Three white-coated academics filed in. *The three wise men,* thought Stuart. *Or the Three Stooges.*

"Ahh, they're here." Dixon began the introductions. "Dr. Rice, this is Arthur Cauldwell from biology; Theresa Monks, pathology; and Peter Chung from archaeology."

In turn they shook Stuart's hand. Cauldwell was as thin and cadaverous as Dixon was fat. He smiled a nervous greeting. Theresa Monk was an unexpressive, bland-looking woman. Her blank, impassive features reminded Stuart of the detached, vacant stare of a schizophrenic. Her handshake was limp and disinterested. But Chung was different. He was short and solid, almost squat. A conspiratorial glint in his eye betrayed his otherwise classically inscrutable oriental features. He pumped Stuart's hand enthusiastically. Stuart liked him immediately.

"Gentlemen," Dixon began when the others were seated—Theresa Monks was obviously genderless—"as you know, Dr. Rice and I are collaborating on a study of—"

"Fuck off, Jelly." Stuart's head snapped around as Chung continued, "Five weeks ago you threw a little piece of wood at us in the lab and told us to fake an AIP on it. 'To keep the plebes in public health happy,' you said. You fed Dr. Rice your pompous too-busy-to-be-bothered routine. But now that we've turned up something interesting in that little piece of wood, you see your name up in lights. So you start sucking up. . . ."

Peter Chung was forty-seven years old and internationally recognized as a genius in fossil research. He had always been outspoken, even in China, where his frequent criticisms had run contrary to the prevailing sociopolitical doctrine of the early sixties. He had left China—escaped, in fact, one step ahead of the Maoist Red Guard—with his doctorate in archaeology and his life and little else. Eventually he arrived in San Francisco with no money, no contacts, and very little English. As an illegal alien he secured two part-time jobs, one buffing cars at a car wash, and the other delivering prescription drugs, or so he was told, for a Chinese pharmacist in the city's bustling Chinatown.

Within six months he had saved enough money and learned enough English to enroll in a university extension course in archaeology. By the end of his first semester his instructors had recognized his talents. He was permitted to advance to graduate studies the next year and to rewrite his doctoral thesis the year after that. Given the quality of his work, the archaeology department eagerly invited him to join the faculty, and eventually to head the section of fossil identification research.

That is where he had crossed paths with Gerard Dixon.

Shortly after Chung had joined the faculty, Dixon was asked to give the keynote address to a visiting team of highly acclaimed research archaeologists. Chung, despite his relatively recent appointment, was to chair the meeting and introduce the speakers. It began as a stiffly formal event. Robotlike, each speaker made his presentation, invited questions that never arose, then sat down to muted applause. Chung was nervous enough as it was, but his nervousness increased even more when, in a well-intentioned effort to soften the atmosphere, he tried to introduce the next speaker, Gerard Dixon, by his familiar first name.

Although by this time he had amassed a formidable vocabulary, under stress Chung still had the characteristically oriental problem of confusing his rs and his ls. His intention was to relax the group. And as he made the introduction the desired effect was achieved, in spades, but at Dixon's expense. The collective mood in the room melted as the guests collapsed in laughter. By everyone's account—everyone but Dixon, that is—more exchange of information was accomplished that day than anyone could remember before or since. The event passed into legend. And from that day Gerry Dixon was known locally and internationally as "Jelly" Dixon.

Dixon had never forgiven Chung for the embarrassment. But that mattered not at all to the archaeologist. He was secure in his work, highly respected by fossil researchers the world over. He really didn't give a damn what Dixon thought of him and rarely missed an opportunity to let him know it.

Theresa Monks remained impassive, unperturbed by the outburst. Dixon's face reddened and he was about to protest when Cauldwell intervened, defusing the situation nicely. He turned to Chung, a mock scowl on his face, his cultivated English accent artificially stern. "Peter, please. Try to be a little more articulate. We do have company, you know." He was obviously accustomed to the animosity between the two men.

Chung looked at Cauldwell and grinned. "Well done, Art. Diplomatic, tactful, effective." Then to Dixon, "Let's just not have any of this collaboration shit, Jelly. This is Dr. Rice's project. We were called in as technicians on this, period." He turned to Stuart and winked. "I like to get the ethnic-minority shit out of the way at the beginning." Then back to Dixon. "Now, Gerrrrry, maybe we can start." It was the closest he would come to a truce.

Dixon's rage subsided, mollified by Cauldwell's distraction and Chung's gesture. "Yes, well, as I was saying, Dr. Rice, your little piece of wood as Chu . . . ah, Peter put it, certainly has a lot more to it than we anticipated."

He lifted the top sheet from the open file on his desk and handed it to Stuart. "This summarizes our findings quite nicely I think."

Stuart read silently:

Specimen: 842771
: submitted for AIP 10/24/84
: Rice, Dr. S.H.; (artifact identified as remnant of infant sleeping crib origin 1943, wood for species identification and ? pathogenic content)

Genus: cedrus
: sp. libani (98), (deodar)

Dendrochronology: 2000+

Carbon 14: 1940 +/- 50 b.p.

Spectrophotometry: 415 (620) n.m.

Paleobiology: hyphae neg., cellulose/lignin normal, tr. limnoria lignorum

Metallurgy: ferrous oxide, calcium silicate (pred.)

Paleopathology: "queery blood" (type/species unk.), cultures neg.

He looked at Dixon.

Chung anticipated his confusion. "Don't worry about it, Dr. Rice. It wouldn't mean a thing to me either." He took the sheet from Stuart. "If we can assume for the moment that you don't know a great deal about fossil research," he paused; Stuart nodded, "then we'll walk you through this report one step at a time.

"But there are a couple of points I'd like to make first. First, when someone brings in an artifact, like your crib slat for example, and asks us to identify it, it's not good enough to just determine that it's a piece of wood, or even that it's a piece of cedar as is the case here. We want to know how old it is; not just when the artifact was created, but how old was the tree when it was cut down. Where did it come from? Where has it been? What was it used for? What else was it used for? Was it cut, or sawn, or worked? How was it cut or worked? Was it painted or stained, and if so, what with, and when? Has it decayed? Why has it decayed, or why not? And on and on it goes.

"So we start with an insignificant little scrap of wood and we piece together the whole history of the world." He smiled. "Not quite, of course. There are limits to our findings, limits which are being pushed further and further as the technology improves. But limits nevertheless. And this is the second point I wish to make before we start. Within those limits," he indicated the sheet Stuart had just read, "we can draw conclusions with near-absolute certainty."

He paused, his voice low, his tone serious. "It is of the utmost importance that you understand the significance of that, Dr. Rice. While we might theorize this or hypothesize that—and we'll be doing a lot of that as well this afternoon—the information summarized on this sheet is gospel. If you took your crib slat to any of the hundred or so other fossil labs in the world, their results would be so similar to these as to be identical.

"This is the truth, Dr. Rice," he said, waving the sheet at Stuart. "It is the total sum of absolute information on which all discussion of this artifact must be based. Conjecture is always fascinating, but as I said earlier, we are simply technicians in this case. We have considered only the hard, documented facts. Do you understand what I'm trying to say?"

Stuart nodded, if not convinced then at least impressed by Chung's seriousness. "From what you've just said along with Dr. Dixon's earlier comments about the kind of stir this crib remnant has produced, I take it that some facts have emerged—not possibilities, but facts—that are, ah, somewhat unusual."

"Probably the understatement of the year, Dr. Rice," Chung continued. "That's correct. It's not what your artifact *might* have been, but what it in fact *is* that is so . . ." he searched for the word, "staggering."

He glanced at the sheet. "All right, let's begin.

"Genus. Okay, your wood is cedar; either Himalayan or Lebanese cedar. Within ninety-eight percent certainty it's Lebanese. If you know anything about wood you'll find that surprising. Cedar is classified as a softwood; good weathering properties under certain conditions, but a softwood nevertheless. Your piece of wood was as hard as a rock. It surprised me too.

"It's old, very old. Dendrochronology two thousand plus means that if the Lebanese cedar tree the slat was made from was still standing it would be more than two thousand years old."

Stuart interrupted, frowning. "Do you mind if I ask questions while we go along? Already I'm skeptical, but since this is all new to me, a lot of my skepticism is born of ignorance. How can you tell from a piece of wood that size how old it is?"

Chung nodded. "Because of its size it wasn't easy. Dendrochronology involves using the annual growth rings to date a tree. It's one thing if we have a full cross-section of timber. But with only a fragment to work with it's something else altogether. We use what's called a floating chronology. We fit it into a sequence of dates already established for pieces of the same type of wood. Yours fits in just over two thousand years ago. It's by the growth rings, incidentally, that we're so sure it's Lebanese rather than Asian cedar. Your wood has fairly indistinct rings, suggesting it grew in an area without a seasonal type of climate; a semiarid, semitropical area like the Middle East, rather than a mountainous area.

"I can see you're still not convinced," Chung added. "Believe it or not, we've used dendrochronology to trace samples of bristle-cone pine right here in California back more than five thousand years. Even Leonardo da Vinci—he first suggested the principle—would have been proud of that. But this isn't the only way we date these things. In fact we use it more as corroboration than anything else. Rather than getting hung up on it, perhaps I'll just reassure you at this point that the date is correct. I think you'll find it easier to accept as we go along.

"Carbon fourteen—radiocarbon dating—ever heard of it?"

Stuart shrugged. "Only vaguely."

Chung continued, "It has to do with a natural decay process that occurs in an organism after it has died. A tree, for example, takes up both isotopes of carbon, twelve and fourteen, while it is alive. When it dies, the carbon fourteen converts to carbon twelve at a fixed rate. By measuring the amount of carbon fourteen remaining in the wood we can tell, usually within fairly narrow limits, when the organism died. In this case, the tree was cut one thousand nine hundred and forty years ago, b.p., plus or minus fifty years."

"Bee pee?" Stuart asked.

"Before present. The half-life of carbon fourteen was recalculated in 1950, which threw all the dates out by about twelve years. A correction factor is built into the calculation now. B.p. simply refers to that change. In fact, all the new dates are also wrong. In my doctoral thesis I recalibrated the standards used to determine the carbon fourteen half-life, so that now the dates are off again by about two and a half years. When I presented the new correction factor I proposed calling the new dates 'b.c.,' before Chung. But my examiners thought that was a bit presumptuous."

He looked up at Stuart, grinning. Stuart couldn't resist a chuckle.

"At any rate, in this case, as you've probably noticed, the limits are rather wide: plus or minus fifty years. That's a half century either way. A lot can happen in a hundred years. We think it was the stain, or what we thought was a stain, that threw the dating process off a bit. Perhaps Theresa can help us with that in a minute.

"So now we have a Lebanese cedar tree being chopped down a little under two thousand years ago. So far so good.

"Spectrophotometry, spectroanalysis. We take a small piece of the wood and do a number of things to it. We can burn it and measure the wave length of the light it gives off. That's emission spectrophotometry. Astronomers use it to determine the composition of stars. Or we bombard it with X rays or some other kind of radiation, atomic absorption or emission spectrophotometry, and measure the composition of the radiation that results. We did both with yours, and got a whole gemish of colours. Which is about what you'd expect from wood. But we also got two spikes on the scanning absorption spectrophotometer, one at four-fifteen nannomicrons, and another at six-twenty. That was a surprise. Four-fifteen is heme pigment, six-twenty is ferricyanide. As Theresa will explain a bit later, both indicate the presence of blood."

Stuart's head snapped up, incredulous. But before he could speak Chung continued, "Yes, blood. But we'll hold that for now. The paleobiology and metallurgy refer to the presence of various organic and inorganic residues in the wood." Turning to Cauldwell: "Art, you're the expert. Why don't you elaborate on this."

Cauldwell cleared his throat and recrossed his legs. "Nice of you to share the stage, Peter."

Dixon fidgeted nervously, misinterpreting Cauldwell's remark. Chung merely enlarged his grin. Sarcasm was obviously standard fare in their relationship. Theresa Monks remained silent, apparently oblivious to the exchange.

Cauldwell began, "Essentially what we're looking for, Dr. Rice, is to see if something, anything, ever took up residence in your little piece of wood. Various types of

moulds or fungus for example. Direct evidence like fungal
hyphae extending into the more central part of the wood;
or indirect evidence, like changes in the expected molecular composition of the wood itself. The report mentions
the cellulose-lignin ratio for example. If it was abnormal
it would suggest that some long-dead creature might have
been nibbling away at the wood. And in fact in your case
we found traces of a little crustacean called a limnoria—a
gribble is the common name for it—which is rather exciting actually. It's usually found along the European shores
of the North Atlantic but has never been reported in the
Mediterranean. Too warm, apparently. Which suggests to
us, and this is part of the conjecture process that Peter
alluded to, that the wood was at some point transported
from the Middle East to northwestern Europe. However,
other than the gribble, and small traces of rust and sand—
all of these were at the notched end of the wood,
incidentally—your wood was remarkably untouched and
well preserved. Unbelievably so, I'd say. You see, contrary to what people usually think, cedar takes preserva-
tives rather poorly. And cedar left exposed to the elements,
like a tree fallen in a forest, ordinarily falls prey to a whole
host of moulds and rots, and in fact decays rather rapidly.
We're not absolutely certain on this, but we're fairly well
convinced that what protected your wood from decay was
the presence of what Theresa has called 'queery blood.' "

Again Stuart was startled by the word. "Queery blood;
you mean you're not sure it's blood?"

"No," Theresa Monks replied. It was the first word she
had said. Her voice was incongruously soft, almost seduc-
tive. "I mean queery—'queer' with a y on the end—blood.
May I, Arthur?"

She glanced at Cauldwell, but even before he nodded
she continued, "Dr. Rice, I'm a forensic pathologist.
Paleopathology isn't exactly my area of expertise, but occasionally I'm called upon by the department for tissue
identification. I wouldn't ordinarily be involved with an
artifact such as yours, and still wouldn't be if Peter hadn't
come up with those unusual spikes on his spectroanalysis.
He suspected immediately, or so he tells me," she gave
the fossil specialist a scurrilous glance, "that it was a

heme pigment residue—blood, that is—and asked me to verify it."

Chung interrupted, "You'll have to excuse Theresa, Dr. Rice. She must be excited. She doesn't usually come this close to a sense of humor."

Monks continued as if he hadn't spoken, "Without belaboring the process, Dr. Rice, what was initially thought to be a stain in the wood turned out to be—I'm not quite sure how to phrase this—more like blood than any other kind of tissue.

"There was a definite hemoglobinlike molecule, and heme iron, and traces of red and white cell membrane on electron microscopy. But it wasn't like any other blood I've ever seen or read of. The specific gravity was too low. Even taking into account the preparation artifact, it was much lower than we'd expect for blood.

"Preparation was quite a problem, incidentally. Ordinarily, removing blood or stains from other materials is a relatively simple matter of saline or chloroform extraction. But in this case some kind of molecular bonding had fused the blood with the wood. It was extremely difficult to separate enough off to run even the basic tissue marker tests. But once we confirmed that it was blood, of course we went ahead with the full identification protocol. And there were several other atypical characteristics besides the specific gravity. For example, an alkyl substitution at the thirteenth carbon of the heme molecule.

"At any rate, we're convinced that it is blood. But what kind of blood we're not sure. It has most of the characteristics of primate blood, highly evolved, and probably human. But since it wouldn't fit into the standard typing format, we can't be certain it's human."

Stuart asked, "You mean it's not type A or B? That kind of typing?"

"I suppose it's more like type O than anything else," Monks replied. "Universal donor blood; you can give it to anyone without fear of a major transfusion reaction. But even in type O blood there are minor antigens, little bits of protein which individualize it. This blood was antigenically neutral. It had no characterizing proteins in it at all.

You could give it to anyone, or anything for that matter, human or not. It wouldn't react with anything at all."

She shifted in her chair, removing her glasses. She polished them on the hem of her lab coat as she continued, "But the most curious aspect of all is its age, or lack of age depending on your perspective. We had just enough left to run through the microcarbon analyzer Peter has been working on. The results were so inconsistent with the age of the wood that we assumed at first that it was lack of sufficient sample, or equipment error, or preparation artifact again. But Peter assures us that his machine has been remarkably adaptable and accurate with every other sample he's run on it. So, if we can accept the results—and I personally don't think we can," she replaced her glasses and glanced at Chung to emphasize her skepticism, "then the blood is old, literally unbelievably old. Older than any human or other life form. In fact it would not date within the calibration of the equipment, which puts it at somewhere more than two billion years.

"In a nutshell, Dr. Rice, your wood is permeated with an ageless, watery, nonreactive, humanoid blood. That's why I called it queery blood, 'queer' with a y on the end." The faintest of smiles crossed her face as she turned again to Chung and added, "Though I suspect that kind of humour is far too subtle for you, Peter."

Again Chung's only response was an ever-widening grin. He flipped through the file. "The only other point of interest, Dr. Rice, concerns the notch at one end of the wood. The wood parenchyma around the notch was compressed, suggesting it is part of what at one point was a square hole, punched rather than cut into the wood. Like a nail hole, although it would have to have been a square nail, similar to one used on a horseshoe. The hole, we believe, acted as a stress riser, weakening the wood enough to cause it to break at that point.

"As he already mentioned, Art found his little gribble at the notch, and the traces of iron rust. The fact that the gribble was superimposed over the rust with quite a thick interface between the two is fairly strong evidence that the hole was created some considerable time before the crustacean actually invaded the wood. Which means, if the Middle East to northwestern Europe scenario is true, the hole was probably created before the wood left the Middle East."

He closed the file, looked around the room at the others, then at Stuart. "As far as hard data is concerned, that's it. An unusually well-preserved piece of two-thousand-year-old Lebanese cedar impregnated with something resembling blood. Old blood, believe me, Theresa." He looked at Monks, his face serious.

"It probably doesn't sound like much to you, Dr. Rice, but from an archaeological perspective these findings are, again, staggering."

He turned to Dixon now. "Jel . . . Gerry, if Mrs. Anderson could be persuaded to bring us some coffee, perhaps we could explain to our epidemiologist friend just what all this means."

Dixon nodded and reached for the intercom.

Chapter Fifteen
November 29

In his study, Stuart slumped in his chair, files and reports strewn across the desk. The notes he had taken that afternoon during his discussion with the four fossil scientists lay open on his lap. Initially he had found it impossible to resist their enthusiasm. As the meeting evolved into a free-ranging discussion of possibilities—what the wood might have been used for, who might have used it, where and when—the excitement and energy in the room had mounted. Each was able to expand on suggestions from the others, sharing and developing theories and hypotheses of the wood's history. Even the antagonism between Dixon and Chung seemed to have faded.

However, well into the second hour he became aware that despite the archaeological significance of the wood, his purpose in launching the investigation in the first place was not being served. He directed specific questions at the researchers, trying to establish some basis for a causal relationship between the wood and the infant deaths. But their responses were consistently negative.

Theresa Monks confirmed that none of the cultures, bacterial, viral, or fungal, grew any pathogenic organisms whatever. The bloodlike stain had been submitted to extensive H.L.A. antigen studies, trying to identify it further. It simply would not react with any known antibody. It was absolutely antigenically sterile. His immune-response theory, that some reactive substance in the wood might be responsible for the deaths, was all but finished.

Cauldwell reassured him that except for the gribble there were no residual traces of microscopic life in the wood. And even the gribble, alive or long dead, was of no pathogenic significance to humans. Lead, arsenic, mercury, cyanide—none of the usual toxins or heavy metals had been found. Even the nonspecific marker tests for other contaminants were negative. They'd be wasting their time to look further.

Any surface markings on the wood were readily accounted for by its recent history. The most superficial scratches bore traces of steel alloy and conformed to the spring in the McEwens' garage door. The surface cutting and sanding flaws revealed by low-power microscopy resulted from the wood being worked and used as a crib slat. None of the serrations or irregularities harboured any unusual organisms or chemicals. "Squeaky clean," Monks had offered.

From an archaeological perspective the wood was a gold mine of exciting possibilities. But for Stuart's purposes it was a dead end. His day, beginning as it had with the optimism generated by Gerard Dixon's intriguing phone call, had ended with disappointment and the realization of defeat.

He tossed the notes onto his desk, scattering four or five of the autopsy reports onto the floor in the process. He leaned back in his chair, crossing his feet on the desk. Marnie called from the kitchen.

"Coffee's on, Stuart. Do you want it in there?"

"Sure, thanks," he replied, distracted. He had investigated the crib deaths from every conceivable angle, drawing a blank every time. Establishing a link between the wood and the deaths had been his last hope. He had hit the final wall, and there wasn't even a crack.

Marnie pushed open the door with her foot, two cups in hand. Seeing Stuart's relaxed posture and the reports scattered on the floor, she joked, "I like your filing system, professor."

Handing him his coffee, she set hers on the desk and knelt down to gather up the files. One was Todd McEwen's. Recognizing the name, she read on. "Are these the PM reports, Stu? The ones on the crib deaths?" she asked.

"Mmhmm," he replied, sipping his coffee. "For what they're worth. Thirteen dead kids, all in the same family. You'd think there'd be a common thread to them. But I can't tie them together with anything. I struck out with the archaeology group. They got pretty excited about the wood apparently being quite old but they weren't much help for my purposes, except in a negative way. They were all keen to run some more tests but they used the whole damn thing up with the first batch. And I told them there was no way they could get any more of it. At least I assume Jill and Brian don't want their crib burned bit by bit all in the interest of science. From the results of the tests they've already done, any more would be a bust anyway."

Marnie settled onto the sofa, scanning the reports she had gathered; names, dates, locations.

"You know, Stu, we've got laws for this and formulas for that. It seems everywhere you turn some researcher somewhere has come up with a logical, mathematical equation, a reason, for everything.

"But these," she waved a hand at the reports, "no one can explain these. Babies dying for no reason, at random almost. I don't believe in divine intervention, yet chaos is the only other explanation for it. Maybe someday someone will organize chaos into a nice neat equation and we'll have things like this all done up in neat, predictable little packages."

Stuart didn't respond. Sensing his mood, Marnie squared the reports on her lap and stood. "You've spent a lot of time on these, Stu. If there was anything there you would have found it by now." Riffling the pages of the files, she added, "These are still in order. Where do you want them?"

"Oh, just on the desk, Marn. Anywhere," he replied, distant, distracted.

She placed them beside the others and turned to leave. "It's after ten; I think I'll head on up." She opened the door. "See you upstairs, honey." The door closed.

Something stirred in Stuart. "Marnie?" Something, muffled, like a branch snapping somewhere in the dark. "Marnie?"

She poked her head back into the room. "More coffee?" she asked.

"No, thanks. What did you say?"

"I asked if you wanted more coffee."

"No, I mean before that."

"I'm going up to . . ."

"No, no. Before that."

"About the chaos, you mean?"

"No. You said something just before you put the files on the desk."

She thought for a moment. "Just that if you haven't solved this thing after all this time and effort you've put into it, then maybe it just can't be solved." She smiled at him. "You're so lost in thought tonight I'm not surprised you didn't hear me the first time. Why?"

"I'm not sure. I guess that was it." His voice trailed off.

She turned to leave again but he stopped her. "No, that's not it, Marnie. You said something else, just before you put the files on the desk. About orders or something."

She thought for a moment. "No, I don't remem . . ." She paused. "Order—just that the files were still in order when I picked them up. I asked you where you wanted them."

"They were still together, you mean?" He had been back and forth through the reports dozens of times. He couldn't recall leaving them in any particular order.

"Well, sure, I put them together. But I just meant the April ones were all together on the floor. I didn't know where you wanted them."

He looked at her, frowning. "What do you mean the April ones?"

"The April reports. Jesus, Stu, where are you tonight? All the reports on the floor were dated in April. I just assumed that since they were all together you must have them arranged by date."

Stuart dropped his feet to the floor and sat forward in his chair. He picked the top file from the stack she had replaced on the desk, reading the date. April. He read the next. April. And the next.

"Son of a bitch," he muttered. "Son of a bitch."

"Stu? Is something wrong?" Marnie's voice betrayed her concern.

Stuart was frantically reading the dates of the rest of the reports. "Son of a bitch. They're all April. Every one. How could I have missed that? Marnie, you're incredible. Every one of these kids died in April. When did Todd die?" Quickly he found the report. "Here, April third, 1983."

He picked up the next file. "Aaron Assad, April fourteenth, 1963." And the next. "Trevor Lasalle, April first, 1956. All of them April, April, April." He looked at his wife, grinning crazily.

Marnie's face was a mixture of amusement and puzzlement. "So what?" she asked.

"So what? I have no fucking idea so what. I've been concentrating so hard on the clinical data in these things I completely ignored anything else. I mean, once you have the age and time of death, who cares about the date?"

He rummaged through the reports until he found the genealogy file with its list of the children's names and their interrelationships and their ages at death. Beside each name he added a new column, the actual date of death. Even as he did this his mind raced back to the results of the computerized searches he had run on the data using the student's program. The persistent, aggravating results listing the sexes and ages and dates of death as being the only consistent data in the reports. *What a fucking idiot,* he thought. *The guy knew what he was talking about all the time.* Once the program was corrected it worked perfectly. Every one of those search results said month of death, month of report, month of autopsy, not date. It had been there all along.

As he proceeded down the list taking the reports at random and correlating the new information with each child's name, another curious pattern emerged. The more recent reports followed a nationally standardized format in which the date of the death was immediately followed on the page by the date of autopsy. He couldn't help but notice the second date as he recorded the first. In each case the autopsy had been held four days after the death. Not one or two, as he knew was the usual case with his epidemiological deaths, but four days. He went back through the older reports. Two were five days later, but in every one the autopsy had been delayed for at least four days after the child died.

He thought back to the events following Todd McEwen's death. He had phoned Novak, worried about the delay in autopsy. But Novak hadn't been concerned. They would only refrigerate the body anyway until after the weekend, he had said.

"Marnie, when did Todd McEwen die?" he asked. "What day was it, I mean? Saturday, wasn't it? Saturday morning. I remember I didn't have to go in to work that day."

"Jesus, Stuart, I thought you'd never forget that. You were so pissed about us having to cancel the last long ski weekend of the season. No, it was Friday. Don't you remember, Good Friday? . . . Stu?"

He knew. There was no logic, no rationale. Yet he knew. Todd McEwen had died on Easter Friday. His autopsy had been delayed until after the long weekend, four days later. He knew. Beyond any doubt he knew that the reason for the rest of the autopsy delays was the same. They had all died on Easter Friday.

"Stu? . . . Stuart?"

Only twice before in his life had he experienced the same tingling in his lips, the constriction in his chest, the dizziness, the inability to breathe. Both times the stresses provoking the hyperventilation symptoms were readily apparent. But now the fear pounding in his chest was infinitely worse; an absolute, irrational panic. His fingers and lips were completely numb. He could hear himself gasping, the nausea choking him, his head spinning and splitting, powerless to stop it. But beyond the numbness framing and pervading the vertigo and the nausea was the cold. Not just a vague chill now. No longer the innocent broken branch in the dark. It was a shivering, freezing breath of ice, enveloping him, terrifying him.

His puzzled, stumbling search had led him to the end of the last hallway. A blank wall. Where there was nothing just moments before, an enormous door had opened; beyond it an endless void, an abyss. The floor behind him had risen, tipped, pushing him through into the chasm, into the cold, blinding light. He was moving down now, the vortex spinning faster, faster. At the bottom, just beyond his reach, beyond his vision, was the crib.

April, the children, the deaths. At the bottom was the answer.

ORIGINS
Part Three

Northern France: A.D. 1551

Friday, April 16, 1551. The citizens of Etretat were about to hang their priest.

Father Jean-Louis Montmartin. Shortly after his ordination he had been sent to this remote village on the north coast of France. The local church held a valuable religious artifact, he had been told, one that needed a resourceful young priest like himself to watch over. Only for a short time, his bishop had reassured him. Just until a parish in Lyons became vacant.

That had been thirty-two years ago. The fire of his faith had long since died. Now, forgotten and embittered, the walls of his cynicism rose as steeply as the cliffs on which his small church stood.

He was the perfect cynic, critical of everything. He distrusted the new pretender in Rome as much as he had disapproved of Pope Julius II. Or the lunatic Italian, Columbus, ranting about a new world, dead now and the better for it. Or Balboa, the typical lying, fornicating Portuguese, claiming to have discovered a new sea. Or the whoring, polygamous Henry of England; the islanders deserved just such a monarch. But he reserved his strongest venom, his most acid bile, for the Protestants, and especially for "the new heretics," the Calvinists.

Hands bound behind him, Montmartin was dragged to the edge of the cliff. There, hundreds of villagers thronged about the base of a tree. A thick, knotted rope swung from its lowest branch. He recognized one of the benches from his church resting on the ground beneath the rope.

Jean Calvin. Montmartin recalled him in Noyon; a young, firebrand theologian. Little more than a lukewarm ecclesiastic, but eager to latch on to any new and controversial theme.

First Erasmus; then Martin Luther with his theses against the indulgences; and now Calvin. Firmly established in Geneva, the Protestant Rome, this blasphemous renegade had taken Luther's ideas to the extreme. He had reduced Christianity to a cold, impersonal system of intellectual arguments. Demystified it. Stripped it bare.

But for all Montmartin's disapproval of the new faith, the people loved it. Calvin's cerebral emphasis on Christian concepts rather than pure faith and Church-oriented materialism translated into lower taxes. Among the swelling numbers of oppressed, disenchanted Catholics, the popularity of the new religion soared.

Rough hands lifted him onto the bench. Montmartin could smell the charred ruins of his church.

It was ironic, he thought. Stories had spread of the Calvinist missionaries, not content with simple blasphemy, resorting to destruction of Church property. But it wasn't the heretics who burned his church. It was the villagers themselves.

A coarse hood was pulled over his head; the rope lowered, tightened around his neck.

What a hoax. What a cynical joke, he thought, comparing his five-hundred-year-old simple parish church to the magnificent cathedrals he could only faintly remember in Lyons. The Calvinists wouldn't even have needed to destroy his church. They would have been welcome to the few tarnished altar ornaments he had: the chalice, the candelabra, the shawl. They could have taken them all. Even the old beam-cask with its fragments of dead leaves

*and rotted leather and cloth. A relic of the Crusades, or
so he had been told.*

*The ancient cask, lashed with rusted chains to a dark,
semipetrified wooden beam, had been hidden in the church
sacristy for almost four hundred years. It was of tremendous religious significance, they told him; the bait that
had lured him to this godforsaken corner of the continent
to begin with. If it was so important, what was it doing
stuck off in some forgotten backwater? Why was it not on
display with the rest at St. Peter's? He had never had his
questions answered. Now it didn't matter.*

*The bench was kicked away. The fall wasn't great enough
to break his neck. The noose simply tightened around his
throat. As he slowly asphyxiated, Montmartin's last thoughts
were of the beam-cask.*

When the Calvinists had arrived in Etretat a month
earlier, Montmartin had been surprised by, and reluctantly admired, their quiet, earnest manner. But where
Montmartin was merely impressed, the effect on the villagers, especially the children, was electric. His congrega-
tion had quickly dwindled. Yesterday evening his Advent
Mass had been attended by less than a dozen of the
faithful. Later that night a group of four village youths
had broken into the church. Inflamed by Protestant rheto-
ric, they were intent on vandalizing its meager contents.
In the morning, just hours ago, he had found the four in
the small, ransacked sacristy, dead.

The collective religious passion of the villagers ignited
into vengeance. The fallen youths were instant martyrs.
Montmartin was dragged before a hastily convened coun-
cil, declared guilty of murder, and sentenced to death.
Never mind that the boys' bodies were unmarked and that
Montmartin himself had reported the deaths. He was guilty.

His church was sacked and burned. The benches, the
altar, anything that could be was thrown off the cliff into
the sea. Many of the villagers wanted to toss Montmartin
himself. When the old beam-cask was heaved into the
waves, the cask itself shattered, spilling its contents over

the cold channel waters. The beam, released from the chains binding it, bobbed to the surface, intact.

Montmartin's tunic slapped at his ankles, his feet only inches from the ground. His body swayed and spun slowly in the breeze. As the last of his life and his bitterness were choked from him he faced the sea. Were it not for the dark hood covering his head, his last vision would have been of the dark wooden beam; the tide, the current, the offshore winds all conspiring to carry it north, across the Channel, to the shores of the island beyond.

The four slain youths of Etretat were buried in a common grave in the village cemetery at the edge of the cliff. A marker was erected at the site detailing the circumstances of their deaths.

On May 2, 1551, a dark, solid beam was tossd by the waves onto the rocks one and a half miles east of the harbour at Portsmouth, England. Save for invasion by the occasional maritime crustacean seeking refuge from the climate, it would remain there undisturbed for the next two hundred years.

In 1553, a solitary priest arrived at Etretat. He left shortly after making a number of hushed inquiries into the events of Easter two years earlier. He seemed more concerned over the fate of an ancient religious artifact than over the demise of Father Jean-Louis Montmartin.

In 1687, from the combined effects of a mid-winter storm and the natural process of erosion, twenty-seven feet of the cliffs of Etretat fell into the sea, including most of an abandoned cemetery. Long forgotten and ignored, the marker and common grave of four martyred youths were never missed.

Chapter Sixteen
November 30

Hunches. Vague, often wild, apparently baseless, instinctive impressions.

Countless times during Stuart's medical training his instructors had drilled into him the importance of hunches in diagnosis. And just as often in his years of clinical practice he had done just that: fixed on some indistinct, illogical diagnostic impression, and traced it through, finally establishing a rational connection between a patient's symptoms and his past medical training and experience. Link-finding, he called it. It was an invaluable tool, the more so as he came to realize that only rarely did disease present itself in an orderly, textbook fashion. Many times in his career these seemingly illogical insights, these hunches, had saved vast amounts of time and expense. Even lives.

As important as training, research, and continuing education were, a highly refined index of suspicion was the prime tool of the best medical diagnosticians. Link-finding. The ability to play a hunch.

It was his index of suspicion that was nagging at him now. The numbness and vertigo, all the hyperventilation symptoms of the night before, had resolved. Now, as he sat in his study trying to explain the symptoms, to rationalize them, justify them, he recognized them as part of a familiar process. Far more dramatic this time, more intense than ever before, but still nothing more than the first stirrings of insight. A hunch.

It was the Easter factor. He had already confirmed the dates with the historical section of the public library. All the infants had died on Easter Friday. A very pleasant Mrs. Trevor-Easton had taken his dates over the phone and within five minutes had called back with the verification. It was left now to find the rational link between the Easter dates and the deaths.

On the surface it was illogical that anything but coincidence was involved. But hunches were rarely logical. Only after the connection was established, if it could be established, would the logic be apparent. Somewhere in his past, in the investigation, this Easter factor had surfaced, briefly, then had sunk back again, hidden. If the link was there, he would have to trace back through the last seven months to find it.

He did find it, four days later and then only by accident.

He had methodically reviewed his files, all the notes he had scribbled and saved. There was no mention of specific dates anywhere. With his penchant for detail—a compulsion, actually, to record every observation, no matter how trivial—if any particular date had arisen earlier in his research, he would have made a note of it. *Sure, Stuart,* he thought ruefully. *Like noticing the April dates of death.*

But if this vaguely familiar Easter factor was not a factual result of the investigation process, then it must have been part of the process itself. He was looking for an event, not a statistic.

"Better hurry up, Stu. Here comes Woody."

Rice and Novak had just finished lunch in the hospital cafeteria. They were about to leave anyway when Novak rose suddenly and made his comment. Stuart looked around. Saul Pezim was winding his way through a maze of tables to where they sat. Pezim's graft-rejection research had run into several snags, and Novak was eager to avoid the agony of listening to a litany of complaints.

As he rose, Stuart was struck by a curious sense of déjà vu. The last time they had been joined for lunch by Pezim, the little researcher had monopolized the conversation, describing how his solution to a research dilemma had been to sacrifice and examine the surviving rats in his graft-rejection study. It was too familiar, examine the survivors.

Another branch broke, another switch was thrown. His elusive Easter factor; it wasn't connected with one of the

dead children. It was one of the survivors. One of the
children who had used the crib and not died.

His mind raced as he walked back to his office. Sixteen
surviving children. He had had no direct contact with any
of them. The questionnaires in his files held all the information he had, and there were no clues there, no mention
of Easter. Or any other date, for that matter. Mentally he
summarized his baseline data: thirteen infants, all male,
all less than one year old, all die in the same crib, at Easter.
Another sixteen infants, twelve girls, four boys, same family, same crib, don't die, at Easter or otherwise. No problems there.

Again, rephrasing it, changing the emphasis: Thirteen
boys, no girls, die only at Easter. None dies at any other
time. True.

Twenty-nine infants use the crib, thirteen die, all at
Easter. True.

Sixteen infants use the crib and don't die, at Easter or
otherwise. True.

Twenty-nine use the crib at Easter, thirteen die. True.

Thirteen die, sixteen survive, at Easter. True.

He stopped, puzzled. *That's wrong. What's wrong with
that? Thirteen die? That's okay. Sixteen survive? True. At
Easter? No, before that.*

It was there. He could feel it.

"Come on Stuart, think." He was talking out loud to
himself now; playing the basic facts over and over, back
and forth like a recorded tape. "Twenty-nine infants use
the fucking crib, thirteen of them die at Easter. Twenty-
nine kids use the crib at Easter, thirteen of them die."

He stopped. That was it. He couldn't say that. All
thirteen deaths had occurred in the crib at Easter, but he
could not say that all twenty-nine infants had actually used
the crib at Easter. Something, some hidden scrap of prior
knowledge, was blocking that statement. His mind was a
kaleidoscope of images: files, reports, conversations, interviews. He was close now. Somewhere, just beneath the
surface of his memory, a forgotten remnant.

The downward rush had halted, the spinning vortex

stopped, silent. Different hallways, different doors lay before him now.

His suspicions had proven correct, the link established, the hunch verified. It was the evening he had spent with the McEwens, with Brian's old uncle, the crib's maker. His story of the crib's origin during the war. How finances had forced his pregnant wife to move back to her parents, away from his Maritime post. He had built the crib for his first child, a boy. But because of the separation he had never seen him sleeping in it. His first encounter with his son was three months after his birth, when he arranged to meet his wife and the boy in Montreal, halfway between their home and his base in the Maritimes, at Easter.

"That kid was with his parents in Montreal at Easter. He was nowhere near the crib."

But even as he said it another specter emerged, more ominous, more chilling. Discovering that brief prior mention of Easter in the investigation not only quelled one suspicion, but raised others. Of the sixteen survivors, he now had one who had not used the crib at Easter.

One that he knew of.

Stuart recognized a familiar anxiety.

Fifteen years ago, while in practice, he had owned a small, single-engine airplane. He had been a careful pilot, always filed a flight plan, checked his charts, the weather, prepared meticulous estimates of fuel consumption, arrival times, alternate landing sites. But more often than not, some unexpected event, weather usually, imposed an enroute detour that forced him off course, over unrehearsed terrain, his whole consciousness dominated then by a pervasive anxiety, a lack of certainty. At takeoff he would always presume but could never be absolutely sure that he would arrive safely at his intended destination. It was that recurring anxious uncertainty that had compelled him eventually to sell the plane. That was twelve years ago. He hadn't flown since, and hadn't missed it.

Now he was flying over unfamiliar territory again. Gone were the usual landmarks of statistics and autopsy reports, medical cause and effect. Connecting the use of a particular crib—at Easter, yet—with the deaths of thirteen in-

fants had no basis in medical fact. He realized this as he
sent letters off to the parents of the surviving children,
asking them for any information they might recall about
their child's first Easter, especially as it pertained to using
the crib. Even as he finished the letters he realized that
the chances of meaningful replies were marginal at best.
Some of the "children" were now adults, with children of
their own. Expecting their parents to recall the events of
an Easter thirty years ago in some cases was not just
unrealistic, it was laughable. He couldn't even remember
his own Easter two years ago.

But even if only four or five of the parents could remember something it would help; one case in particular,
the twins. Scott Jackson had died in April 1952. His brother,
Stephen, was still alive. If the trauma of the event had left
its usual indelible impression in the minds of the parents,
then they more than any of the others would recall that
day, with painful clarity.

As the responses trickled in over the next two weeks
Stuart summarized the information and added it to his
genealogy file. Not unexpectedly, the more remote the
event, the less certain the parents were of any of the
details. Most of them admitted it was purely guesswork on
their part. But some, especially the more recent ones,
were able to state that although they could not recall
the specific Easter in question, given their usual habits
and lifestyles they had no reason to suspect their child had
not used the crib at Easter. Negative affirmatives; better
than nothing. Lynn Thayer, Gwynn Harrison, Corinne
Thayer, Katherine Bucknall, and Judith Thayer—all born
between 1971 and 1979—fell into this category.

Some of the responses were definitely positive. As he
expected, although the event had taken place more than
thirty years ago, the parents of the Jackson twins recalled
the day in exact detail.

Born in July 1951, the two boys had slept together in
the crib for the first four months. But as their size and
activity levels increased, the small crib was simply not big
enough for both of them to use. So a second crib was
purchased; standard fare, beads and glossy paint, but poorly

constructed. Scott, the firstborn by seventeen minutes, remained in the family crib while Stephen was moved to the new one.

In the morning the two would usually awaken simultaneously. And as they grew stronger they would pull themselves to their feet and shake the sides of their respective beds until their mother came for them. As Stephen clambered on the rails of the cheap, store-bought crib it would shake and sway dangerously. His father had dubbed it "the rocker." In contrast, when Scott—in fact even when both boys together—shook and swung from the sides of the family crib, it was so solid it hardly moved. "The rock" he called it.

The "rock" and the "rocker" stood side by side in the nursery. At seven-thirty in the morning on Friday, April 11, 1952, Enid Jackson entered the nursery to find Stephen banging away at the sides of "the rocker." Scott lay still and quiet in "the rock." Dead.

Andrew McEwen's parents also recalled the Easter in question. And as he read their letter Stuart recognized their story as the same one Jill McEwen had told months ago, the race for the crib. Andrew's cousin, Paul Thayer, was born two weeks before him and had "won" the right to use the crib. And had died in it at Easter, three months later. Only then did Andrew get to use the crib, and have his name carved on the side. By his first birthday the following January he had outgrown the little crib and had graduated to a larger one. He was never in the crib at Easter, any Easter.

The rest of the replies prior to 1971 were unreliable guesses, except for Maurice Lasalle's. According to his mother, Maurice was twelve pounds at birth and seemed to double his weight every time she changed him. By the time he was four months old, in September 1958, he had outgrown clothes that his sister had worn when she was eighteen months. He first pulled himself to a standing position when he was seven months. The second time he tried it he was in his crib. He fell out. His father crated it that day and sent it off to a cousin who was expecting early in 1959. A larger replacement crib was borrowed from friends, but within a week Maurice had fallen out of that one as well. He ended up sleeping in a large, homemade wooden box on the floor, surrounded by cushions. He never did spend Easter in a crib. Any crib.

Creatures under his bed, or under the cellar stairs, ready to grab at his ankles as he dashed madly to the top. As a child he had tried to deny their existence. He knew they weren't there, just as surely as he knew they were. Now his fears had regressed, back to that same preadolescent stage. Gone was the mature, rational, bad-weather-detour fear of flying, something he could recognize and rationalize and control.

He reviewed this new information, trying to deny the significance of the pattern that had emerged, trying to ignore the creature grasping at his legs.

Including the "negative affirmatives," nineteen infants had definitely used the crib at Easter: six girls, thirteen boys. The girls were alive; all the boys had died. Only four children had definitely not used the crib at Easter. All were male. All were still alive.

A sudden chill startled across his neck as the cold December wind rattled against the window. Movement? Under the stairs? Under the bed? He struggled with it, desperate, trying to force logic and reason onto it. "Something's got to be contaminating that fucking crib," he said aloud. "But the wood's been studied to death. It's clean. Why only boys? And why only at Easter?"

Chapter Seventeen
December 20

His investigation was taking him further and further from his usual areas of work. He had no charts for the territory he was entering now. No one did.

He had spoken again with Theresa Monks, and again the pathologist had confirmed that all the toxicology and culture examinations of the crib slat had been negative. There had been no traces of any known forms of pathogenic organisms. Stuart picked up on her phraseology immediately.

"What do you mean, 'known forms'?" he asked.

"I mean the culture media and the chemical screens we use are for the strains we might expect to find on such a sample. And quite frankly, we'd pick up ninety-nine percent of the significant pathogens."

"That leaves one percent," he persisted.

"Less than one percent, actually. But you're right, Dr. Rice. If you're implying that we might have missed something, that's entirely possible, though highly unlikely."

"Has it happened before? That you've not detected something? Something that turned up later, I mean?" he asked.

"Yes and no," came the reply, after a brief pause. "It hasn't happened to me, but yes, it has happened before. And no, whatever was missed the first time never did turn up. Not to my knowledge anyway."

"I'm not sure exactly what I'm looking for, Dr. Monks." Stuart was groping now, not even sure what questions to ask. "Would looking into that occurrence help me, do you think?"

The pathologist sighed, her patience thinning. "I'm not at all sure what you're looking for either, Dr. Rice. I would have thought the results of our AIP would have put to rest any thoughts you may have had about some lethal agent contaminating the crib you talked about.

"The incident I'm referring to happened in Sudan in the late sixties. One of the labourers on an archaeological dig died shortly after entering a burial tomb, a tomb which had been sealed for over three thousand years. By the description of his symptoms he died of anaphylaxis, which was confirmed at postmortem. The tissue and serological markers all indicated a fulminant, anaphylactic type of response to some mould or fungus, but all the tissue cultures were negative. And while there were the usual benign, harmless fungi like candida floating around, no traces of any pathogenic organisms were ever found in the tomb."

"And nothing turned up later to explain the death?"

"Nothing definitive. The locals apparently attributed it to a mummy's curse, which I suppose is better than anything the pathology experts could come up with."

"Any theories? I'm sorry to be so persistent with this." In fact, he was getting desperate.

"Nothing that would help, I'm afraid. Although when you read the account of this case, it is interesting that he was the only person to enter the tomb on that particular day.

"Getting back to the moulds, we know that certain forms of mould remain active for years, and even decades. Yeast, for example, in wine casks. All yeasts go through seasonal changes as part of their reproductive process. And so does the yeast in the sediment of wine barrels. It produces all the same buds and hyphae at exactly the same time of the year as the parent yeast in the wild does. It's the reason why some wines, especially the homemade varieties, become cloudy at certain times of the year.

"I remember someone theorizing—remember, there's no proof for this—that just maybe the labourer was unfortunate enough to have entered the tomb at the one time of the year that some fungus in the room was undergoing a normal, mitotic change. And for him, based on some genetic immunological flaw I suppose, breathing in a spore of this altered fungus was all it took to trigger an anaphylactic response. By the time he was found the next day, the mould was back to its normal benign state and never showed up on any of the pathogen screens. It's all just hypothesis of course. One of those patent-medicine theories that sometimes makes you feel better even though it doesn't actually do you any good."

Stuart paused. Monks's comments had raised several intriguing points. "Is there any chance a similar kind of mould or fungus might have been present in the wood I brought in? Remember, it was over two thousand years old. Could anything have survived that long, something you might have missed on the screens?"

Her answer was emphatic. "No. As you'll recall, there were no traces of any kind of growth at all in the wood, normal or abnormal, pathogenic or not. And all the viral cultures are back now and they're all negative."

He paused again, too long this time.

"Dr. Rice," Monks was becoming impatient, "if there's nothing else, I really must be going."

"Yes, yes, thank you for your time, again." Then, almost as an afterthought, he asked, "You wouldn't happen to know what time of the year that was, would you? It wasn't in early spring by any chance, was it?"

"Which? The Sudan incident? As a matter of fact, I remember first reading about it in the newspaper while I was cramming for my pathology orals. That would have been October. Why do you ask?"

"Oh, nothing. Just a thought. Thanks again."

Just a thought, he mused as he hung up. Monks had turned him onto a completely different track. The bacterial and fungal and viral cultures had all been negative for pathogenic strains. But that left the nonpathogens or even the subviral group, which might not show up on the usual screening tests. Some normally benign organism, totally innocuous in its usual form but highly toxic, even lethal at certain stages in its life cycle, at specific times of the year. *Suppose that at some point in its reproductive cycle this organism becomes pathogenic, only to certain individuals, on some age and sex-linked genetic basis, so that it would not affect males and only . . .*

He caught himself. *Stuart, there are so many fucking*

holes in that. He laughed to himself. Yet, at the same time, he realized that again his laughter was a final defense. Again he had nowhere else to turn. As wild as it seemed, this latent-toxin theory was all he had to go on now. He had followed other, equally illogical leads before. One more couldn't hurt.

Chapter Eighteen
December 21

It had been years since Stuart had visited the public library. He had phoned ahead, asking for the historical section, and again speaking to the same Mrs. Trevor-Easton who had confirmed the Easter dates of the infant deaths.

He was met at the entrance to the basement stacks by a plump, white-haired lady.

"Oh, Dr. Rice. It's so nice to see a face attached to the voice. Not many people actually bother to come down here anymore. Against the rules." She motioned upwards with her eyes in obvious disapproval of the library administrators upstairs. "But that's no bother." She pinched his elbow. "Come along then. Roman history you want, is it? And what area did you say? Egypt was it?" She was enormously likable.

"No, Lebanon. Or the area around Lebanon I guess. Whatever it was called in those days."

She led him down two flights of stairs and through a heavy metal door into a massive room. Shelves upon shelves of books crammed the room. Mrs. Trevor-Easton was talking all the while.

"Oh yes, it's had a rather turbulent past hasn't it? What is now Lebanon and Israel and Jordan and parts of Syria was once just referred to as the Levant. Palestine too, though that's usually reserved for a smaller region. So it's the Levant then. Just over here."

Expertly she made her way through the maze to a row of stacks marked QR413. On the shelves were hundreds of thick, dusty, leather-bound tomes, each one identical to the next, with barely legible titles on the bindings.

"Here we are then." She pulled down one of the vol-

umes, blowing dust from the cover and opening it to the
title page. H. Romana: circa 100 B.C.: Egypt.

"Well, it's not Egypt we're after then, is it?" She replaced the book and pulled down the next. "Egypt again.
Well you can see how it works. This whole section has
references to Roman history. Not the originals mind you,
these are just translations of course. But you just go through
them and you'll come across the ones you want. Take your
time now. There's a chair at the end of each row." She
pointed to a small, straight-backed chair in the corner.
"Just browse through the lot and enjoy yourself." She
turned to leave, then stopped and looked back. "You're
sure there's nothing I can help you with, now?"

Stuart's bewilderment must have shown. "I wish there
were, but I'm really not all that sure just what it is I'm
looking for." He looked up at the walls of books before
him. "I knew the Romans kept records, but I had no idea
there'd be so many. All I'm looking for, I think, is some
mention of plagues or epidemics, but I think I'll just have
to go through the indexes and find out."

"Oh you'll find lots of them," she chirped. "Well, good
luck then." She glanced at the watch fob hanging from her
neck. "Eight-thirty. Tea's at eleven. Do join me."

She left him, her humming suddenly muted by the
slamming of the metal door. Stuart glanced again at the
volumes of reference work on the shelves. He shook his
head, pulled down the first book, and began.

A little over two thousand years ago the Romans had
extended their empire into the Middle East, imposing
their customs and their laws on the region, and their
penchant for record-keeping. The earliest reliable recorded
history of the area dated back to the beginning of Roman
rule. All aspects of daily life were written down. Slave
manifests, crop harvests, infestations, population figures,
tax collections, even the locations of the distance markers
on the highways of the day were methodically recorded by
scribes. It was an integral part of Roman order.

Over the millennia most of these records disappeared,
suffering the usual ravages of time and change. But some
survived. These, as they were found, became instant ar-

chaeological treasures, offering glimpses into the rituals
of daily life dozens of centuries earlier. They were preserved and protected, but not until their contents had
been scrutinized, dissected, and translated by scholars.
Copies of these Roman translations were to be found in
virtually every major library in the world.

He was looking for a reference, any reference, to episodes of sudden, unexplained group deaths. Not the mass
deaths associated with pan-epidemics, but smaller, isolated events in which anywhere from one to twenty or so
people died, unexpectedly, with no apparent cause.

Each volume was prefaced by an overview of the information contained in the main body of the book. These
summaries, however, were too general to be of much
value.

The translations themselves were organized by locale
and date rather than by events. They provided a fascinating series of keyhole peeks at the Levant from the Roman
perspective. But to get a chronology of any specific event,
all epidemics for example, he had to pick through volume
after volume, extracting only the information pertaining to
that particular event. Mrs. Trevor-Easton had been right.
There were numerous references to plagues and epidemics—according to the records, some kind of mass death
event occurred at least annually. But in each case the
cause was usually apparent from the scribe's description of
the victims' symptoms. Where the symptoms were equiv-
ocal, the footnotes always provided preresearched diagno-
ses and explanations. None of the books contained any
reference to the kind of unexplained death phenomenon
he was looking for.

One thing had become apparent, though. The quality of
the translations varied dramatically. The majority were
merely literal English translations of the original Latin,
with little attempt at grammatical reconstruction. Reading
them was a slow, arduous task. Others flowed like fluent
prose. Considerable thought and effort had obviously been
spent in making them comfortably readable. Even the
factual data contained in this latter group was more detailed, more accurately displayed.

Out of long-standing habit from his medical reading, he automatically checked the names of the authors and their bibliographies before reading the translations. The poorly constructed ones were usually done by students, no doubt trying to earn a little extra money while practicing their translation skills. The higher-quality works were done by professional scholars. But the best, the most detailed, the most skillfully prepared translations were consistently written by one person: H. L. Maddering. In fact, between 1931 and 1948 Stuart estimated that a full fifteen percent or more of the translations had been performed by that one person. Each was an exhaustingly detailed, exquisitely crafted work of art.

But in the end, good translations and bad, he came up empty. When he finished scanning the last volume he glanced at his watch. It was nearly five in the afternoon; he had been working steadily for more than eight hours. His eyes ached from the dim light, and his neck was stiff and creaking. He had not found anything directly useful, certainly nothing that supported his hypothesis that some mutating organism in the wood might have caused the deaths. When he climbed the stairs he found Mrs. Trevor-Easton arranging files on her desk, preparing to leave. She looked up as he approached.

"Oh, Dr. Rice. Thought we'd lost you down there. I looked in about twoish but you were somewhere back in Palestine I think. So I didn't want to disturb. How did you make out then?"

"Not well, I'm afraid." Stuart stretched, rubbing the back of his neck. "I really don't think the information I'm looking for is down there. Or if it is, the records really aren't organized in a way that makes it very easy to find."

"Yes, I know what you mean," she replied, shaking her head. "I don't much care for the Roman records m'self. Everything's scattered about so. Same with the English, though it hurts to say it. The Germans, though, now they're different. I don't much care for what they did to us in England during the war, but I must admit they do keep good records. All neat and tidy and in order like. Everything just so."

At the mention of Germans, Stuart recalled the superior

translations by H. L. Maddering. "Yes, I noticed one man's translations—or woman's I guess it could be—were conspicuously better than the rest. I think he was German."

"Oh, Maddering you mean?"

Stuart nodded.

"Oh yes, isn't he a dear. He's done work in just about every section down there." She motioned with her thumb towards the stacks. "I do enjoy reading his work. I don't think he's German though. Polish I think. No, they don't make them like he did anymore."

Thinking Maddering might have produced other reference works on the period, Stuart asked, "I noticed all his work was done prior to 1948. You don't know if he produced anything else on the Levant before he died, do you?"

"If we have anything it'll be listed." She moved to the author's index, opening the drawer marked MA. She thumbed through the cards. Maddering's work was listed on more than twenty cards, each bearing twenty-five entries. His output had been prodigious. "My but he has been busy," Mrs. Trevor-Easton remarked. "Tell you what. It's near on closing time now. Why don't I go through this lot first thing in the morning and give you a ring. It's references to epidemics and the like, is it?"

"Yes, that's right," he replied. "But only certain . . ." He stopped. It would be impossible to explain exactly what he was looking for. He would have to review the literature himself. "Actually, anything he might have produced on the region in that time period would be a help. You're being terribly generous with your time on this."

"Oh, it's no bother at all. I enjoy it if you want the truth."

She took one last look at the Maddering file before closing the drawer. "Now there's an odd thing," she said, her face drawn into a puzzled frown.

"What's that?" he asked.

"His birthday." She pulled one of the cards from the drawer, showing it to Stuart. "Here, see?" She pointed to the date beside Maddering's name: "1906–."

"What's wrong with that?" he asked again.

"Oh, nothing's wrong. It's just odd is all. I guess Mr. Maddering must have missed the annual review."

"What is that?"

"Well here, see?" She pointed again to the date. "They've only listed the year he was born and not the year he died."

"How do you know he died?" Stuart had no idea why he asked the question.

"Well, you just said so, didn't you? You asked if he published anything else before he died."

"I'm sorry. I guess I just assumed he was dead because there didn't seem to be anything by him after 1948 in the books. Do you mean he's not dead?"

She sighed with relief. "Well, not according to this one, love." She wagged the card at him. "We're pretty careful about updates. A reference center that's not current isn't worth much now, is it?"

She returned the card to the file and closed the drawer. "I'll get on it first thing tomorrow," she said, a ring of finality in her voice.

Stuart replied, distracted, "Yes, thank you again, Mrs. Trevor-Easton. Will you call me or should I call you?"

"Not to bother. I'll ring you up around nine."

Stuart left the library and mingled with the rush-hour crowd as he made his way to his car. Strange. The day had produced nothing of real value, yet he was less concerned about the lack of progress than about his casual conversation with Mrs. Trevor-Easton: that H. L. Maddering was still alive. He wrote his concern off to fatigue. Eight hours of slogging through ancient Roman history was not his idea of a stimulating day. Any distraction at all would have served as welcome relief.

But the concern remained. All evening and into the night he continued to dwell on the Maddering issue. If he wasn't dead, then why were there no more contributions by him after 1948? He would have been in his early forties then, still a young man. There were countless translations of inferior quality dated after 1948, but none by Maddering himself.

As he drifted in and out of a fretful, restless sleep,

images of doors and hallways appeared and faded and reappeared. He saw himself testing the doors, one by one, looking for a clue, a direction. Just as sleep finally overtook him he heard the quiet opening click of a lock.

At two minutes past nine the next morning his intercom buzzed.

"A Mrs. Trevor-Easton for you, Dr. Rice."

According to the library records, H. L. Maddering had indeed produced several translations and general reviews on the time and area Stuart was concerned with. Unfortunately, there were no specific references to plagues or epidemics in the indexes of any of the volumes currently held by the library.

"I should point out, Dr. Rice," she continued, "that not all the works listed in the files are actually on the shelves here. We have all the better-known ones of course, but there must be another twenty or so listed that we just don't have. Saint Michael's would have the full set, I should think."

"Saint Michael's?" he began.

"Seminary," she finished the sentence for him. "Roman Catholic seminary. They have a lovely reference library there. Oh yes. All theology mind you, but very complete in that. Oh yes, if anyone would have Maddering's work it would be Saint Mike's. I have their number here if you'd like it," she offered.

A Catholic seminary, thought Stuart as he copied the number. *Why not*. He thanked Mrs. Trevor-Easton again for her trouble, and was about to hang up when she called back into the phone.

"Dr. Rice? Oh good, you're still there. It'll be a Brother Thomas you'll be asking for at Saint Mike's. He's the librarian, a cute one that. I've referred a few others off to him in the past, and he's been ever so cooperative.

"But I shouldn't call him till after the holidays if I were you. I'm not at all sure what they do in a seminary over Christmas, but I suspect they'll be rather busy. I should think you'd stand a better chance of getting in to see him once the excitement has died down."

ORIGINS
Part Four

Europe: A.D. 1104

Richard Chieves could read and write, unusual talents for a peasant in twelfth-century France. Because of these abilities he was highly respected by his peers, his advice sought, his opinions valued. Unfortunately, his academic skills did not translate into greater personal income or a higher standard of living. Nor did they offer any protection from "the draft."

Quite the contrary. When his liege lord, Baron Gregoire de Pont-Vezelay, and his army of knights answered the call of Pope Innocent III to fight the infidel in Palestine, Chieves, because of his skills, was conscripted to serve as quartermaster. He and the two eldest of his five sons were to arrange the supplies and coordinate the logistics for the five-month journey to the Holy Land.

The uneasy truce between Christian and Moslem factions in Palestine had broken down, again. Amid rumours of mass Christian slayings, most of them unfounded, the Holy Father in Rome had sent an urgent appeal to the nobility of Roman Catholic Europe. They were being called upon not only to save their Christian brethren but to help re-establish the Church's dominance in Jerusalem.

Thousands responded. In what would come to be known as the Fourth Crusade, countless battle-starved barons and dukes and counts and unaligned knights from all across the continent were to congregate in Venice. From there they would arrange with the Venetian sea merchants for passage to the Levant.

The Venetians, however, were less interested in religious power plays than in establishing their own control over the lucrative eastern trade routes. Their target was Constantinople, not Jerusalem. Lying astride the Bosphorus, the capital of the Eastern Roman Empire effectively dominated the commercial sea lanes from the east. From the merchant's perspective, whoever controlled Constantinople controlled the world.

When approached by this vast, poorly led, poorly organized army from the north for transport, the Venetians saw an opportunity too heaven-sent to waste. They coerced the troops into an impossibly expensive carriage contract. When the leaders of the legions discovered they were unable to pay their fare, it was generously suggested that in lieu of payment they could "work off" their passage by laying siege to the Eastern Roman capital. Ostensibly this was to be done in order to reinstate the recently deposed emperor Isaac. (And quite rightfully deposed. The pro-Venetian ruler was totally insane.) With Isaac back on the throne in Constantinople and the Bosphorus securely under Venetian control, the army would then be taken by sea to Palestine.

Some of the knights, the scrupulous few, were disgusted by this Venetian duplicity. They withdrew from the main force and arranged their own transportation. Most, however, de Pont-Vezelay among them, accepted the arrangements, viewing them as little more than a minor diversion. And, with the fabled Byzantine treasures at stake, a potentially profitable diversion at that. As serfs, Richard Chieves and his sons were totally subservient to the wishes of their lord. They had no choice but to accompany Vezelay to the Bosphorus.

Constantinople fell surprisingly easily. For three days the invaders pillaged the city. After each looting foray they returned to their encampment to cache their plunder and replenish their weapons. Chieves's duties kept him far from the battlefront and from any opportunity to gather riches of his own. It was his responsibility not only to feed the knights and restore their armour but to catalogue and store their bounty for later distribution.

At the end of the third day, with the capital sacked and

beaten, Chieves left his sons in charge of the quarter-
mastering chores to search amid the rubble for passed-
over treasures. He found nothing of value until, sifting
through the smoking ruins of a monastery, he heard muffled voices below him. Clearing aside the debris, he exposed a heavy wooden door that led to a subterranean
crypt. There he found a cluster of three ragged, terrified
monks, huddled together, trying to conceal a small cask
that was heavily bound and chained to a dark wooden
beam.

As Chieves approached, the monks fell back, prostrat-
ing themselves, pleading with him to leave them and their
horde in peace. Though he could make out references to
"the great emperor Constantine" and "eight centuries," he
understood little else of the monks' protests. However,
judging from their desperation and the amount of chain
binding the cask to the wooden beam, he was certain it
must contain something of great value. Over the persistent
wailing of the monks, he loaded cask and beam onto his
wagon and returned to the camp.

The siege of the Bosphorus was successful; the Venetians were safely ensconced in the ancient house of Constantine. But for de Pont-Vezelay the Fourth Crusade was
finished. His spirit was crushed. With most of his knights
slain, he had no stomach left for another battle in Palestine.
He was eager to return to northern France.

Unlike the trip south, however, the journey home, begun in mid-winter, was slow and arduous. Traveling hard
by day, and too tired to prepare a formal encampment
each night, the troops would sleep in their wagons, or
under them, forging what shelter they could from the rain
and snow. In their own wagon, Chieves and his sons
shared their small space with a large portion of the looted
treasures, among it his own plunder, the cask still uno-
pened. The beam, covered with a skin, made a firm but
natural pillow for the boys' heads while they slept.

Of this ragged group, a full third fell to the ravages of
cold and exhaustion. And even with the alpine passes
behind them, as the early spring brought warmer temperatures, so did it bring an abundance of animals, among
them rats, and with the rats an outbreak of plague. Their

numbers dwindled even further. Chieves and his sons, accustomed as they were to hard living, fared better than most. They withstood the journey well.

Until the eleventh day of the fourth month.

The army had stopped for the night. With only two weeks of comparatively easy travel ahead, Chieves and his sons went to sleep in their wagon confident that the worst was behind them. When Chieves awoke the next morning, both his sons lay peacefully beside him, their heads resting against the beam. They were dead.

Death for the peasantry of twelfth century Europe was greeted less as a tragedy than as blessed relief from a lifetime of servility. Chieves had a wife and three more sons at home. He had loved the two eldest, and would miss them, but his mourning would be brief. As he completed the return journey, he thought only fleetingly of the circumstances of the boys' deaths. With typical philosophical resignation he found it more ironic than suspicous that they should both die so suddenly. That they should survive the perils of war and the hardships of travel only to die so near the journey's end, in their sleep. He was only briefly puzzled, and not at all concerned, that their deaths were unexplainable. They had been well and boisterous the night before. They had shared the same pheasant, drunk from the same gourd. Their bodies were unmarked, no sign of violence or the suppurative lesions of the plague. Alas, many events in twelfth-century life remained shrouded in mystery. For Richard Chieves, a peasant who could read and write, the passing of his sons was just one such event.

Once home, the carefully catalogued plunder was distributed among the surviving nobility. As payment for his services, Chieves was permitted to keep the cask and beam he had found and was apportioned a small pouch of coins and semiprecious gems. They would be gone in taxes within a year. When he finally broke the chains binding the cask, all he found inside were the tattered remnants of an old tunic, a pair of rotted sandals, a stained shroud of white muslin, and the fragmented remains of a thorny vine arranged in a crude circle. They were worthless. But, recalling the desperate concern of the Byzantine monks guarding them, he showed the artifacts, the cask and the beam, to the local priest. The priest, equally mystified, or so he said, in turn proposed to show them to his bishop.

It was the last Richard Chieves would see of his treasures.

The Fourth Crusade was a temporary success. The Roman Church's dominance was re-established in Jerusalem, but the irrepressible tide of Islam continued to flow. For millennia, an uneasy marriage would continue to bind Christians and Moslems living in the area.

An emissary from the Holy Father in Rome viewed the cask and beam Chieves had shown to his priest. The priest was instructed to rebind the cask, to replace the chains lashing it to the beam, and to transport the artifacts one hundred miles to the north, to the cliffs of Etretat. No explanation was given for the orders. None was expected.

The priest's counterpart in Etretat received the artifacts and immediately concealed them in his church's sacristy. There they would remain hidden, their presence known only to each successive priest, for the next four hundred years. A quartet of vandalizing youths would eventually discover them, with tragic consequences.

Richard Chieves died eighteen months after returning from the Bosphorus. He died still puzzled over the significance of the cask and the dark wooden beam, still awaiting an answer from his priest. By then the curious deaths of his two sons were long forgotten.

Chapter Nineteen
January 2

Christmas.

Stuart was a creature of habit. But as much as he enjoyed organized regularity—his work, his journal club, his chess and tennis matches with Novak—as much as each contributed its own pulse to the rhythm of his life, he savoured Christmas. Despite the hype, the manic interference, he always found it calming, a soothing eye in the storm. He forgot about the crib deaths, left the investigation idling.

His work slowed. Even the crises, stressful at other times, fell into a peaceful cadence. This year was no different. On December 26, eighteen elderly women in a nursing home fell violently ill with gastroenteritis. Four of them died. With the relatives involved, and the media clamouring for details, it was the kind of catastrophe he would ordinarily dread. But the season was like a balm. Tracing the cause of the outbreak to a turkey contaminated with *Escherichia coli* bacteria, dealing with the press, consoling families, he was hardly aware of the pressure.

On January 2, with the food-poisoning epidemic safely under control, and the holiday sedation fading, his routine gradually resumed its normal pace. He called the librarian at Saint Michael's Seminary, arranging to meet with Mrs. Trevor-Easton's "cute" Brother Thomas two days hence.

Later that same day, he recognized four familiar names in the obituary column of the evening newspaper: the four food-poisoning victims. Each was eulogized with the same anonymous phrases. Like form letters, only the names of the bereaved relatives differed.

*   *   *

While these four death notices were listed in Stuart Rice's evening newspaper, the following entry appeared in the New Year copy of the *Adrian Herald*, the local, weekly newspage of Adrian, Oregon.

BIRTHS

December 29, 1984: To Daniel and Stephanie Harrison; a boy, Gregory Thayer Harrison, eight pounds four ounces. Another grandson for Walter, and a playmate for Shep.

Chapter Twenty
January 4

The drive to Saint Michael's Seminary took Stuart thirty miles farther into the mountains. Visions of heavily robed monks moving solemnly about a walled and dusty courtyard played in his mind as he negotiated the curves and switchbacks. The expectation of rustic simplicity remained with him even as he entered the drive, guided by a discreet brass plate at the gate. But, to his surprise and disappointment, Saint Michael's turned out to be an open sprawling complex of low, tastefully modern structures. The buildings, all glass and cedar and exposed beams, were classic examples of West Coast architecture.

He parked his car in the circular driveway and entered what appeared to be the main building. A black-suited male receptionist pointed him to an open circular staircase leading to the second floor. The library was to the right at the top of the stairs.

It was enormous, easily twice as large as the floor of stacks he had visited at the public library. Carpeted, indirectly lit, the reading chairs plush and upholstered, little expense had been spared in making the facility comfortable and attractive. He coughed gently.

A collared, dark-haired man appeared from among the shelves. He looked at Stuart and smiled immediately.

"Ah. Dr. Rice I presume." He approached, hand extended. "I am Brother Thomas. Just Thomas if you wish. Welcome to Saint Michael's, or Saint Mike's as our dear Mrs. Trevor-Easton prefers."

But as he shook his hand, Stuart felt an uneasy energy flowing from the man. Despite the warm reception, Thomas's casual manner had a vaguely hollow ring to it. A

141

suspicion tainting the charm; a deception hidden just beneath the surface.

Thomas's friendly patter continued. "I must admit, Dr. Rice, when you described your request over the phone I was more puzzled than sympathetic. As Mrs. Trevor-Easton must have told you, this isn't the first time someone outside the Church has expressed an interest in theological literature. But we have never had a request to use the library as part of a medical investigation. And when you mentioned that you are primarily interested in the works of H. L. Maddering, I'm afraid my curiosity went right off the scale." Thomas smiled again.

"Maddering certainly produced most of the quality translations of the era you are interested in, Dr. Rice. But I was thinking about your request since you called, and I really can't recall any of his work dealing specifically with the kind of epidemic topic you described on the phone. In fact, I don't think anyone has published on that as a single issue.

"But as you know, Maddering stopped producing, or publishing rather, in 1948. I'm sure there would be more recent references than his."

Something tugged at Stuart's subconscious. "I'm not ruling out other authors, of course. It's just that there was something about the depth and quality of Maddering's work that makes me feel that he, if anyone, would have what I'm looking for. You corrected yourself there, by the way," he continued. "You said he stopped publishing rather than producing. What did you mean by that?"

A haze settled over Thomas's eyes. He tried to evade the question. "Well, you're right. He is certainly the best theological historian who has ever worked for the Church. In fact, he has produced the highest-quality translations of virtually every original document the Church has in its possession. I'm sure you'll find what you're looking for in his collections."

Sensing something, an intangible, Stuart persisted. "I hope you're right. But you still didn't answer my question, Brother Thomas. And you've raised another. You said, 'is.' He 'is' the best theological historian. Does that mean he's still alive, still working?"

Thomas looked at him, his eyes distant, measuring some unseen scale. Softly—nervously, Stuart thought—he said, "I don't know if he is still producing or not, Dr. Rice. He left the Church in the mid-fifties, but his last completed translation was published in 1949. We have a copy of that here, by the way, if you'd like to see it. To my knowledge he has not published anything since."

Thomas said this with such finality that Stuart decided not to press the issue. He straightened and smiled. "Yes, well, would you mind if I just browsed then? I might be here quite a while, if that's all right."

"By all means." Thomas smiled back, relieved. "Come. I'll show you how the index works and then leave you to your own resources."

Stuart spent the rest of the afternoon scanning indexes and tables of contents and reading in detail the more promising sections. But he could find no references to the kind of phenomenon he was interested in. Until his eye caught on a footnote in Maddering's last published work, an interpretive translation of several neo-Christian documents dating back to A.D. 350. The document itself was an account of the death of a child, the son of the emperor Constantine. The boy had apparently been killed by his mother as they were returning from an extended visit to Palestine. The document went on to describe Constantine's reaction to the infanticide, and his wife's eventual execution. But Maddering, with his customary insistence on accuracy, had subscripted the passage with an explanatory footnote:

Ref: 21. The reader is reminded that while this passage confirms an event well documented elsewhere (74;97;129), the description of the child's wounds is at variance with the recordings of the scribes Tertius Paulus and Certulin (from interviews with the attendants to the emperor's wife) (64;65), who state unanimously that the child's body was "unmarked by blood nor tumor." While Constantine obviously believed his wife to be guilty, the actual cause of the child's death remains open to speculation. Counterinterpretations of this event abound. (81;119;197;203;247)

"Unmarked by blood nor tumor." Stuart reread the footnote, then the translation of the document. The paper described a massive head injury, but eyewitnesses to the event, the mother's attendants, denied the presence of any injuries at all. He copied the list of reference numbers and turned to the bibliography.

He was becoming so familiar with Maddering's work that he recognized four of the five references by their titles. They were all Maddering's own translations. He had already been through them and had found nothing. The fifth was listed as 247: Codex Gnostica XIII, Book II, Ch. VII.

He found Brother Thomas and showed him the footnote and the reference. "Where can I find this . . . what is it? . . . codex?"

Thomas glanced at the entry. "Gnostic Codex thirteen, book two." His brow furrowed. "Is that one or two Is in the numeral?" he asked, squinting closer.

"You were right the first time," Stuart said. "It's a two."

"It must be a typographical error then. They must mean one. The Thirteenth Gnostic Codex contains only one book."

"Okay, book one, then. Would you have it here? Chapter . . . what was it? . . . seven?" He checked the roman numeral.

Thomas began towards the stacks. "They're on the back. . . ." He stopped and returned to his desk. Leaning over the book, concentrating, he mumbled "That does say seven, doesn't it."

Stuart just looked at him.

Thomas looked up. "It's just that there are only two chapters in the thirteenth codex. In fact none of the codices contain more than five chapters per book. This must be a double typo, unusual for one of Maddering's works." He turned to the title page. "Ahh, that explains it. This is the last one, isn't it?" He checked the publishing history. "The 1949 work I mentioned."

"Explains what?" Stuart asked, confused.

The same distant look crossed Thomas's face. He sat back on the edge of his desk, chewing softly on his lower lip, his arms folded. After a moment he spoke, softly again, apologetically.

"I'm sorry, Dr. Rice, I don't mean to be evasive. There's no reason of course why I shouldn't tell you this. It's just that we tend to, how shall I say it, protect our own. I told you this morning that Maddering left the Church in the fifties, and that he hadn't published anything since. That was the truth, but only a part of it.

"In fact, Maddering is still alive, though quite ill I understand. There are many rumours as to why he left the Church, but the truth is that in 1948 he began to show signs of mental deterioration. A precocious type of senility; he was only forty or so at the time. I believe the modern-day equivalent of this is called . . . I'm sorry, I can't recall the name. I believe it starts with an *A*."

"Alzheimer's disease?" Stuart offered.

"Yes, that is probably it. Thank you. In any event, his work apparently became so erratic, so unreliable, that it could not be released." He indicated the book on the desk. "These neo-Christian papers are the last reliably accurate interpretive translations he did. In fact, it's interesting that you found that faulty reference. Two typographical errors side by side would be unheard of in work of Maddering's usual quality. His reference to a second chapter in the thirteenth codex in all likelihood was entirely innocent on his part, simply a product of his diminishing mental capacities. He was working on the entire set of Gnostic Codices when he was relieved."

He paused, smiling warmly at his guest. "And that's all I meant. No big mystery. I'm sorry if I seemed abrupt or secretive earlier. Just an innocent attempt to preserve the reputation of a fallen brother. I hope you'll forgive me."

He extended his hand. "And I'm afraid it's closing time for us. You're more than welcome to return tomorrow, or anytime for that matter."

Stuart shook hands, allowing himself to be guided towards the door.

Thomas continued his patter. "Just give me a call before you come so we'll expect you."

Stuart's mind was a riot of conflicts as he retraced his route, down the stairs, past the receptionist, to his car.

He had found nothing of value except for the Maddering footnote. Yet, when he had confronted Thomas with it, the librarian had skirted the issue, dismissed it, and him, all in one neat diplomatic gesture.

He's lying. As he turned onto the highway, Stuart was shocked at the realization, not sure why he was so certain. In fact, not even sure what it was that Thomas had lied about. The whole story was too pat, too conciliatory. "Preserving the reputation of a fallen brother." What a crock. He recalled Thomas's apologetic handshake, his hand cold, moist, trembling.

"Behind your humble mask, my friend, you're scared shitless," he said aloud. *But of what? Why the hell should he care what I think of Maddering? Christ, I never even heard of the guy three weeks ago. He mentioned there were other rumours as to why Maddering left the Church, but he was pretty damned concerned that I believe the official version, the Alzheimer's disease.*

His concentration was interrupted by a procession of cyclists winding their way down the incline. He braked, touched lightly on his horn, and passed them carefully. They acknowledged his caution with grateful waves as he sped off ahead of them.

Back in the library, Brother Thomas turned out the lights and locked the doors. He didn't feel guilty at all. He had no reason to. He had simply given Stuart the Vatican's reason for H. L. Maddering's departure from the Church. The fear Stuart had detected in his handshake was not the fear of being caught in a lie. Rather, it was the fear that Stuart would question him about the rumours, the alternate explanations that ran so contrary to the official version.

Each man was so concerned with the other's reaction that neither gave a second thought to the most critical contradiction of all. The proof of the rumours for Thomas, and the beginning of an end to Stuart's search. Maddering's footnote. The thirteenth Codex.

Constantine's son. Unmarked by blood nor tumor. It was the closest he had come to a recorded, unexplained, uncaused death. Stuart returned to Saint Michael's the next day, and the next. He ignored the civil though distant attitude Brother Thomas had shown when he returned on the second day, just as he ignored his own feelings of ambivalence towards the friar. He continued to scan volume after volume of translations, looking for another reference to the death of the emperor's son. He found several, but each was little more than a literal translation of the official court version of the incident, nonreferenced, nondocumented. The accounts of the scribes mentioned in Maddering's footnote were not in the seminary library. He did find one interesting and disturbing piece of additional information, however, hidden in one of the less-accomplished translations. The event had taken place "in the fourth lunar cycle, three weeks following the Ides." The first week of April.

By the end of the third day his enthusiasm was waning. Every door he tried remained closed and bolted. He was discouraged and preparing to leave when Thomas approached, consoling.

"You're a very persistent man, Dr. Rice. You have directed so much energy into your search it is truly unfortunate that you haven't found what you're looking for." His voice was too gentle, his words too conciliatory. "But I'm sure not all of your efforts are wasted. Surely something of value will come of it."

Stuart tried to ignore the tone. He hadn't conceded defeat yet.

"In fact, the one reference I did find has turned out to be unavailable. You don't have it here, and I've checked with the public library and the history reference department at the university. Neither of them has even heard of it. It's as though it doesn't even exist."

"Is that the accounts of the Constantine scribes you asked about earlier?" Thomas asked.

"Yes. Maddering seems to be the only one who has ever heard of it."

Thomas nodded. "That's probably quite close to the truth, actually. Many of the translations performed for the Vatican have simply remained there, have never been published or released. Maddering of course had intimate access to all those documents. It's not uncommon to find one or more of his references unavailable for general use."

A door had opened, just a crack.

"Does that mean the account probably does exist?" Stuart asked. "But that someone like myself, or even yourself, couldn't get to read it?" He left the question purposefully vague and ambiguous.

Thomas took the bait. "Myself, perhaps. Someone outside the Church, definitely not. Occasionally they will release a copy of the 'reserve documents,' as they're called, but only with a written submission outlining the reasons for the request. Even then they might refuse."

Thomas's mask had cracked, his guard lowered. Stuart continued to pick away. "I had no idea the hierarchy of the Church included restrictions on information. I suppose they have their reasons though."

Thomas smiled, genuinely now. "Oh yes, Dr. Rice, they always have their reasons. But 'the hierarchy,' as you put it, is much more restrictive than you can imagine. We in the Brotherhood may have a direct line to God, but unfortunately the same is not true of our communication with Rome."

Stuart decided to chance it. He looked straight into Thomas's eyes. "Brother Thomas, what do you think your chances would be of getting me the papers I'm looking for? I'd be more than happy to pay for any mailing or administrative costs involved."

Thomas's eyes softened. "You're really hooked on this, aren't you?" His voice, once distant and cautious, was now warm, concerned.

Stuart only nodded.

Thomas paused for a moment, returning Stuart's gaze. Finally he relented. "Well, I suppose the worst they can do is say no. We send a mail pouch off to Rome every week. I'll draft a request in time for the next one. I'll simply say you'd like the papers as part of a medical investigation and leave it at that.

"I must confess, you have my curiosity piqued on this as well." He smiled warmly, genuinely. "I'll call you when I get a reply. But I should warn you, they're never as prompt as you'd like."

*   *   *

In fact, they were much prompter than anyone expected. The reply arrived five days after the request had been submitted. Over the phone Thomas read Stuart the tersely worded letter, which neither approved nor denied the request.

"'. . . the documents you have requested are no longer in the Church's possession.' That's it, Dr. Rice, verbatim."

Stuart had no idea what it meant. "How do you interpret that, 'no longer in the Church's possession'?" he asked.

"I'm puzzled by it, Dr. Rice. Even when requests for documents are denied they always send an explanatory letter with the refusal. But this contained nothing but what I read to you. No explanation at all. No indication where the documents might be. I checked the indices after you left the other day and I couldn't find any reference other than Maddering's to the scribes' papers either. It makes me think they might never have actually been Church property in the first place. They might have been a part of Maddering's personal collection—it was rumoured to be enormous. He apparently took it with him when he, ah, left the Church."

There it was again. The doubt, the hesitation.

"Which means if I want them I'd have to ask Maddering himself for them?" It was part question, part statement.

Thomas was immediately defensive. "I didn't say Maddering has the papers, Dr. Rice. It was only a presumption."

Stuart hesitated, debating whether to force a confrontation. Thomas was beginning to wall himself off again. Obviously he wasn't going to get anywhere going through official Church channels. Deciding he had nothing to lose, he began.

"Brother Thomas, I'm going to speak candidly. I don't want you to interpret anything I say as being derogatory. Critical yes, but even though it's directed at you I don't mean it as a personal attack."

There was silence on the other end.

He continued, "Ever since my first visit to your library, when I turned up Maddering's reference to that boy's death, I've had the distinct impression that I touched some kind of raw nerve in you. You seemed very distant after that, evasive in your comments, less direct, less frank. I'm specifically avoiding the word *dishonest* because I do think you've been honest, in what you've told me anyway. But for some reason, something in your tone, something in what you're not saying, I get the impression there's a lot more to this Maddering story than what you've told me. And that you know of it but for some reason are reluctant to talk about it.

"You've made several references, very hesitant references, to Maddering's leaving the Church. You even gave me the official version of why he left, the Alzheimer's disease story. Then you told me he is still alive, albeit quite ill, but still alive. Well, that just doesn't wash. You said Maddering last published in 1949 and then left the Church a few years later. That's thirty-five years ago. People don't live for thirty-five years with Alzheimer's disease. Besides, he was only in his mid-forties at the time, and that's too young for Alzheimer's. A presenile dementia or some other neurological disorder might occur that young, but they're even more progressive. He'd have died long ago."

Still nothing but silence.

He continued, "The first day I was there, just before I left you mentioned something about rumours as to why Maddering left the Church. And unless I'm badly mistaken you regretted saying it the moment the words were out of your mouth. Because I think you place a lot more stock in those rumours than you're prepared to admit. You've given me Rome's version of why Maddering left the Church. Truth or not, I'd like to hear the other versions."

The silence continued momentarily. Thomas cleared his throat. Hesitantly he asked, "What difference would it make, Dr. Rice? You're involved in an epidemiological research study. For whatever reason, Maddering left the Church more than thirty years ago. What possible difference could that make to your investigation?"

Stuart's hopes rose fractionally. "In fact, it's not actually Maddering's departure from the Church that really concerns me. It's just that I can't see any other way around this. I've gone through hundreds, perhaps thousands of translations in the past few weeks, and the only definite reference I've come up with to the kind of unexplained death I'm looking for happens to be in one of Maddering's footnotes. I haven't been able to track that reference down through all the usual channels, and now you tell me it doesn't even exist."

Thomas interrupted, objecting. "I didn't say that it doesn't exist. I simply said it might be a part of Maddering's own personal collection."

"You didn't let me finish," Stuart persisted. "Because that's what's so inconsistent. A person with the kind of progressive neurological disease you've suggested wouldn't have a personal collection. Of anything. Even if he had lived this long, which is virtually impossible, with the kind of thing you're talking about he'd have been institutionalized long ago. Given the kind of work he was involved in and the kind of people he was likely surrounded by, any collection he might have had would have been disposed of long ago by his heirs, or trustees or whatever. In fact, it would probably have been simply given back to the Church, or some other historical society. But the Church doesn't have it. And if some other society had it then the libraries would have access to it. But they don't even have a record of its existence. And if neither the Church nor anyone else has those papers, then all that leaves is Maddering himself.

"I have no concrete reason for thinking this, Thomas. Call it a hunch, or an instinct, or whatever, but my gut feeling is that those papers are what I'm looking for. And I learned long ago not to ignore that feeling. It looks like I'm going to have to contact Maddering himself to get what I want, and before I can do that, I need from you, if not the truth about his leaving the Church, then at least where I can find him."

Again Thomas hesitated. The silence was unbearable. After a full minute Stuart pleaded, "Please, Thomas."

Thomas cleared his throat again.

"You ask for the truth about Maddering, Dr. Rice. But just what is the truth? It can take many forms, always depending on your perspective. I am no more than a servant of my masters in Rome. To me, what they declare to be true is indeed the truth, regardless of my personal feelings. Yes, there are other interpretations of why Maddering left the Church, but to me they are nothing more than unfounded rumours. I have accepted my truth, and despite your arguments I continue to accept it."

He paused again, briefly this time. Then more gently, his voice barely audible, "Yet I sympathize with you. My denial of other possibilities, alternate explanations, is a product of my faith; blind faith I'm sure you'll say. Each of us, in our search for truth, walks a different path, each with its own perils. I happen to have overcome my own perils, and am content to have arrived. But you have the right to follow your own path, Dr. Rice, to discover your own truth.

"I can't, or to be more honest I won't help you by discussing this matter further. Maddering lives in Switzerland, in a small village north of Geneva. I don't know the name of the village; believe me, I would tell you if I did. If you wish to pursue this, you will have to do it alone, with him."

He paused, then added, "You have your gut feelings, Dr. Rice. This may sound elitist, but we in the Brotherhood are not immune to those same intuitions. In fact we're rather sensitive to them. And the feeling I have now is one of danger. Not the kind of physical danger you might be familiar with. More of a spiritual danger, the kind of thing that only one of us would recognize. I see a face that you cannot see, Dr. Rice, and that face is terrifying.

"I shall pray for you. Not that you will find what you seek—I'm sure you will. But that you will know how to deal with it when you do find it. Goodbye, Dr. Rice."

ORIGINS
Part Five

Eastern Mediterranean: A.D. 312

A.D. 312. What appeared to be a flaming cross lit the night sky over the Tiber River in what is now central Italy. At that same site the following day the last of a series of battles was waged. The loser, Maxentius, was killed. As a result of the victory, however, the winner, Flavius Valerius Constantinus, was able to consolidate his control over a vast empire. As Constantine the Great, he would eventually rule the entire Roman Empire from Byzantium, its new eastern capital on the Bosphorus.

The heavenly vision that had preceded his final battle was interpreted by Flavius as an omen of triumph. The flaming cross, symbol of a powerful emerging religion, served to strengthen his already-growing belief in Christianity. It is a matter of historical record that his conversion to the faith is often dated from this vision of the cross over the Tiber.

The more important consequence of his conversion, however, was that with it the religion gained a much-needed legitimacy. With this imperial recognition of the faith, the harsh persecution of Christian adherents was instantly eliminated.

As a matter of course, Constantine's entire family—his wife, his four sons, even his mother—converted to the new faith. Of these newly faithful, his mother, Helen, wielded the greatest influence over the emperor, though her position of dominance was rapidly eclipsed by her daughter-in-law. The open and often bitter antagonism between the *two women was an accepted fact of life in the emperor's court.*

In the summer of A.D. 312 an opportunity arose for Helen to regain some of her lost stature. At Constantine's request, she agreed to undertake what is recorded as the first historical pilgrimage to the Holy Land. Although the intent of the trip was to consolidate her son's control over that portion of his empire, Helen in fact hoped to use the voyage to enhance her own reputation and influence. To her great disappointment, Constantine consented to his wife's request that she and their two youngest sons join Helen on her pilgrimage.

Helen reluctantly accepted the company of her daughter-in-law and her grandsons. Supported by a full legion of troops, the party embarked on an eight-month journey. The thousand-mile trek from Byzantium, or Constantinople as it was now called, to Jerusalem was accomplished at a leisurely pace and in sumptuous comfort. The trip was one continuous party of prolonged encampments and lavish receptions with each of the regional Roman governors en route.

On her arrival in Palestine, Helen's principal function was to grant audience to the various local-interest groups, each hoping to curry favour with the new emperor. She accepted gifts and homage on her son's behalf, making many promises, intending to keep none. The most tiresome lobbies were made in Jerusalem by representatives of the various religious groups, Christian sects mainly, each with its own particular interpretation of the newly recognized faith, each seeking royal approval and patronage. She could barely conceal her contempt for the fawning, obsequious manners most of them displayed.

But one group was different. The Gnostics. They stood tall before her, refused to kneel, refused to beg. Self-assured, almost brazen, they claimed to have what they called "the true knowledge," a special understanding of Christ that put them at odds with all the other Christian sects. They had proof of their claims, they said, in the form of artifacts and ancient records that documented the true nature of the Christ.

They led Helen to an inconspicuous burial mound at the

edge of a field outside the walls of the city. From this they unearthed a cache of well-preserved articles: a ragged tunic, a dark wooden beam, a pair of leather sandals, a shroud bearing the faded imprint of a figure, and the brittle remnants of a circlet of vines. As unimpressive as they appeared, these represented the last remaining true evidence of Christ's death.

Helen's curiosity had been roused. She asked to see their documents. But they replied only that the records were well hidden in Egypt, in an area near what today is called Naj Hammadi. They would take her to them only if she would offer them guarantees of royal patronage. She tried to bribe them with lesser rewards but they were adamant: the documents in return for absolute guarantees of official recognition of their sect.

Frustrated and angry, Helen eventually tired of their unyielding demands. She dismissed these "gnostic Christians," but not before she had confiscated their "evidence." These artifacts, along with a mountain of gifts and bounty, would return with her to the Bosphorus.

The homeward journey, begun in mid-winter, was once again punctuated by frequent prolonged interruptions. One such occurred at the end of the third month of the year. For three weeks the party remained in an encampment while the soldiers rested and replenished their supplies.

During these layovers, the royal party lived and slept together in a large compartmentalized tent in the center of the compound. Their aides and attendants slept in more spartan quarters immediately adjacent, with the soldiers arranged in concentric circles on the periphery. For security, the many gifts Helen had received on her son's behalf, including the religious artifacts, were stored in chests and stacked against one wall inside the royal tent.

Constantine's wife slept on large, soft futons in a cubicle next to this wall of treasures. Helen's compartment was against the wall opposite. The two boys, by then ages three and four and growing weary of the constant travel, would as a rule take turns sleeping with the older women. They preferred their mother's soft cushions to their grandmother's hard divan. Constantine's wife would frequently awaken to find both her sons nestled against her, one on each side.

On the fifth morning of the week, she awoke to find the elder boy playing contentedly on the futon nearest the cubicle door. Her youngest son was on her other side, lying between her and the outer wall, his head resting against the stacked religious artifacts. He was dead.

Word of the boy's death spread throughout the encampment. Frantic searches, all in vain, were made for a possible assassin. The royal physician and a priest were called to examine the boy. There were no signs of injury on his body—"nor blood nor tumor" the scribes would write. They had eaten the same food, drunk the same water as everyone else. Poisonous snakes or insects were unknown in the area. The cause of the boy's death was a total mystery.

Constantine's wife was devastated by the loss. But Helen was more concerned over the effect the event would have on her son. The additional concern he would show his wife over the death of their child would certainly add to the considerable influence her daughter-in-law already exerted over the emperor. It threatened to erode even further her own stature. From this additional envy and resentment the beginning of a sinister plan was spawned in Helen's mind.

When the pilgrims finally reached Constantinople, news of the boy's death had preceded them, as had the rumours initiated by Helen herself. Desperate for an accurate account, Constantine summoned his mother immediately. The rumours were true, she told him. She confided to him her false suspicion that his wife had deliberately killed the boy. She supported her claim with fabricated stories of her daughter-in-law's growing hostility and irrationality during the pilgrimage, eventually convincing the emperor that his wife was indeed guilty of infanticide.

Helen's plot succeeded beyond her wildest imagining. Constantine did not question his mother's claims. He passed judgment immediately. His wife was executed.

Certulin and Tertius Paulus, two individual scribes assigned to Helen's pilgrimage, independently recorded the statements of the physician, the priest, the attendants, and the legionnaires, all of whom examined the child's body and all of whom denied the presence of injury or any suspicion of foul play. There is no historical record that Constantine read those reports. If he did, he chose to ignore them. Nor did he question the fact that only the one child had died, the one sleeping against the wall of gifts and religious artifacts.

Helen remained in a position of influence in her son's court until her death a decade later. The bounty collected during her pilgrimage was eventually categorized and distributed. The more valuable of the religious gifts were apportioned among the many prominent new churches in the capital.

The small cache of "gnostic" artifacts was assigned little value. The cask of clothing remnants and the dark wooden beam were relegated to an impoverished monastery where they were stored in an underground crypt. They would remain there, guarded by monks, for the next eight centuries.

Chapter Twenty-one
January 18

Linear progression; slow, sure, safe. Stuart's investigation had followed a standard, unimaginative process, moving in predictable, carefully measured steps, never deviating, never advancing until the base was proven, the platform stable. Until the Easter factor; until H. L. Maddering.

Now everything had changed. "Go with the flow," "roll with the punches," trite idioms; but the intuitive flexibility that he had now adopted was all of these and more, infinitely more. Rational logic had given way completely to reflex and intuition. Six months ago, even one month ago, if anyone had suggested he would be trying to locate a retired Church historian to help him with a crib death investigation, he would have laughed. But he wasn't laughing now. Now it seemed the most natural thing in the world, so complete was his transformation.

It had happened to him once before, when he had made his career change. He had always envisioned himself as a surgical specialist, even going so far as to apply for and be accepted into a residency training program. The entire year before he was to begin was a nightmare of insomnia, unexplained rashes, migraines. At the last minute, thinking better of the four-year commitment, he withdrew his application, abandoning the ideal he had held for years, opting instead for the move to epidemiology.

The relief was overwhelming. All the symptoms vanished almost overnight, replaced by an incredible sense of buoyancy and freedom. Where his time and energy were once dominated by his work—the after-hours on-call, the 4:00 A.M. deliveries—he rediscovered leisure. Not just leisure time but leisure thought. Right-brain thought. Art, music, literature, the creative sphere he had long ignored, suppressed, crashed in on him. At first he was content simply to read and observe, to spectate. But that led quickly to participation. He taught himself to paint, to sculpt. He mastered the piano. He even dabbled at writing, bits of highly entertaining creative fluff published by the local press. And all so easily, so naturally. At the time, he thought his vision and his creative intuition were limitless.

Since then, his years in public health, the insidious influence of procedure and protocol, had gradually stiffened his flexibility. But now something, the Easter factor, Brother Thomas's enigmatic warning, something had released it again. He wasn't involved in just an investigation now, a mere study. Quietly, gradually, the rules had changed. Statistics, genealogy, logical progression, none of the accustomed tools of his profession were valid, or for that matter of any use. His search had undergone a subtle, unseen metamorphosis. Now it was a hunt.

Some elusive prey was just ahead, constantly moving, darting, changing shape and direction. And instinctively, like some highly evolved predator, he stalked it, matching it stride for stride, change for change.

"A village north of Geneva."

Information and communication: on a global basis these were the mainstays of epidemiology. Without current information and the ability to centralize, collate, and distribute it, epidemiologists would be little more than local public-health mandarins, each scrambling to control health events in their own small spheres, never aware of the critical global picture of disease patterns. To fulfill that very function of information dissemination, a highly developed network of technical and personal communication links existed nationwide and across the globe.

Stuart was well integrated into that network. Many of his contacts were anonymous signatures on communications bulletins. But some were faces, men and women he had met at various meetings and conferences. Phillippe Roth was one of those faces.

The principal clearing house for health information on a global basis was the World Health Organization. Roth was its executive secretary and as such was stationed at W.H.O. headquarters in Geneva, Switzerland.

The two men had met at the World Health Congress in New York four years ago. Stuart had delivered a paper on the increasingly complicated process involved in securing information from international health societies such as the W.H.O. No fan of bureaucratic protocol himself, Roth had been arguing the same points with his directors for years. After Stuart's presentation, the two men had talked long into the night. Roth had predicted at the time that Stuart's paper was just the spark he needed to get the changes made. His prophecy proved accurate as Stuart's address galvanized the field support that had been missing from Roth's solitary arguments. As a result, a massive streamlining overhaul had made the entire process of information gathering and dispersal vastly more efficient, and had indebted Roth to Stuart for life, or so the aristo-cratic Frenchman had said. Despite the distance separat-ing them, the two remained in close contact, professionally and personally. Roth was one of the few people Stuart had instinctively felt attracted to. His communication with the Swiss-based organization was always directed through Roth and always included some personal comment along with his requests for information. Roth's replies to his inquiries were invariably prompt, personal, and usually humourous. Stuart recalled the communication he had had with Roth a little over a year ago.

AIDS, the immunity-suppressing mystery illness, had increased alarmingly in his jurisdiction over the previous year. He had forwarded a request to Roth in Geneva for a summary of the world literature on the research and ther-apy of the disease. Roth's preliminary acknowledgment had consisted of a cartoon—a medieval wizard standing over a boiling cauldron—and a condom. Scribbled in Roth's own pen on the cartoon were the words: "The research and the therapy. Stay tuned." Two weeks later, a two-hundred-page summary of the current status of AIDS research arrived on Stuart's desk. The cartoon was still tacked to his notice board. He looked at it now, wonder-ing how Roth would respond to his latest request: to locate one H. L. Maddering, former Vatican linguist and historian, living "in a small village north of Geneva."

He didn't wait long. Ten days later Roth's reply arrived in a hand-printed envelope. The return address in the upper left corner of the envelope said simply; "WHO?" The letter inside contained a full paragraph of good-natured insults and complaints of abused and overworked W.H.O. staff, his kindly nature being taken advantage of, and the like.

But he had found Maddering. Just outside Versoix, a small village on Lake Geneva just north and east of the city itself. He included the address, but concluded his letter with:

My sincerest apologies, but delisting, lack of time, and responsibilities much more mundane prevent me from including Mr. Maddering's telephone number, vehicle license, preference in wines, or hat size.

Truly yours,

Phillipe Roth
Missing Persons
W.H.O.

P.S. In the likely event that your memory has failed as abysmally as the rest of you undoubtedly has by now, may I remind you of my longstanding invitation, and your sworn promise, to visit us here in Geneva.

P.R.

He copied Maddering's address onto an envelope and inserted the letter he had already composed. In it he had briefly outlined the investigation he was involved in, his recent activity in trying to locate historical references to similar kinds of deaths in the past, his discovery of Maddering's reference to one such event (the unexplained death of Constantine's son), and his frustration at not being able to locate copies of the scribes' accounts of that event. He was careful not to exclude other contributions Maddering might be able to make. If the scribes' records were in fact part of Maddering's collection, he would appreciate copies. But at the same time, he would be grateful for any additional references Maddering might be able to provide, if as an historian he was aware of similar incidences of unexplained death during that period. He concluded the letter with an explanation of how he had located Maddering, apologizing for any inconvenience and assuring him of the confidentiality of their communication.

He had rewritten the letter a dozen times, softening and polishing it, rephrasing his requests. Having only Brother Thomas's inconsistent statements to go on, he had no clear idea of Maddering's current health or mental status. The last thing he wanted was to jeopardize what might be his last hope of progress by a lack of diplomacy. Even as he sealed the letter he was filled with doubt, wondering if he should have phrased it differently still.

What happens, happens, he thought as he dropped the letter onto a pile with the rest of the outgoing mail.

Despite the fatalism he had felt when he sent the letter, Stuart was not prepared for the reply.

Dear Dr. Rice:
    . . . The documents to which you refer (Cerus, Ter-tius Paulus) are familiar to me but not in my posses-sion. They were indeed a part of the reference documentation for the neo-Christian translations to which you refer in your letter. However, they were, and to my knowledge continue to be, the property of the Roman Catholic Church.

    As you suspect, they describe eyewitness accounts of the event in question, and are at variance with other historical references. Verbatim translations of these documents are enclosed for your perusal. . . .

Stuart turned immediately to the second page of the letter. It contained two nearly identical descriptions of the death of Constantine's son. He recognized the story immediately. The boy, his brother, his mother, and his grandmother were returning to Constantinople from an ambassadorial pilgrimage to Palestine. At an encampment on their return, he and his brother, as was their custom, had slept in the same room with their mother. In the morning the boy was found dead. But neither the priest nor the physician who examined the boy was able to find any evidence of injury or foul play.

The second report was different only in its choice of words. The content was the same. No alternate explanation for the boy's death was advanced, no evidence given, circumstantial or otherwise. Simple, objective statements of fact.

Disappointed, he turned back to the first page. As he read the final paragraph, his hopes were rekindled.

> Your investigation into the deaths of these infants is at once noble and intriguing. You have given me but the briefest of glimpses into your problem, but with your allusion to what you have called your "Easter factor" you have aroused my curiosity. (You will have noticed that the Constantine event occurred also during the Lenten season.) While your overview does not bring further historical reference to mind, perhaps a more detailed examination of your data would. To that end I would be pleased to review your results and offer what assistance I can.
>
> Yours truly,
>
> H.L. Maddering

Chapter Twenty-two
February 20

Changes. His investigation was hurtling him along an emotional roller-coaster, from resentment during his initial involvement the night of Todd McEwen's death, to indifference as the crisis settled in the early months. Curiosity next, then professional intrigue, and now, finally, a consuming, driving commitment. Even in the absence of concrete progress, where he once would have felt mere professional resignation he was now aware of an aggressive, competitive determination to succeed, to capture a prey. But now, after responding to Maddering's offer, he felt as though his predatory instincts had been tranquilized, put on hold while some bland de-energized muzak kept him entertained. Like a schoolboy waiting for the results of his final exams, his fate was totally in the hands of others.

He had spent most of the two weeks following Maddering's initial response collating and cross-referencing his files. The information he had accumulated on the infant deaths and the subsequent investigation filled more than six hundred pages of notes, tables, reports, memos, none of which would make much sense to anyone looking at them for the first time. A lot of the data he now felt was trivial, incidental. He had been tempted merely to summarize it for Maddering. But it was exactly the kind of trap he knew he had to avoid. Any summaries he prepared would reflect his own observations and biases. Maddering's offer presented an opportunity for a fresh, nonmedical, totally objective assessment of his data, an opportunity he couldn't afford to miss. Maddering must be given the chance to read and interpret the information for himself, from his own perspective. Consequently, he had sent the entire file, trivial data and all. He had enclosed summaries as a courtesy, but also an invitation for Maddering to ignore them if he wished.

By the end of the fourth week his tranquility had dissolved. The passive accept-whatever-fate attitude had eroded, replaced now by a constant, gnawing, subliminal fear. The endless waiting, like a delayed biopsy report, could only mean bad news. Maddering's reply, when it came, did nothing to dispel the anxiety. Quite the contrary. Three terse, cryptic sentences, each one like a razor stropping his fear, honing it. He read them over and over. Each time the blade keened finer, the edge all but invisible, at that dead-sharpened zone between puzzlement and fear.

Dr. Rice:

I cannot, repeat can not, comment on this matter in writing. It is imperative that we meet at your very earliest convenience to discuss your data. I cannot overstress the urgency of this request.

Maddering

Chapter Twenty-three
April 9

". . . begin our final descent shortly. In preparation for landing please extinguish all smoking materials, ensure that your seatbelt is securely fastened and that your back rest is in the upright . . ."

He was only subliminally aware of the flight attendant's message. He responded absently, stowing the unread journal on his lap in his flight bag, adjusting his seat. He glanced to his left. Marnie was busy at the window, craning her neck for a better view. Below them, the monotonous blue-green expanse of the Adriatic slipped quietly away. In the distance the western shoreline; and at the horizon, just visible beneath a smudge of haze, lay Venice.

Despite the frenetic activity of last-minute work and travel changes, the past three weeks had seemed an eternity. His thoughts wandered back. . . .

He had read Maddering's reply dozens of times, analyzing it, dissecting it. No salutation, no closing. Three brief, concise sentences, each an imperative statement, each totally unrevealing. The overall effect had been one of overwhelming urgency. If Maddering's intent had been to create in Stuart an anxious, driven suspense, he had more than succeeded.

Arranging to meet with Maddering had been easier than he expected. With this year's World Health Congress scheduled for the third week of April in Venice, it had been a simple matter to advance his arrival date to allow him time to meet with Maddering in Switzerland before the conference started. The only problem arose with the timing. The airlines were booked solid with holiday travelers. Direct flights to Switzerland were sold out. Transferring to a second flight in Venice was the best option available. But to guarantee two return seats from Geneva to Venice for himself and Marnie he had to settle on a flight a full week before the conference was to begin. His work schedule was flexible enough to accommodate the change, and any concern he had about interim activities was settled by Phillippe Roth's ecstatic reply to his announced planned visit:

. . . though it pales in comparison, I'm sure you will find a week of spring skiing in our humble Alps a reasonable alternative to your North American preference for baseball and fast food.

Ordinarily he would have been overjoyed at the prospect of spending a week at a renowned Swiss alpine resort. But even Roth's understated sarcasm couldn't distract his mood. He was being drawn by some insidious, unseen magnet. His thoughts were riveted on Versoix, on Maddering's cryptic reply.

The two-hour stopover at Venice allowed them barely enough time to collect their baggage, clear customs, and check in at the Swiss Air desk. They arrived at the departure lounge just minutes before the first boarding call was announced.

Two hours later they were descending once more, again over water, this time the cold black stillness of Lake Geneva. A panorama of snowy peaks and village-dotted valleys spread out beyond the northern shoreline. Lost among them was Versoix. It passed unrecognized directly beneath them.

The long flight had exacted a physical toll. Stuart rubbed his fingers against his palms. They were soaked. An uncomfortable, queasy burning churned in the pit of his stomach. He pulled his coat closer around his shoulders. The chill had returned.

Phillippe Roth was even more amiable than Stuart remembered him. He had met them at the airport and chauffeured them back to his home, a large square brownstone less than a block from the lake.

Their initial conversation had been bold, witty. Roth had never met Marnie before, but the two were perfectly matched. Like co-conspirators, they exchanged numerous barbs, with Stuart as their natural target.

Marnie had gone to bed shortly after dinner, exhausted. The men shared a quiet brandy in Roth's den. A log hissed softly in the fireplace. Neither had spoken for several minutes, each content with his own thoughts. Roth stood, gently interrupting the silence.

"Something is troubling the good doctor. Not the conference, and more than just exhaustion from your trip. I rather suspect it involves this meeting you have arranged for tomorrow in Versoix."

He paused. Stuart only nodded. Roth continued, "I'm not prying, my friend. If you think I can help, you'll ask." Part question, part statement. "Meanwhile, your charming wife has had the best idea yet. I'm off to bed. Enjoy the fire, and the brandy. There's more on the mantel. Help yourself."

Stuart looked up at his host, grateful. "Thanks, Phillippe. You're as perceptive as ever. I was just about to apologize for being so detached. It is this business with Maddering. I think it's really just a question of not knowing what to expect." He smiled, adding with more humour than he felt, "Once I've heard what he has to say, you probably won't be able to shut me up."

Roth opened the door, returning the smile. "I think I could handle that." He looked back at his guest, concerned. "You know, Stuart, we reach a point in any crisis where our thoughts come full circle. They double back on themselves, like a snake eating its tail. When that happens, the best-known remedies are action, good brandy, and sleep. The first is for the future, tomorrow in Versoix. The second is past, though you're welcome to more." He waved a hand at the bottle on the mantel. "Which leaves sleep. For the present it's what you need most, my friend." He nodded, brows arched. "Good night."

Once alone, Stuart's mood deepened again. He wasn't

scheduled to meet with Maddering until one-thirty tomorrow, fifteen hours away. He had been traveling continuously for more than twenty hours; physically he was drained. But sleep was the furthest thing from his mind as snatches of some dark somber theme, cold uneasy strains, tugged at his thoughts.

Chapter Twenty-four
Adrian, Oregon: Thursday, April 19

"Rice? You the one Stucco called about?" The state trooper brushed the powdery remnants of a sugared doughnut from his denim vest.

"Stucco?" Stuart answered.

"The desk sergeant in Boise, with all the zit scars on his face. He called shortly after you left, warned us you was comin'. Said you needed help findin' some of our locals."

Stuart nodded; a glimmer of hope emerged. He hadn't given the police in Boise high marks for efficiency or concern. That the slow-witted "Stucco" had called ahead was the first encouragement he'd had for the past four days. He said, "People by the name of Harrison . . ."

The trooper just looked at him, a faint smile forming on his lips. From the back of the room a deeper, gravelly voice asked, "Dan and Steffie?"

Stuart looked towards the voice. An overweight, greying, marginally uniformed policeman was folding a sheet of paper. He stuffed it into the pocket of his down vest as he lowered his feet to the floor and pressed himself to a standing position. His first few steps were lurches, his gait evening out as he crossed the floor to where Stuart was standing. He looked at the younger trooper. "Don't get old, Donny. At least if you do, move somewhere where it's so hot your shit comes out cooked like a sausage." He looked at Stuart. "Arthritis. Every time it storms I feel like my hips 'n' knees is made 'a sandpaper."

The young trooper clucked at him. "Sure, Ed. Wake up in the morning, every joint stiff but the right one."

The older man ignored the comment. "That Dan and Steffie Harrison you're lookin' for?" he asked.

Stuart nodded again. "That's right. I understand they

live about half an hour away, up towards the, ah, Ohyoway? dam."

The younger trooper snickered in the background. The older man looked at Stuart. "Owyhee," he said, picking something from between his teeth.

"I got the *O* right," Stuart said, half-apologetically.

"Oh, Donny wasn't laughin' at that. Nobody gets the name right." He looked at the snow gathered on the window sill. "It's the half-hour he was laughin' at. That right, Donny?"

"You got it, Sarge." The trooper squared a sheaf of papers on the counter. "They're only fifteen or so miles out, but in this shit," he cocked his head sideways at the window, "they might as well be in fuckin' Portland. Jeff said he was pushin' drifts two 'n' three feet high off the highway between here and Boise. Shit. You go another five hundred feet up and you're lookin' at twice that. The Harrison place, shit, they're halfway to the dam. Even in your four-by-four, Ed, it'd take three hours anyway."

The older man had been watching Stuart while the trooper spoke. "Ed Lauder, by the way," he said, extending his hand.

Stuart took it, the glimmer of hope fading. "Stuart Rice. I take it all this snow isn't quite what you expect this time of year."

Lauder shook his head. "Ain't she a bitch. Middle of April, you'd think we'd be seein' a little sunshine for a change. Every few years though we get stung with a howler." He paused for a moment, eyeing Stuart. "Stucco said you sounded pretty desperate to get here. There a problem?"

Stuart looked at Lauder, debating how much to tell him, how much he'd believe. These were simple, uncomplicated men. He could never expect them to believe his story. Worse, if he told them the real reason for his coming, they would be just as likely to detain him, lock him away in some softly padded room. He decided to half-lie.

"More of a promise than a problem actually. Unless I don't get there before midnight, then it's a problem for me." He laughed, hoping to divert Lauder's curiosity.

"I'm a friend of a cousin of Stephanie's, from California. He should be making this trip, not me. It's kind of a message, is all. Something to do with the family, her father in fact. And it has to get to them tonight. Their living in the bush without electricity or phone service doesn't make the job any easier."

Lauder's face creased at the mention of Stephanie Harrison's father. "You talkin' about old Walt?" There was genuine concern in his voice now.

"Do you know Walter?" Stuart asked, welcoming the diversion but still afraid of being trapped in a lie.

"Old Walt? He's a tough old fart to forget. Was up to see Steffie and Dan back last July or August. In fact, said he was comin' up from California at the time, now that you mention it. We don't get a lot of tourists through here. Don't like 'em usually. But if they was all like Walter we'd have the doormats out. Stood right where you're standin' now and asked me for directions. We ended up havin' a beer over at the hotel. That man could charm the socks off my wife. And anyone knows my wife knows that's damn near impossible. You got hard news on Walter?"

Stuart's mind was racing. He had to make this sound plausible. "Ah, no. Nothing bad. It has to do with an heirloom, from Walter for the baby. It's a traditional family thing, something to do with Easter. We're the closest to here geographically, so Walter tried to get Stephanie's cousin to bring it up. But they've gone off for the holidays so he phoned me. And like you said, with Walter doing the talking it's tough to say no. So here I am." He tried to keep the story at least half-true, playing down his own role. The last thing he wanted was a lot of delaying questions.

Lauder was looking at him curiously. "Another heirloom, eh? Last time Walt brought along a crib for the baby. Said that was an heirloom too."

Stuart started at the word. If Lauder noticed his reaction, he gave no indication.

The conversation had stalled. Stuart was eager to leave. "If it's going to take me three hours to get there, I'd better get started. You don't happen to have someone going that way, do you?"

Lauder looked at Donny. The young trooper's face was incredulous. "Up the dam road? Sarge, you're jokin'. There's only you and me on tonight. And hydro'll only have a skeleton crew on for the weekend. There's no way they'll have that road cleared off before Monday at the earliest."

Lauder turned to Stuart. " 'Fraid not."

"Can you point me in the right direction then?" Stuart's urgency was growing. With the increase in traveling time his margin for error was closing rapidly.

Lauder pulled a wrinkled AAA motorist map out of a drawer and unfolded it on the counter. He indicated the start and finish points of Stuart's intended trip, his voice strangely calm and subdued. When he finished, he folded the map with the section containing the route exposed. He handed it to Stuart. "Better take this with you." He paused again, the same uneasy concern in his eye. "Whatcha drivin'?"

"I rented a Mustang at the airport in Boise. I guess I didn't consider the possibility of backroad driving when I got it. Is that going to be a problem?"

Donny snorted. "Backroad? Christ, you'll be lucky if you find even that. That 'Stang'll get you about two miles outta town."

Lauder's head cocked slightly as he looked directly at Stuart, measuring. He nodded slowly, then shrugged as he pulled a set of keys from his pocket.

"I wouldn't ordinarily be doin' this," he said. "Still wouldn't be if you hadn't said you was a friend of Walter's. You'll need at least a four-wheeler to make it there tonight. A goddamn snowmobile'd be more like it, but you'd like as not freeze yer ass off before you got halfway. Follow me."

He walked Stuart out of the station to a red and white Jeep Cherokee parked beside the police cars. Stuart watched as he knelt beside the two front wheels, adjusting something on the hubs. He stood up again, stiffly, brushing snow from his knees. "Someday I'm gonna get rid of this son of a bitch and get me one with the controls inside." He blew into his hands. "Don't touch them hubs. They're all set to go."

He handed Stuart the keys and pulled the paper from

his vest pocket. It was a single sheet of telex copy. Waving it at Stuart, he yelled over the noise of the wind, "I'm not too worried about ya' drivin' off with my Jeep, Dr. Stuart Rice, public health officer in Davis, California, two-ninety Ellis Crescent, wife, no kids, two parkin' violations outstandin'. First you tell me you got a message, then you tell me it's an heirloom. It's probably a little bit of both, but then why confuse us poor country crackers with details."

Stuart was about to protest, but Lauder continued, "Ya ain't told me the truth yet about why you need to see Dan and Steff in such a hurry, but I get the feelin' ya ain't lied to me neither. There's somethin' goin' on up at Dan's place. I ain't sure what the hell it is, but it's got you scared. And if a smart guy like you, Dr. Stuart Rice from Davis, California, figures there's somethin' to be scared of, then that's all I gotta know.

"I sure as shit ain't goin' up there on a night like this; and if I asked Donny to go he'd just go jerkin' off for four hours and come back and tell me he couldn't get through. Which leaves you—just the way it probably should be anyways."

He opened the door. "You be off now. Don't stand on the clutch. The damn thing's just about wore out as it is. And stay in the middle of the road. I mean right in the middle. There won't be anyone comin' at you; no one else fool enough to be out in this shit. There's no shoulders once you're on the dam road. You slip off the edge and we won't find ya till July. So stay in the middle."

He slammed the driver's door, slapping twice on the side as if to say "good luck."

Or "crazy bastard," Stuart thought as he started the engine. It whirred twice, then caught. He gunned it gently, testing the feel of the accelerator. It had been a long time since he'd driven a standard. He depressed the clutch, cautiously moving the shift lever into low. The gears scraped gently, then meshed. The pitch of the engine changed slightly as he released the clutch. The Jeep edged forward. He pulled out of the parking lot and onto the highway and added speed.

Eighteen inches of snow had fallen in the past twenty-four hours, with no let-up forecast for the next eight hours at least. The wind cascading through the mountain passes had piled the snow in sculpted drifts. Stretched across the road at irregular intervals, white dunes would appear suddenly in his headlights, too suddenly to brake. And no need to, he soon found. As ominous as the mounds appeared, the Jeep passed through them as easily as through fog.

By the time he reached the turn-off onto the dam road, he had the feel of the car and the driving conditions. He relaxed a bit, smiling at his underestimation of Lauder. "Simple, uncomplicated men," he said aloud to himself. "What did he say? Poor country cracker?"

As he headed up the first incline, the conditions were no better, but certainly no worse. The Jeep was surefooted and stable. He relaxed even more, allowing his mind to wander back. Nine days ago he had met with Maddering in Switzerland; tonight he was driving up a mountain road in a blizzard. Nine days. Not quite an eternity, but a lot had happened in the interim.

Chapter Twenty-five
April 10

Despite the exhaustion from traveling halfway around the globe, his first night's sleep in Geneva had been fretful, interrupted by frequent starts and awakenings. Not the usual sluggish disruption of jet lag. His internal clock was wound too tightly, filling him with a distracting, disorganizing energy. But now, as he drove the short distance to Versoix, his concentration returned. What last night had insinuated itself as a sinister veil between his thoughts and sleep had been replaced by an eagerness, a return of his predator's instinct.

Maddering's residence was located on a low rise of treed land on the shores of Lake Geneva. The house itself was invisible from the road. Visitors had first to locate the nearly illegible sign marking a common road leading to several separate estates, then choose the correct drive leading from the road to Maddering's house. Contrary to what Stuart presumed would be a Swiss penchant for numerical tidiness, most of the estates in the area had names rather than numbers. And where they did, there did not seem to be any logical sequence to the numbers.

He missed it on the first pass. When he reached the cul-de-sac at the end of the road he doubled back, checking the drive posts more carefully. He almost missed it again the second time, just catching the initials H.L.M. under the draping branches of an overgrown hedge. He turned into a narrow drive. Encroaching evergreens brushed his car as he passed. Facing full onto the lake at the end of the driveway stood an imposing three-story stone house. Except for a faint glow of light barely visible through a heavily shaded window near the back, the house looked deserted. The outer skin of his optimism flaked off as he parked the car and walked towards the house. Had Maddering forgotten about the meeting?

As he approached the front door he noticed that half the stairs had been replaced by a ramp. He climbed the stairs. Looking back at the drive, at the two-acre plot of treed land surrounding the house, the overwhelming impression was one of isolation and disuse. The place had an untended, almost wild feel about it. The house itself, grey and monolithic with its dark, curtained windows, looked abandoned. There were no signs of life anywhere. He looked for the doorbell. It was set into an incongruously bright metal intercom panel beside the door. As he pressed it a muted ring sounded somewhere distant beyond the door. It was answered immediately by the unmistakable buzz of an electric door lock. Stuart hesitated, surprised by the urgency and inconsistency of the sound. The noise persisted, waiting for him. He turned the brass doorknob and opened the door. The lock was silenced.

He was standing in a small, dimly lit foyer. As his eyes adjusted to the light, static crackled to his right. He looked up at the source of the sound. A small intercom speaker was inset into the paneling of the foyer. A soft-sanded, low-pitched voice said, "Good morning, Dr. Rice. Thank you for coming so promptly. Forgive me for not greeting you at the door. I'm sure you'll understand once we have met. The foyer you are standing in leads to a hall. Kindly follow the hall to the end, to the last door on the right."

The speaker became silent. *Interesting reception,* he thought as he walked slowly down the hall. He passed several doors. On his right the doors were closed, the knobs removed, the holes through which the knobs once passed sealed over. On the left all the doors were open, the rooms beyond nearly empty, dark, uninviting. Most of what little furniture remained was covered with white sheets. Any exposed furniture, and in fact the rest of the decor in general, was drab and tattered. The wall coverings, light fixtures, carpets: everything was decades old, postwar. The only visible concessions to progress appeared to be the electric door lock and intercom systems, and a stainless steel handrail running the length of the hall. He ran a finger along the rail. Judging from the dust, it hadn't been used for months, perhaps years.

Unlike the rest, the last door on the right had a knob—a push plate rather, the type found on institution doors. He knocked softly. The same low voice, closer now, invited him to enter. He pressed gently against the plate. A hiss of air and the quiet hum of a hydraulic mechanism broke the silence as the door opened automatically. He stepped through. The door closed behind him.

The enormity of the room was staggering. The reason for the closed doors along the right side of the hall was immediately apparent. The partition walls separating the rooms on this side of the house had been removed. The entire half of the house had been converted into one enormous room. While the lighting was still dim and the interior decor as dated as what he had seen from the hall, at least this side of the house was clean, lived in. He looked around more closely. The room was a completely self-contained suite. A single, unmade bed stood against one wall. A toilet, guarded on three sides by a rounded metal rail, was visible through an open door to his left. A condominium-style kitchen and eating area occupied the corner to his right.

But two features dominated the room. The first was the number of books. Everywhere. Lining the walls on over-crowded shelves, stacked in piles on the floor and on windowsills, crammed onto every available surface. The second was the desk. The huge mahogany piece, itself piled high with books, loomed at the far end of the room. From behind it a small, huddled form maneuvered itself. A self-propelled wheelchair rolled smoothly across the tile. As it neared, he formed his first impression of H. L. Maddering.

Brother Thomas was right, Stuart thought. *This man is sick, very sick.* Maddering was a shrunken, emaciated shell. Even sitting, his posture was stooped and slumped. His right hand rested limply against the chair's control lever. His left was lost somewhere in the folds of the evening jacket that hung loosely from his shoulders. With the withered frame, the dry, wrinkled face, the pate bald save for an occasional wisp of grey at the temples, he reminded Stuart of a gnome. Except for the eyes. Pale blue, partially hooded by redundant folds of lid, they radiated a soft, calming tranquility. Paradoxes in that hollow, cachectic frame. But at the same time they seemed to hide a fiery energy, just under the surface, a spark about to explode.

When he spoke, the rough baritone voice, like the eyes, seemed misplaced coming from such an emaciated source. "Good morning again, Dr. Rice. And welcome to Switzerland." He didn't offer his hand.

"Thank you, Mr. Maddering." Stuart nodded. "I haven't had time to see much of your country yet, but I am impressed with what I've seen so far." This gnome of a man, the wheelchair, the eerie sense of desertion and desolation surrounding the house, the entire ambience should have imposed on him a sense of mystery and unease. Instead, he felt calmed, reassured.

Maddering turned his chair halfway, keeping his head turned towards Stuart. "Dr. Rice, as you can see, my mobility is rather limited. Unfortunately, my energy level is likewise quite restricted. If you'll forgive what must seem terribly impolite I would prefer to dispense with the pleasantries and preserve my strength for, ah, more important matters."

"Of course," Stuart said, noting Maddering's hesitation. "Can I help you with that?"

Maddering's chair moved towards the far end of the room. "Not at all, thank you. Please, sit there beside the desk." He motioned to a large, overstuffed armchair. He positioned himself behind the desk, his chair angled to the side facing Stuart. "To answer the question in your eyes, Dr. Rice, yes I am ill. I have been for a long time. Thirty-five years to be exact."

Brother Thomas wasn't lying then, Stuart thought.

"I have a variant of A.L.S., amyotrophic lateral sclerosis. I believe you call it Lou Gehrig's disease in your country. As you know, it is a chronic, degenerative neurological disorder. I happen to share it with a very brilliant—and tragically young—British physicist. However, unlike his, my own illness has been in and out of remission for the last three decades. Unusual for this disorder, as I'm sure you know. But that is the last I will speak of it. We have far more important things to discuss."

A file lay open on the desk in front of Maddering. Stuart recognized some of the papers he had sent. The old man pointed at the file.

"I have studied your findings, Dr. Rice, and your summaries—thank you for your thoughtfulness in providing them. Again I shall apologize for appearing so abrupt, but I would like to go over your data with you without committing myself to any kind of comment at this point. I would like you to review your investigation for me verbally, chronologically. Occasionally small details too seemingly irrelevant to record in writing will be recalled which might cast a, ah, different light on a subject. I'm interested not so much in factual data. You have that very well documented here." He waved at the desk. "What I'm looking for is . . . is," he paused, groping for the word, "something . . . less tangible. I'm not sure I can describe what I mean without limiting your responses.

"When we become involved in a task, truly involved, and especially in a task such as yours, we begin to experience things. Reactions if you will, visceral responses to the input we are receiving. Feelings but not just feelings in the accepted sense. And more than just insights, or flashes. More in the realm of the paraphysical or parapsychological. Sensations or symptoms you may have had in the course of your, ah, search, but didn't think to record, perhaps were not even consciously aware of enough to comment on. I'm not sure I can explain clearly exactly what I mean, or really whether I should for fear of restricting your memory to only a certain category of symptoms. Perhaps if you just begin, describe the process of your investigation from the beginning, the very beginning, I'll be able to prompt from you the kind of thing I'm referring to."

He slumped even further in his chair, his fingers steepled in front of him, his eyes fixed intently on Stuart, waiting. Stuart reached for the summaries to jog his memory, disturbed by Maddering's gaze. *He's waiting for something*, he thought. *More than waiting. He's hoping*.

Stuart paused to collect his thoughts for a moment, then

began. "I guess the first time I became suspicious that something other than a routine crib death was involved here was an incidental comment I happened to overhear our neighbour make, the mother of the baby who died last April."

Maddering interrupted immediately. "Excuse me. If I recall the postmortem report on that child, you were the pronouncing physician, is that not correct?"

Stuart nodded. "Yes, but I didn't suspect anything until . . ."

Maddering continued, "Then your first exposure to the events in this, ah, study was when you actually examined the body of Todd McEwen, on April first, 1983. Is that correct?"

Stuart was impressed with Maddering's familiarity with the detail, but still puzzled. "That's right, but again, it was a good two months later before . . ."

Maddering interrupted again. "I'm sorry for being so persistent, Dr. Rice, but you must start at the beginning. The very beginning. How were you first made aware of the infant's death? Start there."

Stuart began. He tried to recall the events in order of occurrence. Todd McEwen's death, Jill's comment on the patio. His initial surprise at the number of crib deaths in the family and how his surprise turned to suspicion and intrigue as more and more deaths arose in the genealogy. He tried to concentrate on sequence rather than consequence, the process of the investigation rather than the results. With Maddering's continual prompting and probing, he was amazed at how much detail he could recall. The unpacked boxes in the McEwen nursery, the static shock when he first touched the crib, the topsoil he and Brian had shoveled, his initial reaction to "Too Right" Hamilton and her computer science student, his summer cold, Saul Pezim's rats . . .

At each step in the process Maddering would interrupt with: "What did you feel when that happened?" or "Did you feel anything, physically or emotionally feel anything?" But Stuart was never certain. He was amazed at how small a role his own emotional and physical feelings had actually played in the investigation. As Maddering continued to press for these reactions, Stuart's frustration began to show.

"For a lot of these events I can recall conventional responses like surprise and anger and disappointment. But I get the impression you're looking for something else. And I'm not really sure just what it is I should be trying to recall. To be honest, I'm not even sure what difference it'll make even if I could remember."

Maddering nodded. His voice took on a soothing, confessional tone. "I don't expect any of what you've been saying to make much sense to you yet, Dr. Rice. It does to me, believe me. Part of this exercise, the greater part, is to dredge the deeper parts of your memory, the parts you would ordinarily ignore, simply lock away and forget about." His voice deepened again, more serious, almost a tinge of regret to his words now. "If the original impression I have of your work is accurate, then what I'm looking for is there. In fact, you have hinted at it many times. We just haven't found the key yet, the key which will unlock that part of your memory and allow us to probe those deeper parts. We'll find it. If it's there, we'll find it. Please continue."

They found it, two hours later as Stuart was describing his wife's accidental discovery of all the deaths occurring in the same month. As he recalled the rapid onset of his hyperventilation symptoms, Maddering's body seemed to stiffen.

"Tell me more about these symptoms, Dr. Rice." Maddering's eyes had deepened, and his voice had an expectant timbre to it. "Have you ever experienced them before?"

Stuart tried to describe the breathlessness he had felt, the numbness and dizziness, the chill, the nausea. He went on to relate the two other times he had suffered those symptoms, both times related to identifiable stress.

"Was there anything different about the symptoms this time?"

"Only the fact that there didn't seem to be any specific cause for them. I'd been working fairly long hours on this by then. I wrote it off to a combination of fatigue and the surprise of Marnie's discovery. I didn't think too much more about it, actually. It didn't last long, an hour at the most."

"But the symptoms themselves, as a package if I may call it that. Was this package of symptoms the same as the package you experienced earlier, during your final medical examinations and during the, ah, sexual experience you alluded to? Try to play back the three episodes in your mind, concentrate on the physical images."

"I'm not sure I can do that," Stuart protested. "I don't usually somaticize my problems. And when I do I don't usually make a big deal out of it."

"Try, Dr. Rice. This is extremely important. Take each symptom in turn, each episode. The breathlessness, for example. Did you have that during your exams? Try to rewind the tapes."

Stuart closed his eyes, concentrating, trying to form a mental image, trying to recapture the sensual details of long-forgotten chapters in his life, experiences trivialized even at the time. Which symptoms correlated with which event? Maddering was right. There was something there, just below the surface. As he replayed the events, a pattern emerged. It came to him slowly, dawning gradually, like a late October sunrise. He opened his eyes. Maddering was watching him, nodding slowly, his mouth set, his body trembling slightly.

"You knew it was there," Stuart said softly. "How did you know? And better yet, what does it mean?"

The old man replied slowly, "I suspected, Dr. Rice, but I didn't know, not for certain. This is why it was so imperative that we meet in person, to determine whether or not it was there. I'll explain the significance of this shortly, but before you lose it I want you to trace the investigation backwards now. Try to identify the same sensation at other times during your study."

This time it was easy. As though a perceptual floodgate had opened, Stuart was able to recall several prior and subsequent occasions during the investigation when he had been aware of the same discomfort. He had written it off variously to improper air-conditioning, to a summer flu, to an unseasonably cold evening. "But what does it mean?" he asked.

Maddering replied, "First, Dr. Rice, let me reassure you that the symptom you felt was real. And it is a remarkably common experience, at least to those of us involved in, ah, 'ecclesiastical pursuits' will do I suppose. You won't find it referred to in any medical or neuropsychiatric text, although the French psychiatrist Marques referred to it as *la mystique gelee.*' If you recall from your medical-school days the explanation and description of the hyperventilation syndrome, it is a largely psychogenic overbreathing phenomenon resulting in a lowering of the carbon dioxide content in the blood, and a subsequent distortion of calcium distribution. That in turn gives rise to a variable but relatively predictable combination of symptoms, many of which you have described. The vertigo, the numbness and tingling, the nausea, chest tightness: all these can be explained by the disturbed physiology. Even feelings of suffocation and unbearable warmth. Warmth, Dr. Rice. The hyperventilation victim feels warm, not cold. The chill that you recall feeling over and over during your investigation is not a hyperventilation symptom. It is *la mystique gelee,* 'the frozen mystique,' and its cause for you is based on something more fundamental than mere physiology. Something more profound than you can imagine.

"But I am getting ahead of myself. Please, we have the rest of your investigation to examine. There are certain, ah, facts which you have uncovered which you must clarify for me. The genealogy, for example. The table you prepared of the children in the extended Thayer-McEwen family was quite detailed, but I want you to review it with me now."

Maddering ticked off entries from a long list he had prepared of apparently trivial details. Stuart tried to clarify and expand on each. But after two hours of interrogation his fatigue and frustration were once again evident. *I'm looking for a reason to explain thirteen crib deaths,* he thought. *This is getting us nowhere.*

Sensing his frustration, Maddering said, "Bear with me, Dr. Rice. We're almost finished. I would like to go over the information on the scrap of wood which you had analyzed. Is there any chance that the age and identification of the wood might be mistaken?"

Stuart was puzzled. He was convinced that the wood did not harbour any pathogenic organisms. The age and type of the wood were secondary, unimportant.

"No. The archaeologists at Davis were quite definite on the wood. In fact, they went to great lengths to convince me that by any one of several different typing and dating methods the results would have been the same. But I should point out that the final cultures—I think they're in the file—all came back negative. No moulds, fungus, viruses. Nothing."

Maddering ignored his comment. "And the, ah, stain in the wood? They are convinced that it is blood?"

"I think so. The pathologist who did the work on it wasn't at all sure what type of blood it was, or even what species. Apparently it wouldn't match with any known blood antigens, or anything else for that matter. But she found enough cellular remnants that she was convinced in the end that it was blood of some kind. The comment I made in the file about the age of the blood is a bit specious, I'm sure you realize. They couldn't date it accurately for a number of reasons. At least, they presumed that since the age they were getting on it was so inconsistent with the age of the wood that it must have been some kind of preparation artifact or equipment error. I don't think we can rely on it."

Maddering simply nodded. He was looking at him now with an unwilling but resigned acceptance. He put his right hand to his forehead, covering his eyes, his head tilted forward as if asleep. After he had held this posture for two minutes, Stuart coughed softly, concerned. Maddering simply turned his palm out but remained silent.

Stuart persisted. "Look, Mr. Maddering. You mentioned that you tire easily. We've been at this for over seven hours now. If you prefer, I can come back later today, or tomorrow."

The old man shook his head. When he looked back up at Stuart his eyes were moist.

"Are you a religious man, Dr. Rice?" he asked. He wiped his eyes with a trembling hand.

"No, I'm afraid not," Stuart replied, lost at the sudden change of direction.

"Well, I am. Always have been. Probably even more since I left the Church." He shifted in his chair. He smiled gently at Stuart. "How could I be more religious than that? As a priest—you were not aware that at one time I was in the clergy—anyway, like any young priest I was consumed by the passion of Christ. The pure ecstasy, the spiritual explosions that filled us then, nothing could surpass that. We could have conquered the world with our faith. Yes, how could I possibly be more religious than that?"

Stuart only shrugged, even more puzzled.

"Yet, I haven't a fraction of the faith I shall need to accept what you have brought to me. I'm an old man, Dr. Rice. I've seen many changes, most of them good. I have had experiences, met people, acquired information and knowledge until sometimes I thought there could not possibly be more to see, more to learn.

"And now you have brought to me something new. Oh, I know your own emphasis has been on solving an unusually high incidence of crib deaths in this one family." As he said this he rocked his hand back and forth dismissingly. "And this something new is something I have never seen before, would never have seen had it not been for your investigation. Yet, though I have never seen or heard of your problem before, Dr. Rice, though I have no intimate knowledge of the families involved or of the phenomenon of sudden infant death, I know the answer to your puzzle. I know it as certainly as anything I have ever known.

"You are involved in something of such enormous dimensions, something of such unimaginable importance. Yet, if I simply told you the answer, you would not believe me. I don't mean in a distrusting way. I mean that without some kind of historical reference you would not be able to believe me.

"I must caution you, Dr. Rice. You will find that accepting the answer is infinitely harder than searching for it. I am going to tell you a story. Every word of it is true. And when I have finished, you will have your answer. I can only trust God that you will know what to do with it."

*   *   *

The state trooper had been right. The higher Stuart climbed into the mountains, the greater the snowfall. The drifts came at him out of the dark now like huge threatening waves, slowing his momentum each time the Cherokee crashed into them.

He glanced at the odometer, then at his watch. Nine-fifty. He had covered seven miles in the past hour and a half, and his pace was slowing as the altitude increased. At this rate he would make it before midnight, but his margin of safety had narrowed alarmingly. Instead of arriving in the early evening, as he had planned, he now had about forty-five minutes to spare. The road arched out along the crest of a broad plateau. The wind had scoured the pavement almost bare, the road too straight and clean to support any significant drift formation. As he relaxed his grip on the wheel and increased his speed marginally, his thoughts faded back to Maddering's story.

Chapter Twenty-six

Poland. Her label as the paranoid schizophrenic of Europe was well deserved. Her history was a continuum of occupations and partitions; her political system a mosaic of feuding, foreign-influenced, regional states. She had every reason to question her existence as a nation, to create for herself a delusional framework of supportive, self-reinforcing convictions, much the way the schizophrenic protects himself by withdrawing into his own world of delusion and fantasy.

The fervor with which the Poles embraced their religion was interpreted as an integral part of this national paranoia. Through the ages their unshakable faith in Roman Catholicism was undeterred by the forces of Islam from the south and east, or more recently by the Protestants from the west. Neurosis, psychosis, whatever, it was their bond. Their adhesive. No foreign political or religious force could alter it. Religion was the glue holding together the essential fabric of Poland.

When Helmut Leiter Maddering was born in 1901 in the German-dominated area of northern Poland, his Prussian father found himself trapped in that glue. As willful and domineering as he was, the staunch Lutheran could not change his Polish wife's decision. Her son would be raised a Catholic. And much to his father's continuing disappointment, as the boy grew linearly his faith expanded exponentially. From the age of five, there was never a doubt in anyone's mind that H. L. Maddering would grow up to be anything but a priest.

His early years as a seminary student only reinforced his beliefs. To the concern of his masters he fairly exploded with faith. In a new and troubled postwar Europe they preferred their aspiring clergy to have a clear grasp of the greater picture, of the political and fiscal realities of the times. Maddering's blinding faith, his singleness of purpose, was at once his greatest strength and his greatest weakness.

As his training continued, however, he became aware, subtly at first and then more obviously, of a second passion, a second religion in his life. History. Where his initial studies involved endless intensive examinations and interpretations of the Scriptures, it wasn't until his third year as a student that his reading concentrated less on theology and biblical analysis and more on the history of Catholicism and Christianity.

Blessed with a photographic memory, he absorbed text after text of historical, geographical, and archaeological data, most of it aimed at establishing the physical authenticity of Christ. He became obsessed with accuracy of detail in his reading. All the books he read were translations of the original documents. But after discovering different and conflicting facts emerging from two different translations of the same Hebrew text, he taught himself Hebrew, then Coptic, then Aramaic, enabling himself to analyze scriptural material written in its original language. By the time he had finished his formal training it was widely recognized and accepted that Maddering's knowledge and understanding of historical Christian detail was unmatched anywhere outside the Vatican—and very possibly within. But when it came time to leave the seminary he gently but adamantly resisted the pressure from his superiors to accept a position in Rome as an historical theologian. He would serve his Church as a parish priest.

"I should have taken their advice," Maddering said. "Oh, I looked and played the priest role quite well, but in the end, the concerns that my seminary masters had voiced about the lack of rounding to my character proved correct. I lacked the emotional prerequisites for the job. For compassion I felt only sympathy, for acceptance only tolerance. Even love for me was a kind of platonic admiration.

"But the deciding blow came when it suddenly became clear to me that even my faith, my life force, had been replaced by simple belief. My initial enthusiasm as a priest had given way to a resigned cynicism. I knew it. My bishop knew it. It was time to move on. When I received a second invitation to join the historical section in the Vatican I accepted it. Gladly."

The Jeep skidded on a patch of black ice as it rounded a curve. Stuart adjusted his speed, steering automatically in the direction of the skid. Once more exposed to the channels of rock and wind, dunes of snow had collected on the road, slowing his progress to a crawl. He checked his watch again. With the straight-road reprieve he had gained fifteen minutes. His thoughts relaxed once more.

Chapter Twenty-seven

Maddering's real life in the Church began in Rome. Despite the ingrained depth of his religion, his disappointing experience as a practicing member of the clergy was enough to convince him that his faith was strictly his own. A private, nontransferable conviction. With that revelation made and accepted, he eagerly set about serving his Church in what he called his ministry of history. It didn't take long for him to realize that this was where he had always belonged.

Because of his fluency in the major languages of the early Christian period, his work at first consisted mainly of reviewing and revising existing translations of ancient Hebraic and Coptic documents. During the 1930s, while the rest of the world drifted inexorably towards war, Maddering was slowly, methodically re-establishing the historical authenticity of the very beginnings of Christianity.

The war broadened. For Maddering, as the conflict raged across North Africa it brought an ironic benefit. As a result of troop movements and field burials, countless priceless artifacts and documents were uncovered. Doubtless many were destroyed, but enough were salvaged to provide Maddering with a constant stream of new material for authentication. Even when the battle lines withdrew to southern Europe, the renewed archaeological interest in North Africa and the Middle East guaranteed a continuing supply of new documents for translation.

"Mind you," he said, "most of it was trivial and very badly preserved. Slave manifests, grain-harvest tables, that sort of thing. The Romans especially kept records of everything. But a lot of it was barely legible, much less translatable."

And so Maddering's work proceeded. With his photo-

graphic memory, his fluency with language, and his absolute insistence on accuracy, he was soon recognized
internationally as the world's premier historical theologian. His published works ran into the thousands, with as
many again reserved for private circulation within the
Vatican. His reputation was unassailable, his position secure. Until December 1945.

One month after the armistice was signed, a remarkable
set of documents crossed Maddering's desk.

"It was apparent from the beginning, as soon as I saw
them, that these weren't the usual clerical records I'd
grown accustomed to. The quality of the preservation,
even the style of the writing was superior. I can still recall
the excitement I felt when I first laid eyes on them."

The discovery of these documents was shrouded in mystery at the time. Inevitably, rumours of the find began to
circulate. But the more persistent the archaeological community's attempts to gain access to them, the more they
were thwarted by an impenetrable tangle of political and
legal roadblocks. The official story of this discovery was
not released until 1975, thirty years later.

"These documents are extremely controversial, Dr. Rice.
So controversial in fact that they threatened to undermine
the very foundations of the Church. And they are inextri-
cably bound up in the answer to your problem. It is
imperative that you hear both the official and the true
versions of their discovery."

In 1975, a detailed statement was released concerning
the by-then-long-forgotten discovery of this cache of religious documents. According to that press release, an Egyptian peasant by the name of Muhammad Ali al Samman
was digging topsoil near the settlement of Naj Hammadi
in upper Egypt when he uncovered a large red earthen-
ware jar. Although he was afraid at first of releasing a
spirit, he eventually broke open the jar, in the hope that it
might contain gold. Instead, to his disappointment, he
found thirteen leather-bound books and numerous loose
sheets of script-covered papyrus.

He returned home with his find, dumping the papers in
a pile beside the stone oven. His mother used the loose

leaves of parchment for fuel. But al Samman, thinking the books might be of some value, showed one of them to a local scholar. The scholar in turn informed a friend in the antiquities section of the government. The government then purchased one of the books and confiscated eleven others. The thirteenth book, or codex as it was called, the smallest of the lot, al Samman managed to hide and eventually smuggle out of Egypt, to be sold illegally in Europe or North America.

In time this contraband document was purchased by the Jung Foundation in Switzerland and returned to the Egyptian authorities. Today the entire original collection of thirteen books is preserved in the Coptic Museum in Cairo. They are the subject of over four thousand books, essays, and critiques. Collectively they are known as the Gnostic Gospels.

"As I said, Dr. Rice, this was the official version, released some thirty years after the discovery. In fact, the actual events transpired very differently.

"Because of my talents, the Vatican frequently rented my services out to various Middle Eastern governments, for a fee of course." Maddering smiled at this. "The number of discoveries at the time was truly staggering. The various Mediterranean governments of the day had neither the time nor the resources to develop their own authentication departments. They were only to happy to pay for our service.

"It was a routine matter then for these particular documents, these Gnostic Gospels, to be shipped from Egypt, where they were indeed found, to Rome, and then to my office for translation. The package I received contained thirteen codices—not twelve as the official story claims—and a carefully preserved stack of loose papyrus leaves. There were fifty-two separate chapters in the codices. They were written in Aramaic, most of them in the first two centuries A.D. They were remarkable in that they represented the first significant evidence of the beginnings of what we today call gnosticism. Are you familiar with the term, Dr. Rice?"

Stuart shrugged, shook his head. Other than during his

brief encounter with Brother Thomas he had never heard of the word. Nor had he any idea where Maddering's story was heading.

Sensing his guest's confusion, Maddering continued, "Be patient, Dr. Rice. I know this seems exhaustive, but without the historical background you can never begin to understand the significance of what you have discovered.

"Early Christianity, you see, was a new and tremendously powerful phenomenon, but it was much more diverse than most people suspect. It was open to interpretation in many different ways. Eventually, what is now called orthodox Christianity prevailed. But of the alternate interpretations of Christ, one of the earliest was that of gnosticism. Their basic belief was that Jesus was more of a spiritual guide than a divine Messiah. That He was gifted with some special kind of insight, but that He simply led others, more like a guide than a Messiah, to his own spiritual plain. Once there, all others were his equal. This concept of Christ as a mere human versus Christ the Son of God was a fundamental, irreconcilable difference between the gnostics and the orthodox Christians."

With death the penalty for heresy, the earliest Christians literally risked their lives to practice their religion. This morbid uncertainty led the adherents of each of the different sects—including the gnostics and the orthodox Christians—to not only carry out their religious rites in secret, but also to record their beliefs and most importantly to hide their records. Never knowing when more lenient conditions might prevail, they preserved their records very carefully, not just for years, but for decades and centuries. Even millennia. As events transpired, when Constantine the Great converted to orthodox Christianity around A.D. 300, the gnostics and all other fringe sects were threatened with annihilation. They had done well to hide their documents.

Maddering continued in his quiet, soothing voice, "In the Vatican, the reaction to these newly discovered codices was quite mixed. Historically and theologically they were controversial, even disturbing to some extent. They contained references to several aspects of Christ's personal life not mentioned in the New Testament. His sexuality, for example. You are familiar with Mary Magdalene, Dr. Rice? The so-called whore of Christian orthodoxy?"

Stuart nodded.

"Contained in the Gnostic Codices is 'the Gospel of Mary,' written by her and claiming to be an account of her, ah, domestic relationship with Jesus. There are others: the Gospel of Philip, the Apocalypses of Peter and Paul, the Apocryphon of John, secret books these last three, alluding to homosexual relationships between Jesus and his disciples. One, the Gospel of Judas Thomas, claims to be an account of His life written by Christ's own twin brother.

"Oh yes, they were controversial. But by the time of the Naj Hammadi discovery the Church had matured. Gnosticism was dismissed by then as a petty irritant. Despite the fears of the more conservative members, as novel and controversial as this new historical information appeared, from a theological perspective it presented no great threat. In fact, many within the Vatican viewed it as a healthy counterpoint to orthodox doctrine.

"But this applies only to the main body of the codices, the first twelve books. These were accepted as being interesting but rather benign. However, the loose sheets of papyrus, the ones supposedly burned by al Samman's mother, and the thirteenth codex, the one apparently smuggled out of Egypt: these were different. Unacceptably different. Half of the thirteenth codex, the part now in the Coptic Museum, is the Gospel of Judas Thomas, the twin brother of Christ. The other half, the half which we are concerned with, was the Gospel of Jesus Christ, Himself."

Stuart looked up, unbelieving.

"You have every right to be skeptical, Dr. Rice. I would not believe it had I not translated it myself. It was an extremely accurate account of the life of Christ, more accurate in fact than any of the synoptic gospels of the New Testament. It contained information that could only have been written before A.D. 50 by someone, a collaborator, with an intimate knowledge of Christ's life. But more important, this gospel contained a summary, a synopsis if you will, of the writings on the loose papyrus which was found in the jar with the bound books. That papyrus and the ink used were traced and dated with absolute certainty to within a ten-year span between A.D. 25 and 35. The script on the papyrus was different from the rest of the codices; the ink and parchment themselves were different; the grammatical construction was different. Those documents, those loose sheets of parchment, were the original writings of Christ Himself."

Stuart began to rise. "With all respect, Mr. Maddering, you are asking me to accept a pretty unbelievable—"

"Yes I am, Dr. Rice. Indeed I am. But perhaps I should remind you that if my colleagues and peers are to be believed, I am an acknowledged authority in these matters, perhaps the foremost world authority. It is not important that you believe what I am telling you; only that you accept that I myself believe it."

Stuart settled back in his chair, strangely comforted. His concern and intrigue grew as the enormity of what Maddering was saying crashed in on him, and that somehow it involved him and his search.

Maddering continued, "When we read the synoptic Gospels of Matthew and Mark in the New Testament, Dr. Rice, we invariably form an image of Christ as an infinitely benevolent Messiah, an all-loving Saviour. But, in distinct contrast, the man described in the Gospel of Jesus, and again in his own writings, is totally different. Certainly the writings confirmed what we already knew of his earlier life. That He was a member of the Essenes, one of the three original Hebrew sects, the Sect of the Scrolls. That He was educated by them, shared their pious, moralistic, communal lifestyle. But according to his own records, by the time He was seventeen or eighteen He was aware of a special nature in Himself—a 'unique aura' the gospel calls it. And He was fully prepared to explore and exploit that special aura, even at the expense of others. He could no longer accept the Essenian ideals, or their insistence on self-denial at the expense of his own advancement. So He left them—in fact He was expelled from their community—to establish his own following.

"Why? Why did He feel He was different? What did He

have that the rest of the sect did not? His gospel gives us clues.

"If nothing else He was a supremely gifted showman. If you understood society in biblical times, the preoccupation with the occult and the so-called black arts, you would understand that any modernday illusionist would have been accepted then as some kind of Messiah. Apparently—and this was well-described in his own writings—He would frequently use simple sleight-of-hand tricks or stage-managed miracles to impress and influence the masses. Much the same as a traveling patent-medicine salesman might have done in the early days of your own country. Or worse. The intensely humane Christ described in the Bible, the Saviour we have come to love and worship, would—again, from his own records—routinely resort to more pragmatic and even sinister methods to gain attention and respect. With curses, for example. Yes, curses. Oh, usually impersonal threats involving crop failures or climate changes and the like, impossible to verify or deny. But curses nevertheless, and tremendously effective given the gullibility of the population and the spiritual charisma He appeared to possess.

"But why? Why, for example, would a man of such obvious stature deliver the sermon of the Beatitudes and then attempt to drive it home with a curse of pestilence on anyone who refused to accept his teaching? Full of love one minute, hate the next. Was He that unsure of Himself? Was He insane? Certainly, if they are translated literally his writings would be interpreted today as those of a schizophrenic megalomaniac. A biblical Jim Jones.

"But in fairness there was more to his writings than simply their literal translation. Hidden between the lines, a message which I could feel but could not quite define. Woven in with the paradoxes and the contradictions, an invisible yet totally distinct, almost palpable thread. There was some unspoken strength there, a conviction. Despite the curses and the other questionably scrupulous methods He used, I got the distinct impression of a completely unique, infinitely superior man who if not the Son of God then He might as well have been, because his effect would have been the same. With my own familiarity with the ancient language and its idioms I was able to detect this undercurrent despite the literal translation. Unfortunately, none of my colleagues in Rome could see it. Nor, given the factual material in the writings, were they inclined to believe it.

"As you so correctly commented in your initial correspondence with me, Dr. Rice, I have an absolute penchant for historical accuracy. But here I had this terrible dilemma. How was I to translate these remarkable documents? On the basis of which religion? Literally, in the worship of historical accuracy? Or figuratively, based on my own ability to perceive this hidden message of supremacy? Do I preserve the faith by excusing His apparent faults, ascribing these darker methods of his ministry to contemporary showmanship and rhetorical style? Or do I translate them word for word, and damn the results? What would you have done?"

Maddering's tone had changed. A sadness had crept into his voice, a resignation. Stuart had no idea what he would have done in the circumstances, but one look into the old man's eyes told him with absolute certainty what Maddering had done.

Softly, fearfully, Stuart whispered, "You destroyed it."

Maddering closed his eyes.

The Church was more than capable of defending itself against most of the information contained in these new documents. Despite the apparent contradictions, the bulk of the Gnostic Gospels represented no more than a different ecclesiastical interpretation of the events described in the Scriptures.

But it had no defense against the second chapter of the thirteenth codex or the writings of Jesus. These were authenticated documents that, in their most truthful interpretation, categorically refuted and disproved everything on which the very fundamentals of Christianity were based. They could not be released.

The procedural difficulties that prevented outsiders from seeing the documents were organized by the Vatican while a very small and very secret committee of elite theologians debated the fate of the thirteenth codex and the writings of Christ. It was the decision of that committee to destroy the documents rather than risk their exposure. A suitably intriguing set of circumstances was created to explain the delay in returning the final, controversial document to Egypt. It was arranged through this committee that the censored thirteenth codex, containing only the Gospel of Judas Thomas, would be made surreptitiously available to the Jung Foundation, which in turn would donate it to the Egyptian authorities.

H. L. Maddering's was the only dissenting voice on the final vote. He was also now the only surviving member of the committee.

"Yes, they destroyed them. They burned them, and all the notes and copies. I say 'they' because my own resistance to the destruction of such monumentally important documents was absolute. Under no circumstances could I condone such an act. But my voice on the committee was negligible compared to the combined influence of the cardinals. I openly rebelled against their decision, going so far as to question the infallibility of the Holy Father himself, who ultimately agreed with the committee's recommendation.

"My disillusionment was total. I was absolutely unable to accept the decision. Even after the documents were burned I couldn't accept it. For the first time in my life I felt vengeance. At first I tried to have my opinion published, but by then I had become a pariah, an outcast. All my work was rigidly censored. Any reference I made to the Gospel of Jesus or his writings was simply deleted. I was cut off from my usual channels of communication. I tried to sneak small snippets of controversial information into my translations, hoping someone would take note and begin an inquiry. But few noticed, and when they did the apparently contradictory information was explained away as either typographical error or the result of my own diminished capacity.

"They were stage-managing my departure from the Church, and quite successfully. It wasn't long before conditions were so intolerable that I could no longer remain. A suitable illness had already been created to explain my departure. I renounced my vows and settled into semivoluntary exile here in Switzerland. Once separated from the Church, I was no threat to them. My reputation within the international historical community had been destroyed by rumours of my mental deterioration. I tried to threaten them with my intimate exposure to the codices and my talent for photographic recall, but they confidently and correctly reminded me that without the original documents as proof, any public exposé I might make could be easily refuted, written off as a flight of fancy by a tragically, precociously demented former priest.

"Yes, the documents are gone, Dr. Rice. I have long ago forgotten the anger I felt over their destruction, and have even forgiven the committee for its actions. But even after all these years I still see them in my mind, as clearly as these files in front of me. Constantly."

Ten forty-five. The lights of the Jeep glinted off the reflective sides of a mailbox, barely visible above the bank of snow. Stuart stopped the car and squinted through the window. The name on the box stared back: Harrison. He shut off the engine and stepped out into the storm, shielding his eyes from the wind. At first he could see no sign of a house or driveway. But from a perch on the hood of the Jeep he could just make out the outline of a building several hundred yards to his right, and leading to it the faint outline of a road barely showed under the massive drifts. But even for the Cherokee it was impassable. The rest of the journey would have to be taken on foot. He pulled his coat tighter around him and stepped off the road, immediately sinking to his thighs in soft snow. After a dozen stumbling strides he settled into an awkward rhythmic gait, lifting his feet high to clear the drifts, swinging his legs off to the side and then forward. He looked up at the house, a darkened silhouette in the distance. At this rate it would take him another fifteen minutes to reach it. One hour's grace.

He lurched forward slowly, like an automaton, his legs lifting and lowering of their own separate volition. The wind, the cold, the hypnotic regularity of his movements all combined to lull him, ease him into a trance. He returned to Versoix. . . .

Chapter Twenty-eight

Maddering guided his chair around the desk. "So you see, Dr. Rice, if the writings of Jesus Himself are to be believed, and I am absolutely convinced that they can be, then we are left with a Christ who was radically different from the one portrayed in the Bible. But what does it all mean? And more important, what could this remarkable revelation of a man who lived almost two thousand years ago possibly have to do with the deaths of your infants?"

He stopped in front of a pile of books on the floor. Reaching forward, he removed the top book, read the title, and replaced it. He scanned the rest of the pile, cocking his head sideways to read the bindings. Not finding what he was looking for, he turned his chair towards the far wall. He arched his neck backwards, straining to see the topmost shelf of an overloaded wall unit.

"Would you be kind enough to reach a book for me, Dr. Rice. Just there, on the top shelf."

Stuart followed the old man's finger to a large leather-bound volume. As he reached for it, Maddering stopped him.

"No, just to the right. Yes, that's it."

He pulled down a much narrower book. He looked at the title, *Art and Ecclesiastical Doctrine,* then handed it to Maddering. The chair glided back to the desk.

"Do you know anything about art, Dr. Rice? I don't mean technically. More the social significance and impact of art."

Stuart shook his head. "Nothing."

Maddering explained, "Well, without belabouring it, we usually like to think that art in its various forms is a fairly accurate reflection of the society in which it is produced. But in fact—and this is especially true since the Renaissance—artists are, as a rule, quite liberal in their interpretation of social values or events. So the resulting picture or sculpture or whatever is usually just one man's interpretation of what happened. And not usually a very reliable interpretation, given the often-eccentric nature of the artist."

He held up the book. "Religious art, however, is another matter, especially early religious art. Unlike the patronage system in which an artist would be free to paint whatever his intellect and talents dictated while some wealthy patron supported him, religious art was ordinarily produced on a commission basis. A specific religious group or society would commission and pay a specific artist to produce a specific painting, or sculpture as the case may be, of a specific subject. But before being hired the artist would first have to satisfy his sponsor that he would represent the subject accurately—that is, according to the sponsor's interpretation. Remember, at the time the various Christian denominations were vying for recognition. They were not about to commission a portrayal of someone else's beliefs. So we find that although various Christian religious events like the birth of Christ, or the Sermon on the Mount, or the Crucifixion, or the Last Supper are all matters of record, the artistic interpretation of that record varies enormously, depending not on the vision of the artist but on the theological doctrine of the sponsor. So the orthodox Christians would insist on an orthodox interpretation by the artist, the gnostics a gnostic interpretation, and so on. Look."

He flipped through the book. The pages were filled with reproductions, with the occasional paragraph of text. He stopped at a picture of the Last Supper.

"Classically orthodox," he said, pointing to the various details in the drawing. "Christ in the center, peaceful, intense. The disciples arranged on each side in order of priority, Judas always on the left. Linear arrangement, no one in the background. The chalice of wine here, representing his blood, and the bread over here, his body. The background, the foreground. The picture looks quite natural, a credit really to the artist's talents. But in fact, despite the natural appearance, everything is carefully, rigidly dictated."

He turned the page. "Now look at this one. Same event, but the differences are obvious. The number of people, the women, the variety of foods on the table, the Romans in the background, the look on Christ's face: everything is different. No symbolic wine or bread. Even the colours used are different. But look here." He pointed to the name of the artist. "And here." He turned back to the first painting. "The same artist. Same event, same artist, yet two radically different pictures. The first one is orthodox, the second gnostic."

He moved forward in the book.

"I could show you a dozen more pictures of the Last Supper and they would all be basically the same. But we're not interested in the Last Supper. Ah, here we are." He flattened the book on the desk.

"No single event in Christian history has been represented more frequently than the Crucifixion. There are literally hundreds of thousands of paintings and etchings and carvings and lithographs and mosaics depicting this one event, yet under orthodox Christian doctrine they all contain the same ecclesiastical information. This is a good example. Here, the Cross itself, tall, taller than the crosses used for the two criminals. Everything to the right of the Cross represents 'the new': the Church, Mary, the disciples, the repentent criminal on this cross. And everything to His left is 'the old': the synagogue here in the background, the Romans, the thief who refused to acknowledge Him. And here, one of the Romans, the one who stabbed Him, mounted on a horse. The skull at the base of the Cross—all orthodox Crucifixion scenes show it, an allegorical reference to the skull of Adam. And the Cross itself, always a muted grey, almost unnoticeable. And look at Christ, the wreath on his head, eyes open, gazing upward, the serene, beatific look on his face, no sign of suffering—it wasn't until the ninth century, incidentally, that orthodox belief acknowledged that He actually died on the Cross. Paintings after that show Him with his eyes closed." He pointed to the torso. "Note the blood, Dr. Rice, from the wound in his side. Its colour. And note the name of the artist."

He turned several pages to another portrayal of the

Crucifixion, by the same artist. Stuart studied it. The differences were striking. The crowd was larger, some of the spectators were laughing, others crying. The Romans mingled with them, jeered with them. In the background, beyond the Crucifixion site, was a market where business appeared to be carrying on as usual. There was no organization to the scene, no mounted Roman, no symbolic skull. Christ's Cross was the same size as those used for the thieves, and lower, much lower than the one in the previous picture. Even the number of thieves was different. Here, five criminals hung from crosses arranged erratically around Christ. The Cross itself was dark brown in colour, much more obvious. But the most obvious difference, the most sinister, was the appearance of Christ Himself. He was strained forward, His face contorted with agony and rage, His mouth open as though screaming at the crowd.

"Again note the blood, Dr. Rice." Maddering pointed to Christ's side and hands and feet. Streaks of pale brown pigment covered his side and limbs and spilled onto the Cross."

Stuart nodded, not sure what he was supposed to be noticing.

"This is a gnostic interpretation of the Crucifixion," Maddering continued. "Same artist, same technique, same canvas, same pigments; in fact, both of these paintings are remarkably well preserved, and these reproductions are very faithful to the originals. Yet each shows a radically different event taking place. So which one do we believe? We know the Crucifixion took place, but which of these two interpretations is more likely to be historically accurate?

"Well, what do we know about crucifixions?" Maddering shifted awkwardly in his chair, lecturing now. "We know they started with the ancient Syrians and Abyssinians, eventually refined by the Greeks and then the Romans. The Romans originally used crucifixion as a form of entertainment. Slaves would be fastened to heavy Y-shaped beams so they couldn't move too quickly, then a crowd would chase them down and beat them to death. Or in large arenas like the Coliseum the beams would be attached to low uprights with the prisoners' feet suspended just off the ground. Wild animals would then be released into the ring to kill and eat the slaves. It was enormously popular as a spectator sport. Nero himself, in fact, is reported to have entertained his guests by dressing up in animal skins and personally hacking to death many of these cross-immobilized prisoners.

"But in time it came to be used more and more as a form of capital punishment, especially for political or religious agitators. Since the whole idea of crucifixion was a delayed, agonizing death, you can imagine its tremendous deterrent potential. And as it became more and more popular as a form of punishment—there were literally thousands of crucifixions being performed in some weeks—in true Roman fashion they soon devised more efficient ways of performing the task. The Y-shaped device was replaced by a more easily constructed straight beam. To eliminate the inevitable attempts at escape, the guards would usually scourge or whip the victim to weaken him, then make him carry his own platibulum—the cross-beam—to the execution site. There, they would nail his hands—his wrists actually—to the beam and hoist it up onto the top of an upright. These upright beams, like these extra poles in the gnostic painting," Maddering waved his hand at the book, "were permanently implanted, and could be used for any number of crucifixions. For important criminals they would use a tall upright so more people could see him. But the vast majority of the victims were lesser criminals. And since the executioners would often be required to perform two or three hundred crucifixions in an average day, it was much easier and more efficient to use the low uprights.

"These were public events. And certainly with any given execution a certain number of spectators would be expected. But they were so common and so approved of by both the Romans and the largely collaborative population that any one crucifixion rarely disturbed the usual day-to-day processes of life.

"So, given that information, what can we conclude about the crucifixion of Jesus? He was, remember, little more than a petty irritant to the Romans; certainly not a prominent or important criminal. All things considered, we can conclude that the gnostic interpretation, with its low cross, the milling crowds, the standing Roman infantry, the additional crucified prisoners, the busy market in the background, is probably much closer to the truth. But if the historical details in the gnostic painting are more accurate, then what about the ecclesiastical details?"

Maddering flipped back and forth between the pictures as he continued.

"The Cross itself, was it light grey or was it dark brown? Remember, it's the same artist, Dr. Rice, same technique, same pigments. Was Christ serene, oblivious to pain, or was He in agony and screaming at his executioners?"

His voice suddenly changed, softened. "But look here, Stuart." It was the first time he had used his first name. He was pointing at the wound in Christ's side. "The answer is in the blood, this pale brown hemorrhage. Look at his hands and feet, and here on the Cross itself, the same watery-looking liquid. But the blood from the criminals on the other crosses, bright red." He turned the page. "And here, in the gnostic painting? The same. An anemic-looking brown substance coming from Jesus, and red blood from the convicts."

He looked up at Stuart, a distant resignation in his eyes. "Despite all these differences, that one similarity, the blood of Christ, has been the subject of more debate among ecclesiastical scholars than any other single detail of the Crucifixion. There is still no agreement on what it means, but there are countless references in classical literature to the differences in the blood of men and gods. Homeric legend, for example, contends that gods have a mixture of blood and water in their veins. In that respect, the accepted opinion among theologians is that the gnostics, despite their insistence that Jesus was just a man, must have recognized some kind of divinity in Him. Not that He was just a special man, but that He in fact was a nonhuman being, a god-person if you will. But now if the gnostics recognize and concede that Jesus was in fact a godlike being, what about the most striking difference in the paintings, the radically different appearance of Christ on their cross compared to the orthodox cross? What does the violence and anger on his face mean?"

Maddering could sense Stuart's confusion. "Let me put

it another way. If we have proved that some of the gnostic version is correct, then it is likely that the entire gnostic version is correct. If Jesus was portrayed as just another criminal, with red blood, then his facial appearance in the gnostic painting could be written off as human suffering. But the gnostics have represented Him as a god, not just another man. So what does the expression on his face mean if He's a god? Look at his face. What is He screaming at the crowd?"

Without waiting for an answer Maddering continued, "The New Testament quotes Jesus as making two statements while He was on the Cross. Loosely translated, they are a forgiveness: 'Father forgive them for they know not what they do,' and a lament: 'Father, why hast thou forsaken me?'

"But the Gospel of Jesus, that half of the thirteenth codex which was destroyed, though it confirms the forgiveness it describes the lament very differently. According to this gospel, the Romans and the spectators wanted to cut Christ down from the Cross before He was dead in order to prolong his agony. Even the New Testament concedes that He died very quickly, in five or six hours instead of the usual day or day and a half. But Jesus, tortured as he was, would have none of it. He insisted that his body be left on the Cross indefinitely, that He would never die. And how did He convince them to leave Him there? With the same methods He had always used. He threatened them.

"He's screaming a curse, Stuart. A curse. Translated literally from the Coptic, He said, 'Have not this ark . . .' "

Stuart groped for the first step with his foot. His prediction had been remarkably accurate. It had taken him just over fourteen minutes to reach the house. And not a moment too soon, he thought, as he stood on the porch trying to stamp feeling back into his near-frozen feet. He knocked on the door, cautiously at first, then louder. A dog barked inside, followed by fainter stirrings and a softened murmur of voices. A muffled shuffling of feet crossed the floor. Somewhere inside, a clock announced the hour. He glanced at his watch. Eleven o'clock. On the fourth chime the door opened, spilling a crack of light onto the porch. His real task was just beginning.

Chapter Twenty-nine

"Daniel Harrison?"

Harrison wasn't tall, but even through the loose robe Stuart could tell he was solid. He had long, light-brown hair tousled from sleep. His face was square, angular, softened by a rough-trimmed beard. His eyes fixed on Stuart with a mixture of suspicion and puzzled concern.

"Where the hell did you come from?" He looked at Stuart, then beyond him at the porch and the storm. "You alone?" he asked.

Stuart nodded. "Yes."

"Better come in, then. No sense heating half of Oregon."

The clock finished its chimes as the door closed behind him. A vague unease teased at him, more than the strangeness of the encounter or the immediacy of his mission. Something just off center, out of tune.

"I'm sorry about the late arrival. Actually I planned to be here about five hours ago, but with the storm and all . . ." Stuart stopped.

Harrison just looked at him, head cocked, eyebrows raised.

"I'm sorry." Stuart shook his head, backtracking. "I'm way ahead of myself. My name is Rice, Stuart Rice. I'm a close friend of a cousin of yours, Brian McEwen. We're neighbours actually, in Davis, California. And the reason I'm here is, ah, kind of complicated, and kind of crazy too, actually, and, and maybe we should sit down and I'll try to explain."

Harrison led him into the living room, where the last remnants of a fire glowed in a large, stone fireplace. He pulled an enormous piece of split birch from a barrel and placed it on the embers, stirring them in the process. The bark caught immediately. Stuart chose a low stool next to the flames, holding his hands forward to catch the warmth.

"Danny? Is anything wrong?" a woman's voice asked from the top of the stairs.

Harrison looked at Stuart, who shook his head gently. "I don't think so, hon. We've got company from California. Come on down."

Soft woman-steps padded on the stairs, followed by the tapping-scraping of nails. A petite, radiant, healthy-looking woman emerged from the doorway, and behind her, head high, tail wagging furiously, was the largest, blackest dog Stuart had ever seen. The sight of such an enormous animal so close and unrestrained frightened him. The woman detected his nervousness immediately. She reached for the dog's collar.

"Shep, down," she said gently.

The dog immediately reclined at her feet, his large friendly eyes constantly on the visitor.

"Stay," she added before moving into the room.

"Hello." She smiled at Stuart. "You're a long way from California."

Stuart was standing now, trying to concentrate on the woman, trying to ignore the dog.

"I know all dog owners say the same thing, but don't worry about him," she said, serious but grinning. "We had to train him this well to keep him from licking people to death." She held out her hand. "I'm Stephie Harrison."

Stuart took her hand gently. "Stuart Rice, and that's got to be just about the biggest thing I've seen that still qualifies as a dog." He returned the woman's smile, reassured.

"He's a Newfoundland. And you're right, he's a lot bigger than most. But he's a big wimp actually." She looked at her husband.

Harrison just shrugged. "Stuart here says he's a friend of Brian and . . ." He looked at Stuart. "Jo is it?"

"Jill," Stuart replied.

"Brian and Jill McEwen from Davis," Dan finished.

Stephie looked alternately from her husband to Stuart. "McEwen? We don't know anyone . . . the ones Dad brought the crib up from?"

"That's right," Stuart answered. Her mention of the crib created a natural opening for him. "I met your father in fact while he was in Davis visiting Jill and Brian. And believe it or not, it's the crib that I'm here to talk to you about." He paused. "You still have it, don't you?"

"Oh yes, it's upstairs, full of trouble," Dan said, smiling.

"Trouble?" Stuart's inner alarm sounded.

Dan chuckled. "No. The baby's in it. Asleep. He's only trouble when he's awake."

Stephie was curious now. "What about the crib?" she asked.

Stuart's alarm quieted but did not silence. The unease he had felt when he first arrived had returned, stronger now, closer. He tried to ignore it as he explained his reason for coming.

"It's a long and rather complex story," he said, glancing again at his watch. "Maybe I should start at the end first and explain why I'm here, I mean me rather than Brian or Jill. Then I can fill in the background.

"It has to do with a study I've been doing over the last year of some, ah, health problems in Brian's family. I'm a doctor by the way, an epidemiologist, public health. Anyway, after a rather, ah, convoluted search I ended up just last week tracking down some information in Switzerland. Information which I felt you should have as soon as possible."

The Harrrisons looked at each other, then back at Stuart.

Stuart smiled. "Well, I warned you it was kind of crazy."

He went on to describe how it was necessary that he reach them by the weekend, but after his meeting with Maddering he had no way to get through to them from Switzerland. His only contacts were the McEwens, and they were unavailable, gone for the holidays. His only recourse was to return to Davis, find out where they lived, and try to contact them.

Getting into the McEwens' house was expedited by the emergency keys they had exchanged. Marnie knew where Jill's address books were kept, but even with the address they quickly learned that the Harrisons lived on an isolated homestead without power or telephone or radio communication.

Heavily booked holiday air traffic had already delayed and extended their traveling time from Europe. By the time they had finally arrived home it was early Thursday morning. A telephoned request to the police in Adrian to convey information in person had been firmly refused. The worst storm in twenty years had been raging for the past twenty-four hours. With the still-deteriorating weather conditions they had neither the time nor the resources to be carrying personal messages to anyone. The only way he could contact them was to do it himself. Thus, the hastily arranged flight to Boise, Idaho, and the harrowing drive to Adrian and beyond.

"But I made it," Stuart concluded.

"Which explains how you got here," Dan said. "And in weather like this I'd say you deserve a medal. But you still haven't told us why."

Before Stuart could answer, a low rumbling growl erupted from Shep. The three turned to look at the dog. He was still lying at the door, but his head was erect now, turned towards the bottom of the stairs. The fur at his nape had stiffened. His lips curled slightly, the tips of his canines barely exposed.

Stephie looked at her husband, then at Stuart. "I've never seen him do that, never," she said. Then to the dog: "Shep, come over here. Come on."

The dog rose, his attention torn between the stairs and his master. He growled again, followed by a puzzled whimper before he finally entered the room.

"Down," she ordered. "Good boy. What's the matter?" She ruffed the dog's neck, tugging gently at his ears. "Dan, he's really spooked. He's shaking like a leaf. Easy, boy."

The dog lay beside her. Not sprawled this time; on his haunches, legs coiled tightly, ready to spring. A constant deep bass rumbled in his throat. He ignored Stuart and his masters. His eyes were riveted on the doorway and the stairs beyond.

Harrison looked at Stuart, half-smiling, half-concerned. "I'm sure this doesn't have anything to do with you, Stuart. It's just so unusual to see him upset about anything. He'll settle down in a minute." He felt less convinced than he sounded. "You were going to tell us . . ."

But the logical, acceptable explanation Stuart had prepared had vanished. Even the intention had evaporated.

Perhaps the dog's restless behaviour had precipitated it, but what he felt now was more than the simple fear of being so close to a large, angry, unrestrained dog. The unease he had felt when he first arrived had grown, magnified. And at the edges, surrounding the fear, twisting, worming its way to the center, a too-familiar discomfort had returned. *La mystique gelee*. Maddering's story, his urgency, his warning, all flashed before him. He looked again at his watch. Eleven thirty-five. He still had twenty-five minutes. Why the panic?

Harrison stood and moved behind Stuart to the wood barrel. He extracted another log and added it to the fire. As he watched him, Stuart noticed for the first time the rustic interior of the house. Natural moss and bark packing wedged between as insulation accented the soft-rounded waves of the log walls. Three or four large, woven scatter rugs covered the trafficked portions of the plank floors. The furniture was old and overstuffed, but comfortable, permeated with the relaxed smell-memories of countless birch fires. A large maple rocking chair guarded one end of the hearth; an empty baby bottle leaned, asleep, against one of the curved rockers. As the log burst into flame a glint of movement behind the chair caught his eye. In the corner, lost in the gloom, stood a grandfather clock. Its brass pendulum, beating in time to some unheard tune, caught and polished and returned the firelight with each swing. Stuart remembered the chimes when he had first knocked on the door. He turned back to his hosts, relaxed marginally by his visual tour.

But as Stuart's anxiety eased, the dog's seemed to increase. He was half-standing now, his growl louder, lines of foam beginning to form at the rims of his lips.

"Danny, this is weird." Stephanie's voice was cautious. "There must be something out there."

"It's probably just a moose or a deer, Steph," he tried to console her, "tricked around by the storm."

"He's not looking at the front door, Dan. He's looking at the stairs." The caution in her voice was tinged with fear now.

Harrison grabbed a handful of the dog's mane, pulling him gently towards himself. "What's got into you, fellah."

He looked up at Stuart and smiled as he pushed the dog's rump onto the carpet. "Midnight madness," he said. "Must be past his bedtime."

Watching the dog, sensing the Harrisons' mounting concern, Stuart's own anxiety had grown again. He could feel the first faint tingling in his lips, the first suggestion of breathlessness returning. And behind them, lurking, ever-present . . . His senses sharpened. The fire was suddenly too warm, the stool too hard, the sweet smell and crackling of the fire too sharp, too loud. And behind it, behind everything, like some all-governing metronome, the regular ticking of the grandfather clock.

"What did you say?" Stuart asked, panic edged into his voice. He looked around the room.

"It's okay, Stuart. He's just spooked about something. He probably thinks he should be upstairs in bed." Dan continued to scratch behind the dog's ears.

Stuart continued his search. "You said midnight madness. What did you mean?" His eyes locked on the grandfather clock, the pendulum swinging like the tail of some malevolent beast. He looked at the face, his breath catching in his throat. The chimes he had heard rang in the far reaches of his memory. How many were there? He turned back, eyes wide. He looked again at his watch. "That clock. Does it always run fast?"

Stephie answered. "No. My dad made that too, by the way. In fact it loses about ten minutes a month."

Again Stuart checked his watch against the clock. "It's an hour fast!"

"It's never been out by that much. Has it, Dan?" She looked up at her husband.

He thought for a moment, puzzled, then asked, "You coming straight up from California, Stuart?"

Stuart just nodded.

"That explains it then. Most of Oregon is on Pacific time, and geographically we should be too. But with Boise so close, commerce-wise we're tied in more to Idaho than Oregon. So there's an extension of Mountain time projecting into the eastern part of Oregon, centered around Adrian. We're an hour head of you here."

It had reached him now. Stripped away the last of his

protection. It pryed at his collar, scraped its way over his neck and down his back. It gained entry at his waist, spreading out within him, icing his colon, turning his blood to slush.

Like the protective flight response of a startled herd, an unseen pulse passed between them. Only Stuart knew the exact nature of the danger, yet instantly, instinctively, the others were aware of its presence, its magnitude.

"The baby," Stuart whispered.

Shep was on his feet, bared snarling fangs amplifying the now-constant growl. Harrison was thrown to the floor as the dog broke free. It lunged for the stairs, howling, nails tearing at the exposed planks.

"Danny, what the hell is going on?" screamed Stephanie. And to Stuart: "Who the hell are you? And what did you say about the baby?"

Dan was on his feet now. He scrambled after the dog, taking the stairs three and four at a time. From the upstairs landing he could hear the dog barking and snarling at the far end of the hall. "Oh Jesus no. *Shep!*" he screamed, as he ran, desperate and terrified, towards the noise. "Get away from him. *Shep!*"

The other two were on the landing now. Together they raced to the end of the hall, stumbled into the room. The dog stood square in the center of the room, his huge body twisting, lunging, his jaws snapping and slashing at some unseen prey. He ran towards his masters, barked, howling some panicked message, then back to the center of the room.

Stuart stood at the doorway, not daring to approach. A sinking despair settled over him as he surveyed the room beyond the dog. It was a nursery. Bright curtains, home-made rock and driftwood mobiles suspended from the ceiling, a hand-carved hobby horse standing sentry in one corner, and in the other, dark and familiar . . .

A veil descended, blurring his vision, muffling the sounds. From his slumped position he only faintly saw Harrison restraining the dog. Blurred shapes behind a misted window. Stephanie, no more than a ghostly outline as she crossed the room to the crib, her gasp and scream barely audible.

Epilogue

Snow continued to fall, vertically now, the wind all but calm. The state trooper's warning echoed in his memory as Stuart turned the Jeep around. He backed cautiously to where he judged the edge of the road to be, then forward, then back again. It required seven separate movements before he was facing in the opposite direction. The tracks he had made only three hours ago were gone, vanished completely under the blanket of white. He glanced to his right, at the Harrisons crowded into the front seat beside him, Stephanie in the middle huddled into her husband, the small, carefully wrapped bundle between them. The car moved forward, quiet on the soft-padded road.

With the wind silenced, the snow accumulated steadily on the windshield. As the Jeep glided slowly down the mountain, the hypnotic regularity of the wipers rewound the tapes of his memory. The events of the past two hours were too traumatic, a sound too painful to hear again so soon. Without willing it he was back in Versoix, listening to the final terrible chapter of Maddering's story.

"Have not this ark lest this day thy sons be forfeit." Maddering repeated Christ's curse. "The Romans threatened to take Him down from the Cross, so He threatened them back. 'Don't touch this Cross or else,' He said. But we know that He did die on the Cross. And that his body was taken down and his Cross dismantled, just as they all were.

"In 1945 when we discussed this passage in the Gospel of Jesus, we interpreted this curse in the context of gnostic doctrine. That is, we wrote it off as a final desperate gesture by Jesus using the same methods He had used so successfully in the past. True, this curse seemed more

216

direct, more immediate; that is, He seemed to be making a specific threat against specific people at a specific time. But this was to be explained by the immediacy of his circumstances.

"That was my interpretation, Stuart. And in this case, the rest of the committee agreed with me; at least they conceded my greater fluency in historical translation and interpretation.

"But I was wrong. Until you wrote to me, until you sent me your data on the crib deaths, I had no way of knowing just how wrong I was." Maddering's voice was faltering now. He was shaking his head, apologetic, almost sobbing. He looked up at Stuart.

Stuart could only stare.

"Don't you see, Stuart," he said desperately. "The curse. If we interpret it literally, then of course it can be written off as his last dying attempt at manipulation. But what if He intended it as a noncontemporaneous curse? Like all the other curses described in his writings. An oblique, nonspecific, eternal threat. A 'mummy's curse.' Then it all fits."

Rice was still confused.

"Stuart, you still don't understand. You have traced and studied the history of a family tragedy: thirteen infants, all of them sons, all dying in the same dark wooden crib at Easter, the anniversary of Christ's death. You have traced the origin of the crib to a soldier scavenging wood from the artillery shaft of a fort in the Canadian Maritimes. How the wood got there—across the Atlantic, out of the Middle East, across Europe—is unimportant. The point is you have traced and dated that same wood to the cedar forests of biblical Lebanon. The unusually thin, unmeasurably old blood permeating the wood, the total lack of contaminating organisms, the square hole in the broken crib slat, punched by a nail rather than cut.

"Have not this ark lest this day thy sons be forfeit," Maddering whispered. "The ark is his Cross, Stuart. The day is Easter, eternally Easter. How many others have possessed his ark on the anniversary of his death? How many sons have died through the centuries as the result of his curse?

"Your crib, Stuart. It is the ark. The ageless blood is the blood of Christ. Your crib is made from the wood of his Cross."

It had stopped snowing now. Almost stopped. Occasional flakes appeared suddenly, caught in the glare of the headlights. Horizontal tracers of white, aimed at the grille, only to veer at the last second and disappear in the swirl as they passed.

He turned off the wipers. The face of the woman beside him reflected in the mirror of the windshield. A stranger. Yet her eyes, the desolation, the quiet form in her arms; the tragedy so familiar now. When had it begun? Last year? A thousand, two thousand years ago?